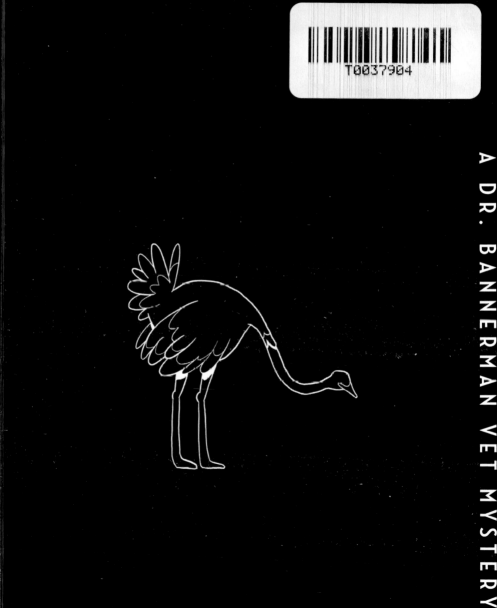

A DR. BANNERMAN VET MYSTERY

PRAISE FOR
PHILIPP SCHOTT

Fifty-Four Pigs

"A charming mystery, the first in a series featuring Peter Bannerman, an amiable, introverted, tea-drinking, obsessive vet, who converses more with his dog, Pippin, than with his wife, Laura, or anyone else . . . James Herriot fans will want to check out this one."

— *Publishers Weekly*

"Original, well-constructed, with a cast of interesting characters — I hope this isn't the last we'll read about Dr. Peter Bannerman and Pippin."

— Ian Hamilton, author of the Ava Lee series

The Accidental Veterinarian

"Few books . . . approach the combination of fine writing, radical honesty, and endless optimism found in Winnipeg practitioner Schott's . . . Laugh until you cry — and believe, as he says, that all that really matters is that the heart of the pet (and its owner) is pure."

— *Booklist*, starred review

"Schott's writing is engagingly conversational and showcases his colorful sense of humor . . . Educational, entertaining, and compassionate, this confluence of happy accidents is a must-read for anyone who is, loves, or works with a veterinarian."

— *Shelf Awareness*

How to Examine a Wolverine

"An engaging study of the behaviors of pets and the people who care for them. Schott's tone is warm, friendly, and folksy in his storytelling and his conversations with pet owners; even in the most stressful times, he's a compassionate and level-headed guide. *How to Examine a Wolverine* is an essay collection that celebrates the love of animals."

— *Foreword Reviews*

The Battle Cry of the Siamese Kitten

"While some pieces offer LOLs and some are sad, it's all just plain entertaining, with clients like bush dogs Doobie and Gator, a gorgeous snow leopard due for an ultrasound, and yellow lab Man Hampton. Animal owners will find lots of welcome — and readily dispersed — factoids."

— *Booklist*

"Philipp Schott is not James Herriot. This book isn't about creatures great and small in pre-war Yorkshire — but the pets that come to this Winnipeg clinic are just as entertaining."

— *Chesil Magazine*

The Willow Wren

"Philipp Schott pulls off the considerable feat of creating empathy for his characters without ever resorting to easy excuses for their sometimes indefensible choices . . . a fine, nuanced storytelling achievement."

— Frederick Taylor, historian and bestselling author of *Exorcising Hitler: The Occupation and Denazification of Germany*

"This beautifully written tale alternates between displays of sardonic humour and setting some truly poignant and heart-wrenching scenes. Morally complex and nuanced, this book is a must-read for anyone who wants to understand a difficult period in German history."

— Dr. Perry Biddiscombe, historian, author of *The Last Nazis: SS Werewolf Guerrilla Resistance in Europe 1944–1947*

WORKS BY PHILIPP SCHOTT

DR. BANNERMAN VET MYSTERIES

Fifty-Four Pigs: A Dr. Bannerman Vet Mystery #1

Six Ostriches: A Dr. Bannerman Vet Mystery #2

THE ACCIDENTAL VETERINARIAN SERIES

The Accidental Veterinarian: Tales from a Pet Practice

*How to Examine a Wolverine: More Tales from
the Accidental Veterinarian*

*The Battle Cry of the Siamese Kitten: Even More Tales from
the Accidental Veterinarian*

OTHER

The Willow Wren: A Novel

SIX
Ostriches

A DR. BANNERMAN VET MYSTERY

PHILIPP SCHOTT DVM

Published by ECW Press
665 Gerrard Street East
Toronto, Ontario, Canada M4M 1Y2
416-694-3348 / info@ecwpress.com

Cover design: David A. Gee
Cover artwork © Joey Gao / www.joey-gao.com

LIBRARY AND ARCHIVES CANADA CATALOGUING IN PUBLICATION

Title: Six ostriches : a Dr. Bannerman vet mystery / Philipp Schott, DVM.

Names: Schott, Philipp, author.

Identifiers: Canadiana (print) 20230145663 | Canadiana (ebook) 2023014568X

ISBN 978-1-77041-725-0 (softcover)
ISBN 978-1-77852-112-6 (PDF)
ISBN 978-1-77852-111-9 (ePub)
ISBN 978-1-77852-113-3 (Kindle)

Classification: LCC PS8637.C5645 S59 2023 | DDC C813/.6—dc23

This book is funded in part by the Government of Canada. *Ce livre est financé en partie par le gouvernement du Canada.* We acknowledge the support of the Canada Council for the Arts. *Nous remercions le Conseil des arts du Canada de son soutien.* We acknowledge the funding support of the Ontario Arts Council (OAC), an agency of the Government of Ontario. We also acknowledge the support of the Government of Ontario through the Ontario Book Publishing Tax Credit, and through Ontario Creates.

For Lorraine

PROLOGUE

The fence was gone. Yesterday it was there, but this morning it was gone. He ran toward the opening. Maybe the man took it away. Maybe it disappeared. Much was unfamiliar in this country, so everything was possible. The others stood back. They were cowards. He was the leader for a reason. There was no danger. He knew this. This was an opportunity, that's what it was. Let the cowards miss out. He crossed into the new territory and looked about him. The grass was much longer here. And it whirred and clicked and buzzed with many different kinds of insects. Tasty insects. Tasty plants. Paradise. Toward the shrubs it was wetter and there were even more insects and tender-looking shoots. He trotted to this spot and began to peck at everything, gorging like a child let loose in a world made of candy. Then something caught his eye. It glinted in a shallow pond. It was like a piece of the sun. He was so clever for coming here. The cowards would not get this delicious morsel. But it was not delicious. The piece of the sun was beautiful, but it tasted of nothing as it went down his long throat. It should have been warm and soft, but it was cold and hard. It had unpleasant edges and corners. This was surprising. It was nothing like what he imagined eating a piece of the sun would be like. He began to consider the impossible: that he, the leader, had made a mistake.

CHAPTER
One

Dr. Peter Bannerman and the ostrich stared at each other.

Even though Peter was six foot five, the ostrich was still taller than him, so Peter had to tilt his head upwards to get a good look at the bird's eyes. Caution was warranted around ostriches, but there was a strong fence between them, so he was safe from kicks. A quick sharp peck was not out of the question though. Peter didn't get any closer than necessary.

"How long has he been off his food, Dan?"

"At least a week, and he's hardly been passing any droppings. I think it started when I let them into the new pasture on the north side." Dan Favel, a powerfully built middle-aged Métis man with an iron-grey brush cut and an impressive moustache, looked mournful as he said this. Dan had recently taken early retirement from the Royal Canadian Air Force to start his dream exotic livestock farm on the edge of New Selfoss. "I thought I was doing them a favour. The grass and bugs were so good over there. Too good, do you think? Did he overdo it?"

"Maybe," Peter said as he continued to consider his patient from a safe distance. "I'll be honest, Dan, this is my first ostrich patient, so I'm going to have to do some reading before I assume that I can just extrapolate from chickens and ducks."

"Do you hear that Big Bird? The doctor is going to do some studying and then he'll fix you up." Dan's gentle, childlike singsong was in comical contrast with his military bearing.

"Big Bird? Is that his actual name?" Peter asked.

"Yes!" Dan beamed. "And that's Ernie, Bert, Mr. Hooper, Oscar, and The Count over there." He indicated to a corral on the far side of the house where five ostrich heads bobbed above the high wooden fence. "But they're all girls except Big Bird and Mr. Hooper. I figured ostriches don't care about gender identity. And my granddaughter loves their names!"

"No, I don't think they care." Peter chuckled.

"Is there anything you can do today while you're here?"

"Well, it doesn't hurt to take an x-ray of the proventriculus."

"The what?"

"It's sort of his first stomach. 'Pro' means 'before,' and 'ventriculus' means 'stomach.' It's the first place the food comes after travelling down the esophagus, and it's a common place for blockages to occur — at least in other bird species. The gizzard is the next stomach, and that's where all the grinding happens. Because birds don't have teeth, big chunks can go down and get stuck before they reach the gizzard."

Dan rubbed his chin. "Sounds like a design flaw. The gizzard should be first."

"Ha! I suppose you could argue that, but the proventriculus secretes digestive juices that soften the food and make the gizzard's work easier."

"Oh, OK. So, you can x-ray here?"

"For sure. I'll just run to the truck and grab my portable unit. In the meantime, can you round Big Bird up, hood him, and get him in a position where I can approach his lower neck from both sides?"

"Will do. I'll get Kim out to help us."

Peter walked back to his truck, which was parked in the muddy yard between the paddock and the house. He enjoyed the momentary break to think. He also enjoyed the soft breeze and the novel sensation of warmth on his face from the late afternoon sun. It was mid-April, and the sun was finally something other than just a source of light. He wasn't a sun worshipper — far from it, in fact — but as much as he loved the challenge and invigorating bite of a Manitoba winter, by April he was ready for a change.

As he opened the compartment on the side of his New Selfoss Veterinary Service truck where the x-ray unit was stored, he paused to listen to the trill of a red-winged blackbird among the cattails in the small pond beside the drive. This was the soundtrack of spring. *And it's going to be a good spring*, he thought. This was not just wishful thinking. It was logical because the winter had been so difficult due to everything that happened after the explosion of Tom Pearson's swine barn. The principle of regression to the mean dictated that it was likely that spring would be more average than winter had been and therefore, by comparison, good.

The x-ray machine was compact and came in what looked like a large black cooler on wheels. He grabbed that and the flat grey x-ray cassette before walking back to where Dan and Kim were herding Big Bird into a squeeze chute by waving blankets at him. This was a funnel of fences where the parallel ones in the "spout" could be adjusted to keep an animal snugly in place. Platforms on either side allowed access from above.

"OK, I've got the hook ready," Kim shouted. She was considerably smaller than either Peter or Dan, but she had been an Olympic gymnast as a teen, and from having seen her work with her ponies, Peter knew that she was still exceptionally strong and quick. She was wielding a long pole with a blunt-ended hook at the end. While Dan stood behind Big Bird to prevent him from backing up, Kim snagged the ostrich's neck. She managed to make this look both forceful and gentle. And then in a split second she put a hood over Big Bird's head and released the hook. This had the desired effect as the 250-pound bird immediately became calmer, no longer flapping his stubby wings against the sides of the chute or flailing his head about.

Peter was impressed. It was like something out of Marlin Perkins and *Mutual of Omaha's Wild Kingdom* with Kim in Jim's role.

"Good job, Kim!" he called as he approached. "Now please get him to shuffle forward so he's tight in the squeeze."

This took a little more doing as Dan and Kim manoeuvred Big Bird back and forth until they had the squeeze chute settings exactly right to keep him in place. The chute was made of steel tubing, and fortunately the gaps were perfectly spaced to allow access to the area Peter wanted to x-ray.

Peter was proud of his new x-ray equipment. It was digital, so he could review the results instantly, without having to develop films. This was not only more efficient, but it saved stress on the animals.

In a matter of seconds, the black and white images appeared on his monitor.

"It's good! You can let him go!" Peter called up from his crouched position beside the machine.

"OK!"

This was followed by banging and flapping noises as the chute was opened and Big Bird ran off, presumably in a foul temper.

"What does it show?" Kim asked as she bent down beside Peter and squinted. Dan joined her a second later.

"See this?" Peter pointed to a whitish blob at the bottom of what was obviously, even to a layperson's eyes, the neck.

"Yes."

"That's the proventriculus. All the white stuff is food — mostly leaves and grass, I'm guessing. It's jammed full. The whiteness shows the density, so it's quite impacted."

"Silly, greedy bugger," Dan said.

"But what's that?" Kim asked, pointing at a bright white T-shaped object.

"Good eye. I was just about to get to that." Peter tapped the screen to zoom in on the object. The crossbar of the T was shaped liked a squashed pentagon, with the point opposite the stem. "It's metal and about the size of your thumb."

"Wow," Kim said.

Peter tapped some more, zooming further, and then adjusted the contrast. "Now look, you can see that there's some sort of symmetrical etching or design on it. There's no way to make out exactly what with x-ray, but this obviously isn't a natural object."

"Crazy. I guess he'll need surgery, eh?" Dan said this quietly. He looked over to where Big Bird was now standing, preening, presumably to get the human taint off his feathers. Peter thought he noticed Dan's eyes moisten.

"Yes, I'm afraid so. But it's not a difficult one."

"The previous owner of this property had young kids. They must have lost some sort of toy," Kim said as she and Dan walked Peter back to his truck.

"We'll find out soon," Peter replied as he swiped through the calendar on his phone. "Day after tomorrow good? That's Wednesday. First thing in the morning?"

"Perfect! See you then."

Big Bird was Peter's last patient for the day, so he drove directly home. For the first half of the drive, he worried about some of the technical aspects of the planned surgery. He had never operated on an ostrich before. The general principles of surgery were more or less universal, but he fretted over the potential non-universal aspects. By the second half of the drive, however, he had switched to analyzing the probability that the object in Big Bird's proventriculus had belonged to a child. He didn't know much about children, but it struck him as being an odd toy. Perhaps it was some other sort of trinket that had been picked up somewhere else by a raven or magpie and then dropped?

He was still lost in this reverie as he parked the truck, entered the house, and absent-mindedly petted Pippin, their enthusiastic black and white lab-husky-collie mix, so it took him a second to properly orient himself when Laura greeted him loudly from the living room.

"How was your day?"

"Good. Interesting case at the end." After giving Pippin two treats from his pocket and letting Merry, their tortoiseshell cat, rub up against his leg, Peter took off his boots and went into the living room.

"Oh?" Laura said, looking up from her knitting. Laura was in many ways the physical opposite of her husband. Where he was tall, she was short. Where he was dark complexioned, she was fair. Where he had unruly brown hair, she had tidy trademark Gudmundurson bright red hair, from which the tops of her ears protruded slightly, like an elf, Peter often said, which he meant as a compliment. "Like interesting for vets, or interesting for regular humans?"

"Ha! The latter. An ostrich at Dan and Kim Favel's place."

"Did it disembowel you with its claws?" Laura asked, grinning broadly.

"Nope."

"OK, only mildly interesting so far."

"Looks like it swallowed some kind of toy or piece of jewellery or knick-knack. It's a weird T-shaped metal object with a design on it."

"Hmm, that is interesting." Laura set her knitting aside and put her hand out. "Let's see . . ."

Peter found the x-ray images on his phone and handed it over. Laura squinted at the screen.

"Hmm," she said. "I'm going to adjust the greyscale and try flipping to negative."

Peter watched from over her shoulder as Laura tapped a few times and then pinched and zoomed.

"What do you think?" he said.

"This is a mjolnir," she answered without looking up from the screen.

"A myaw . . . what?"

"Mjolnir. *Myawl-near.*" She drew out the syllables for emphasis. "Thor's hammer. A Norse religious symbol worn as a pendant. See the little hole at the end of the stem?"

"That's a weird toy. But maybe a tie-in to the movie?"

"No," Laura said, adopting an authoritative tone. She was a professional knitter whose niche was bespoke geek-wear, such as Lord of the Rings sweaters, Star Wars mitts, Doctor Who socks, and Harry Potter toques. She was very familiar with Marvel's product lines. "They used a cheesy rectangular mallet-type hammer in the movie and their merch, rather than a true mjolnir."

"Ah. So, a tourist souvenir from Reykjavik then."

"I suppose." Laura continued to look at the screen, evidently lost in thought. Then she handed the phone back to Peter and said, "A bit of an odd souvenir though. Mostly people were buying expensive wool sweaters or cheap plastic Viking helmets last time I was there. As I said, it's actually a religious symbol."

"But someone could just think it's cool. In Nepal, non-Buddhist tourists buy all kinds of Buddhist related stuff, like prayer wheels and paintings of Tibetan demons. I can picture just the type to pick up a Thor's hammer pendant — spiky black hair, leather wrists bands, bleeding eyeball tattoos, like Darcy down at the garage."

Laura snorted. "Maybe. Real pagans probably dress in business suits."

"Real pagans?"

"That's the point I was going to make. I've heard that Norse paganism is making a comeback, so for them it's not just a cool trinket." She paused and picked up her own phone. "You have me curious now. I'm going to research this a little."

Laura was proud of her Icelandic heritage, her parents having emigrated from there in the 1970s, part of the second wave of

Icelanders to come over, a hundred years after the first. Peter knew that when Laura said she was going to "research this a little," it meant that she was going to read everything she could find on mjolnirs, new pagans, and probably the Icelandic souvenir trade as well. If it had to do with Iceland, she had to know about it.

In the meantime, he had research of his own to do — ostrich surgery. This was too big a job for his phone, so he got up, stepped around Pippin, who was snoozing on the floor between them, and retrieved his laptop from the rolltop desk. He logged on to an online veterinary surgery database and sighed heavily. There was no straightforward "this is how you perform surgery to remove a foreign body from an ostrich" information. This was going to take hours of digging and reading and extrapolating. He sighed again.

"This is impossible," he grumbled.

"Mm-hmm," Laura said, not taking her eyes off her phone.

"Ostrich surgery. How am I supposed to figure out how to . . ." and then he trailed off. It was obvious that Laura wasn't listening. She was deep in some Icelandic lore rabbit hole. She sometimes seemed to have no idea how stressful his job was. He was about to say something louder to try to elicit a reaction from her when an image suddenly floated into his mind's eye. It was of a tall slender woman with waist-length wavy black hair, high cheekbones, and blue eyes vivid against her olive skin. She was wearing a lab coat and smiling at him.

Alicia.

CHAPTER

Two

"**M**ay I please speak to Dr. Alicia Loewenstein?"

"Who may I say is calling?"

"Dr. Peter Bannerman, in Manitoba."

"And may I tell her what it's regarding?"

"Ostrich surgery."

There was the briefest pause before the receptionist said, "OK, please hold for a moment."

The Toronto Zoo's on-hold message consisted of a series of exhortations to take advantage of various exciting special events in the coming months. Peter tuned these out and allowed his mind to wander back 20 years to vet school in Saskatoon, where he and Alicia had been classmates. She was a strikingly beautiful woman of mixed Jewish and Indonesian parentage. She was also the top student in their class year after year, winning armloads of awards at graduation. Even though he and Laura, who was studying paleobiology across campus, were already dating then, Peter couldn't help but have a crush on Alicia. She always had talented and attractive boyfriends, so the crush was abstract. He didn't think he would have dumped Laura for her, but nonetheless he felt awkward and guilty about it for years.

This line of thought was interrupted by a familiar bright voice. "Peter! It's been years! How are you?" Alicia was always perky without taking it to an irritating extreme.

"I'm great, thanks! How about you?"

"Oh, you know, busy, busy, busy, but doing well. So, what's this about an ostrich?"

"He's got an impacted proventriculus. I've never done a proventriculotomy on a bird this size before. The surgery looks straightforward, but I'm uncomfortable with bird anaesthesia at the best of times, let alone when the bird is 120 kilos! As you can imagine, we don't see too many ostriches in Manitoba."

"Ha! I'm surprised you see any at all. But you're in luck. The size actually makes the anaesthesia simpler because they are so much easier to intubate than smaller birds. I would pre-med him with ket-val and then maintain him on iso. Keep a line in and some more valium handy because their recoveries can be rocky."

"I'm trying to picture what a rocky ostrich recovery looks like . . ."

"Oh yeah, look out! It can get wicked ugly when they start flailing those giant claws around! Do you have good techs?"

"Only one, Kat, and yeah, she's good with just about anything. One of the owners is excellent too, so I'll get her to help with restraint."

"Well, call me on the day of the procedure if anything comes up. You can get them to page me as urgent."

"I really appreciate it. I wasn't sure who else to call. Reading up on VIN forums only takes you so far, and the local zoo doesn't have any ostriches. And now that it's been so long since we were in school, I wasn't sure anymore who I'd call at the college."

"No problem at all, Peter. It's great to talk to you! Practice going well?" Her tone was warm, and her interest sounded sincere. Peter had an odd feeling in the pit of his stomach. Suddenly it was 20 years ago and Alicia was flashing him a smile from across the cafeteria.

Keep it professional, Peter reminded himself. "Booming. It took a few years for everyone to forget the old guy and get used to me, but now it's going really well."

"And you were in the news a few months ago! Exploding pig barns! Smuggler gangs! That must have been terrifying."

"Oh, that." Peter tried to sound casual. He wasn't sure whether he had succeeded.

"That was so crazy! Like you were some kind of private detective figuring it out!"

Peter was pleased by her admiring tone. There was a time when he would have used that as a springboard to tell stories to make himself look even better, but he had learned that people actually preferred modesty. "A lot of the credit has to go to Pippin, my dog."

"Ha! Credit to your dog! You've always been funny, Peter. Well, I'm dying to hear more about that. My sister's moved to Winnipeg, and I'm coming out to visit her in a couple weeks. I'll text you, and we'll have to get together for coffee or dinner then."

"Sounds great! And I'll let you know how things go with the ostrich."

"Please do. I've got to go now, I'm being paged. Apparently one of the gibbons managed to split open a rubber ball and get his head stuck inside. Take care, Peter!"

"Yes, you too!"

Peter hung up and set the phone down. The clinic was quiet. He sat back in his well-worn old brown office chair and stared off into the middle distance. Alicia Loewenstein. He wondered what she looked like now. He realized that he didn't even know if she was married or had kids. Maybe even divorced by now and married again. Twenty years is a long time. He gave his head a slight shake. It didn't matter. He had gotten the information he needed. That was what mattered. But Alicia Loewenstein. He snapped out of this reverie when Theresa, the receptionist, popped her head into the office.

"Sparky's set up and ready, Peter!"

"OK, thanks. Be right there." Sparky was a chihuahua with only two teeth left, so his tongue always lolled comically out of his mouth. He was ancient too, maybe 17 or 18, and had become one of Peter's favourites over the years. Peter smiled to himself at the thought of seeing Sparky with his bony little tail wagging manically.

Wednesday morning was bright and clear again. April weather on the Canadian Prairies can resemble a wheel of fortune, spinning back and forth between wintery and summery and various states in between, sometimes hourly. Peter liked the challenge this presented. It made him feel more intrepid. However, from a practical perspective, he had to admit that summery was preferable.

Peter and Kat squinted in the sun as they watched Kim and Dan lead Big Bird out of the trailer in the parking lot behind the clinic. A couple of passersby stopped to watch. Big Bird had been hooded back at the farm to make the transportation less traumatic, so he walked down the ramp very gingerly, taking big slow steps like a child tiptoeing theatrically. Everyone involved, presumably including Big Bird, would have preferred to have the procedure done at the farm, but Alicia had recommended gas anaesthesia, and that could only be safely managed at the clinic. The passersby took pictures while Dan smiled and waved. Then Big Bird was taken in through the back door, after being made to duck slightly by Kim.

They had set up the treatment room as a temporary operating room as the actual OR was too small. The radio was turned off, the phone's ringer was turned down, and no other appointments were booked for the morning to keep the environment as calm as possible. The procedure itself should be quick, but Peter didn't know how long he'd need to supervise the recovery. He didn't know as much about ostriches as he would like, but he did know that they had such a keen sense of hearing that zebras and antelope sometimes relied on them to give early warning of an approaching lion. Also, Big Bird gave off an especially alert and apprehensive vibe, as if a dropped paper clip could send him into a frenzy of flailing kicks.

As it happened, Big Bird was a model patient. Perhaps he had been stunned into passive mode by the novelty of the situation, or perhaps Kim and Kat were just that good at handling him. Either way, he submitted to the induction of the anaesthesia with nary a twitch of a toe.

After their phone call, Alicia had sent an email with specific doses and more ostrich anaesthesia tips. Her advice was good because the procedure went very smoothly. As Peter began closing up the incision, he could imagine himself doing more of these, maybe even expanding into emus. Not that there was any demand for that. As anticipated, the proventriculus had been jammed with densely packed semi-digested fibrous vegetation. Peter didn't want to take the time to pick through it while Big Bird was under, so he handed the gooey wad to Theresa, his receptionist, who was acting as an assistant while Kat monitored the anaesthetic.

"Peter, you're right!" Theresa called from the far side of the room.

"About what?"

"There *is* a Thor's hammer in here!"

"What does it look like?"

"Like a flattened little mallet with a wider bit at the end of the handle. And it's covered in a carved design!"

"Laura and I thought we saw a design on the x-ray, but we couldn't make out any details."

"It's very intricate. Lots of circles and swirls. It's beautiful."

"Can you tell what kind of metal?" Peter was almost done stitching. He nodded to Kat, who understood the signal to mean that she could begin reducing the percentage of gas mixed in the oxygen.

"I'm not an expert, but I think bronze?"

"Huh." Peter was concentrating now on knotting the last suture.

"But it must be pretty new because it's so shiny. Copper and bronze turn green when they get old, don't they?"

"Yes, that's true. Pretty weird thing for an ostrich to find."

"African bird eats Scandinavian object on Canadian farm," Kat said, and chuckled as she adjusted the anaesthetic further.

Big Bird's recovery was just as smooth and uneventful as his induction. To everyone's relief, he did not thrash his legs about and disembowel anyone, nor did he flail his long neck back and forth and whack his head, rendering him even more addled. Instead, he gradually returned to consciousness, looking dazed, and did not try to stand until Peter deemed it safe and Kim coaxed him to his feet. When it was time to go, he staggered slightly, like a tipsy bar-hopper, as he was led to the back door.

When they were settling the bill, Dan fished in his jacket pocket and pulled out the mjolnir, which Theresa had given him earlier. He put it on the reception counter in front of Peter.

"You keep this, Peter — consider it a tip."

"Really? Are you sure? It's beautiful."

"Absolutely sure. Not really my kind of thing anyway."

"Thanks!" Peter looked at the shiny little hammer, excited that he could take it home to show Laura.

"But" — Dan broke into a broad smile — "if it ends up being valuable, we'll go halfers on it, eh?"

"It's a deal!" Peter paused as he picked the mjolnir up and looked at it closely. "Still no idea how it got there?"

"Nope, but we just bought that section from Jim Thorkelson's estate a month ago. It was lucky that came available so soon after buying our home quarter section. His son, Jim Junior, contacted us to see if we were interested. I don't think Thorkelson was doing anything with that land for years. You'd have to call Jim Junior in Calgary to find out more."

"Yeah, I know Jim Junior. We went to high school together. He played D&D with us for a while."

"Small world."

"Small town," Peter laughed. He looked at the mjolnir again. "This can't have been there very long. There's no corrosion."

"Stomach acid clean it up?" Dan offered as he put his receipt away and zipped up his jacket.

"Maybe, but I doubt it was in there long enough for that."

"Oh well." Dan shrugged and stepped away from the counter. "Thanks again, Peter! Have a great day."

Peter sometimes had trouble taking the hint when a conversation was finished. "Do you know if Jim Senior went back to the old country and maybe brought back souvenirs?" He held up the little bronze hammer and smiled.

"No idea, Peter. Never met the guy. But that makes as much sense as anything. Doesn't look much like a kid's toy."

While Peter was in surgery with Big Bird, Laura was at home, pacing. She wasn't normally a pacer. Normally, if she had something on her mind, or felt anxious or nervous, she knitted. The rhythmic motion of her fingers and the distraction of keeping track of the stitches and pattern always calmed her, but not today. Petting Merry also sometimes helped, but not today either.

Peter's birthday was coming up on Saturday, and she didn't have a present yet. Moreover, something had been off between them for months, and it had felt even worse in the last couple days. He seemed more distracted and distant than normal, and even a bit irritable around her, which was not at all like him. As far as she knew, work was going well, so that couldn't be the reason. She had even planned this great party for him at The Flying Beaver, and while he seemed pleased by that, he wasn't as excited as she had hoped he would be.

She needed to come up with a really good present. She knew it was childish to hope that an awesome gift could make right whatever was wrong, but it couldn't hurt. It was tough though. With Peter's mild Asperger's, or autism spectrum disorder, or whatever she was supposed to understand his mental wiring to be, he could be really intensely interested and excited about some things and completely dismissive of other things with very little middle ground. A gift was typically either a massive hit or an epic fail.

Laura sighed, stopped pacing, and sat down. Pippin was fast asleep on the hearth rug, but Merry came over and hopped on her. Merry had the loudest purr of any cat Laura had ever met. It did help a little.

Laura pondered what Peter had been excited about lately. And then it came to her. It was obvious. The mjolnir!

She knew what to get him.

She pulled out her phone and searched for hobby stores in Winnipeg. This was going to be a winner!

CHAPTER

Three

Usually, the best part of Peter's day was walking into his house after a day at the clinic. This was not because he was happy to have escaped work, nor was it because he really looked forward to supper, nor even, if he was honest with himself, because he was so keen to see Laura. All of these things were true, but it was not what made opening his front door the best part of his day. Pippin made this the best part of his day. More specifically, it was Pippin's never-fail, over-the-moon greeting. Laura would call a cheery hello from somewhere in the house, and that was nice, and Merry would occasionally wander by and give him a friendly glance, and that was nice too, but Pippin made Peter feel like he was the most important person on Earth. Which he was, to Pippin.

Pippin was always right there behind the door. Regardless of whether Peter had walked or driven, Pippin knew that it was Peter, and he was ready for him. The greeting began with a few quick barks before Peter had even opened the door. These were happy yip-yip barks, not the low arf-arf barks he made when strangers approached. As soon as Peter opened the door, Pippin would begin bouncing on his feet, smiling a huge, tongue-dangling smile, and wagging his whole hind end. Pippin would continue doing this while waiting for Peter to hang his coat, take off his shoes, and put down anything he was carrying. Then he knew he'd get his ears vigorously scratched and be asked how his "dog day" had been. Finally, there came the best part of Pippin's day — being permitted to smell Peter's pants. Pippin had an extraordinary sense of smell. Anyone who had spent any time at all with Peter knew this because he would always find a way to slide into the conversation the fact that Pippin had won gold at the Western Canadian Scent Dog Association championships in Moose Jaw the previous year. From his pants Peter assumed Pippin was able to deduce which animals Peter had seen that day, in which order and, in many cases, what kind of condition they had been in. It was Pippin's daily newspaper delivery.

While Peter stood there, smiling at his dog, waiting for him to finish the inspection, Laura came out of the kitchen. She gave him a peck on the cheek and asked how his day had been. He described a few other cases and then, pretending he had forgotten until that moment, he said, "And oh, Big Bird's surgery was today."

"I knew that. Why do I think I waited through the beagle anal gland story? So, what did you find?"

"You're right, there was a mjolnir in there!" Peter pulled a small terry cloth bundle out of his backpack and handed it to his wife. Laura didn't say anything as she pushed her red hair out of her eyes and carefully unfolded the towel. She stared at the gleaming little hammer for a long moment, turning it over several times.

"It's so beautiful," she finally said, almost in a whisper.

"Isn't it?" Peter bent over to look at it with her.

"Doesn't say 'Made in China' anywhere on it," Laura said.

"No, or 'Made in Japan' if it's a little older," Peter said, chuckling. "Pretty cool though, eh? I figure old Jim Thorkelson brought it back from Iceland and it fell out of his pocket or something."

"Jim Thorkelson, the real estate guy?"

"No, his dad. You're thinking of Jim Junior. Remember him from high school? A couple years younger than us? He moved to

Calgary. Jim Senior owned the parcel of land just north of Kim and Dan Favel's place."

"And he went to Iceland?"

"That's just an educated guess. It's the most logical explanation if you examine the probabilities."

Laura smiled. Peter was always "examining the probabilities," and if there was any way at all to assign a number to those probabilities and calculate them, he would. To Peter, the world was nothing more than a series of giant interlocking math problems. Only the data was too often lacking.

"You just need more data, right?"

"Right." Peter smiled back at her.

Pippin had been sitting quietly beside them in the front hall, his eyes going back and forth as each person spoke. He had one ear down and one up, highlighting the border collie in his lab-husky-collie mix.

"Has he had his dinner yet?" Peter asked, cocking his head toward Pippin.

"Nope, I've been busy in the kitchen, but I guess it's time."

"I'll do it. By the way, what are we having?"

"Chana dal."

"China doll?"

"Yes, you goof, China doll in a playdough sauce with a Lego side salad. No. *Chah-nah* dal," she dragged out each syllable. "Curried lentils."

"Oh, right. Cool."

Peter filled Pippin's bowl with kibble while the dog watched, every muscle tense, unblinking eyes focused on the bowl. Peter waited for five seconds before saying, "OK." Pippin's rigid intensity during those five long seconds never failed to impress Peter. He felt a tiny bit mean making him wait like that, but it was an important discipline. In the long list of things that irritated Peter, poorly behaved dogs ranked high. Pippin hadn't so much as nibbled on a shoe as a puppy, so they had gotten lucky with him, but Peter strongly believed in the power of routine. If something was objectively the right thing to do, you just did it and you kept doing it. Laura viewed this approach as being overly rigid at times, but they had somehow achieved a homeostatic balance between them wherein Laura's more flexible nature helped pull Peter out of some of his deeper behavioural grooves when they were no longer helpful.

One harmless groove, however, was the perfectly brewed cup of decaf tea after work. There had been a time when Peter would drink regular tea, but the best medical advice was to stay away from caffeine after midday, so he did. The choice of tea depended on his mood and the weather. Sunny days like today put him in a South African rooibos frame of mind, unless he was feeling melancholy, in which case a cheap English blend such as Taylors Yorkshire was more suitable. Rooibos needed to be steeped longer than black teas, at least four minutes, so while he waited, Peter went to the lovely old rolltop desk in the corner of the living room. Laura had done such a good job restoring it. Peter always admired manual skills like that as he could be inept and awkward with his hands himself, unless he really concentrated hard, like in surgery, and that was too exhausting for any hobby. From the desk drawer he pulled out a large faux-antique magnifying glass, like the kind Sherlock Holmes is pictured using. He took it over to his favourite green armchair where the tea (two minutes and twenty seconds left to steep) and the mjolnir were waiting on a small round side table. He adjusted the angle of the reading lamp behind the chair and then set about examining the little bronze object in minute detail. It was astonishingly beautiful. He was so absorbed in this that he accidentally let the rooibos steep five minutes and he didn't notice that Laura was standing beside him until he reached for the tea.

"Pick up any more clues where that came from?" Laura said.

"No, but I'm wondering why it didn't corrode. Old Jim's been dead a couple years. It only takes a few weeks for bronze to start to show green spots. Assuming it really is bronze, of course."

Laura picked up the little hammer and the magnifying glass. "I'm pretty sure it's bronze. It's darker than copper or brass and a little less shiny. But copper and brass would also tarnish or corrode, although brass more slowly. Where does Dan think the ostrich picked it up?"

"In a marshy area at the edge of some bush, just inside the new property north of their farm."

"Hmm, what kind of plants were around there?" Laura's educational background in paleobiology, a combination of biology, archeology, and geology, was coming in handy. Knitting was more satisfying though, and there were no jobs in paleobiology in New Selfoss, or even Winnipeg.

Peter was quiet for a moment as he tried to recall. "Well, I didn't go over there, but from a distance I could see a large aspen stand between the house and the marsh. Right around the marsh there was quite a bit of tamarack and some birch."

"Thought so. The soil, and any standing water, is probably quite acidic there. That could protect bronze against corrosion."

Peter nodded. "So we can't use that as a way to figure out how old it is."

"No. It could have been there weeks, months, or decades."

"Centuries!" Peter laughed.

"Ha! Yes, Vikings sailing through the Davis Strait, across the bay, down the Nelson to the lake!"

They both laughed. Pippin had been snoozing by the hearth and looked up, startled by the noise.

"However, that reminds me that you should show this to Grimur at the U of M," Laura added.

"Sturluson? The archeology prof? Yeah, I suppose I could. Even though it's a tourist knick-knack, it's well enough made that he might get a kick out of it. He was in the *Globe* a couple weeks ago. Another Viking dig in Newfoundland."

"If anyone around here can give you more information about this thing, it's him."

"For sure. And I should see if Dan will let me take Pippin out there to have a sniff around." At the sound of his name, Pippin sat up and looked expectantly at Peter and Laura, his head cocked to one side.

Laura smiled at Pippin. "I suppose where there's one weird object, there could be more. But can you smell metal, Pippin?"

Pippin stretched and walked over to Laura, tail wagging. "I'm sorry, boy, nothing special is happening. We're just talking about you." Laura reached down and gave the dog a scratch behind his ears.

"You're right to question that. Metal doesn't have a smell as it doesn't release molecules in the air. That metallic smell on our fingers after handling pennies or rusty nails comes from the sweat and oil in our skin reacting with the metal."

"Thank you, Professor Bannerman," she said, grinning at her husband. "But what then are you going to train Pippin to find out there?"

"I don't know yet. Maybe nothing specific. Some dogs are specialist sniffers that just find drugs or corpses, but Pippin's a generalist. He's great at finding anything out of the ordinary in a given environment."

"Like your car keys that time in the Jarvinen Forest when you didn't even know yet that you had lost them!" Laura gave Pippin a pat on the head, murmuring "good boy" as she did, and then stood up and walked toward the kitchen.

"Like my car keys that time, exactly." Peter pulled his face into a stagey grimace when he said this, and then switched to a smile and called after her, "Speaking of smells, that chana dal smells delicious."

Laura lifted the pot lid and gave the stew a stir. "Of course it does," she said, and flashed him a smile from the kitchen.

CHAPTER

Four

Unlike many rural Manitobans, Peter enjoyed coming into the city. Winnipeg fascinated him. As he drove down Highway 59 from New Selfoss he would decide whether to stay on the east side of the Red River and come through the city on Henderson, or whether he would cross to the west and drive down Main. He could also go farther east to Lagimodiere, or farther west to McPhillips or even Brookside. Each offered something different to look at and think about. Of course, it also depended on where he was going, and efficiency was important to Peter, but when he had the time, he liked to mix it up. Main Street was today's pick. It was mid-morning on Thursday, after his early farm calls, and he didn't have to be back in the clinic for appointments until after three, so he had plenty of time.

Main Street was like one long open-air museum. There were modern structures at the upper-middle-class northern edge and again where the government splashed money around downtown, but in-between, the working-class ethnic history of the city was on display out his car window as he rolled along, annoying the other drivers by going the speed limit. The Winnipeg of a hundred years ago with Jewish delis, Polish veterans' clubs, and Ukrainian churches mingled with the Winnipeg of today of Indigenous gospel churches, African grocery stores, and Vietnamese restaurants. Among these was an astonishing array of pawn shops, spanning every era. It was not beautiful in the way the word is normally used, yet to Peter it had a kind of beauty nonetheless. He was careful not to romanticize poverty, but he felt strongly that the Japanese were onto something with their concept of wabi-sabi — the beauty inherent in the imperfect and impermanent. Asymmetry, roughness, and modesty are prized in that aesthetic.

His phone rang as he passed the boarded up Special Times Romanian Café and Disco, with the "Disco" in faded rainbow letters. He always refused to answer it while driving. On the truck's LCD console, he could see that it was Laura's brother, Kevin Gudmundurson, an RCMP officer in New Selfoss. He wondered what Kevin wanted, but let it go to voicemail. He'd check when he parked at the university.

Normally parking at the university was an ordeal, but this time he was lucky and managed to slip into the last remaining spot in front of the archeology building. His appointment with Grimur Sturluson was for eleven thirty and he was 15 minutes early, having allowed ample time to find parking. He tapped on voicemail and opened Kevin's message.

"Hey Pete, Laura mentioned you had picked something up from the old Thorkelson place. This could be of interest to an investigation. Give me a call when you get a chance, eh? Thanks."

Kevin, who was the only person allowed to call Peter "Pete," met Laura for breakfast every Friday morning at Rita's Coffee Shop in New Selfoss. Kevin often also came over on Sunday nights for dinner, if it didn't interfere with his dating life.

Peter still had plenty of time, so he called Kevin back, picturing his burly brother-in-law with the fiery red hair and full beard behind the wheel of his Mountie cruiser somewhere.

"Hey Kevin, Peter here, calling you back."

"Hi, yeah, thanks. Look, this little hammer thing Laura mentioned — any chance you could bring it by the station?"

"Sure. Can I ask why?"

"I can't say."

"Has there been a crime committed on the property?"

"I can't say." Kevin's tone was not unfriendly, but not conversational either.

"Ha! I suppose not. OK, have it your way then."

"I will." This was said with a chuckle. Peter and Kevin knew each other very well, so it was impossible for Kevin to maintain his all-business demeanour right to the end of the conversation.

They made arrangements for Peter to come to the station after he was done at the clinic that day. As Peter stepped out of the truck and walked toward the archeology building, he smiled at Kevin's manner on the phone. It must have taken every ounce of his brother-in-law's willpower to force him to make that call. Kevin hated to involve Peter in any way in a criminal investigation. Peter had a pattern of being more curious than Kevin considered appropriate and then somehow, even if inadvertently, involving himself in the process. It was embarrassing for Kevin. The other officers teased him about his brother-in-law acting like a junior private eye or, worse still, showing Kevin up. From Peter's perspective, these incidents, such as the murdered cat lady or the blown-up pig barn, just happened to fall in his lap. What was he supposed to do? Ignore his knowledge and logical facilities? Ignore Pippin's nose? Anyway, being curious about a Norse trinket was not in the same league as what had happened before. Not at all.

There was a quiet voice in the back of his mind telling Peter that he should cancel the appointment with Sturluson now that he knew the police were interested in the mjolnir. On the one hand, he should just let Kevin do his job himself and figure out what this object really was and if it related to whatever he was investigating. But on the other hand, he was here already, and it would be rude to cancel on such short notice, wouldn't it? Moreover, he would just pass along to Kevin whatever he learned anyway. He was doing him a favour, really. Saving him time. Peter pondered for a moment. The other hand won.

Dr. Grimur Sturluson's office was at the end of the hall, past a notice board filled with the requisite *Far Side* comics and long-past-dated notices for meetings and events. Peter had met Grimur once at a mutual friend's birthday party, and Grimur had remembered him when Peter called. The door was half ajar, so Peter knocked and then stepped in. Sturluson was middle-aged and of medium height and build. His blond hair was slicked back into a small ponytail, revealing a high domed forehead. His frameless square glasses, pale blue eyes, and neatly trimmed goatee and moustache gave him a severe look, but this was allayed by his large friendly smile. He was practically beaming. Peter noted that he was very stylishly dressed in narrow dark jeans turned up at the cuff to reveal bright purple socks and what looked like expensive brown leather shoes with pointed toes that curved slightly upwards at the tip. He wore an untucked subtly patterned pink dress shirt with a contrasting navy collar. Peter normally paid no attention whatsoever to clothing and fashion, but this was so out of keeping with his preconceived stereotype of what an archeology professor would wear to work that he couldn't help but notice.

"Good to see you again, Dr. Sturluson," Peter said, shaking his hand after the other man stood up and stepped around his desk.

"Grim, please. Good to see you too, Peter! Have a seat." He gestured to a wooden chair in front of the desk that Peter imagined was normally occupied by nervous penitent students.

Peter looked around, impressed by the floor-to-ceiling bookcases filled with both books and artefacts. The most interesting looking artefacts and oldest looking leather-bound books were in a locked glass-fronted case to the left of the desk, beside the small leaded glass window looking out on campus.

"Nice collection!"

"Thank you. It's taken many years! Now what have you got to show me?"

Peter reached into his inside jacket pocket and pulled out the carefully wrapped item.

"A mjolnir, I believe."

The professor leaned forward and aimed a desk lamp at the object, which now lay in the middle of his otherwise empty wooden desk. He slid his glasses down his nose slightly and bent forward.

"Mjölnir is the name of one specific hammer, wielded by Thor. We wouldn't refer to any copies as Mjölnir. There is only one. It's always *the* Mjölnir, never *a* mjolnir. Not if you want to be correct. You could say 'Thor's hammer' though. That would be fine." He said this quietly as he turned it over slowly in his hand.

"Kind of like *the* True Cross versus just *a* crucifix?" Peter offered.

Grim nodded without looking up and said, "Yes, similar to that."

Peter didn't say anything further as Grim continued to study the hammer. He radiated an odd kind of intensity that might have unnerved someone else, but Peter was used to odd and intense people. In fact, he was one himself. He liked Grim. Natty clothing aside, he seemed like a kindred nerd.

Then Grim flashed Peter a smile and opened a desk drawer to pull out a large rectangular magnifier on a stand with a built-in light. "This is quite something you've brought me. Please explain again where and how you found it."

Peter went through Big Bird's story in as much detail as seemed relevant while the archeologist examined the hammer through the magnifier. Grim nodded from time to time as Peter spoke but was otherwise intent on his work. When Peter was done, Grim stood up, smiled at Peter, and said, "Thank you. Please follow me now. I want to show you something." He wrapped the hammer again and then ushered Peter through the door and down the hall. Two students walked by, talking to each other, but otherwise the building was quiet and empty. Peter followed him through a door and then down a flight of stairs to the basement level and a hallway that mirrored the one above.

"Lab's down here," Grim said over his shoulder. He stopped at a door and fished in his pocket for keys. Finding the right one, he opened the door and flicked on a light. Peter was astonished to see about half of a blackened human skeleton laid out under a clear plastic tarp, each of the bones neatly labelled.

"Who's that?"

"I don't know yet, but if my hunch is right, you'll find out in the news." He winked at Peter.

"Not a recent murder victim though?" Peter said, smiling to show that he was joking.

"No, not at all recent. But that's not what I want to show you or talk about." Grim smiled back.

Grim pulled two stools over to a microscope at a side counter under shelves filled with plastic tubs labelled with dates and locations. Peter noted that most of the locations were in Newfoundland, Nunavut, Greenland, or Iceland. Grim unwrapped the hammer and placed it under the microscope. He adjusted the light and the magnification and then asked Peter to come and have a look.

"See that?"

Peter was looking at a greatly magnified portion of one of the carved spirals. "Yes," he said cautiously, unsure what exactly he was supposed to be seeing.

"That faint oval is a sprue mark."

"Sprue mark?"

"The channel where the molten bronze was poured into the mould. The style and position tell me that the maker used what's called the lost wax process, which takes twelve laborious steps."

"OK, wow. That's interesting."

"It is, and it also tells us that this isn't just a cheap tourist bauble. Furthermore, the fact that the sprue mark is visible and is not a perfect circle tells us that this is quite old. From these clues, and from my guess at the copper to tin ratio, because that varied over time, and from the style of the designs, I'm going to say that this little pendant dates from between the mid-ninth century to the late eleventh." He paused before adding, "A.D. of course."

Peter looked up from the microscope. "Are you serious?"

"One hundred percent serious."

"But how is that possible? Was old man Thorkelson a careless collector?"

Grim smiled and adjusted his glasses. "I have some theories, but a good scientist doesn't speculate out loud without more data."

"A man after my own heart." Peter laughed. "But how cool is this?"

"Very cool."

Grim measured and photographed the pendant before giving it back to Peter, who gingerly slid it into his inside jacket pocket, which he then fully zipped up.

CHAPTER
Five

Peter's phone rang on the walk back to the truck.

"Hi, where are you now?" It was Laura.

"Just leaving Sturluson's office."

"What did he say?"

"Believe it or not, he thinks the pendant is really old, probably from the Viking age!"

"Seriously? Wow. Maybe a Thorkelson family heirloom . . . but what a weird place to lose it. Anyway, I called about Rose." Laura had a quaver in her voice when she mentioned Rose. His wife was normally one of the most unflappable people Peter knew, so this immediately got his attention.

"Hang on a sec." Peter was climbing back into his truck and shifted the phone from one hand to the other as he did so. "Rose Baldwin?" Rose was a sheep farmer and good friend of Laura's who supplied Laura with a lot of the wool she used in her knitting business.

"Yes. Patrick's been killed."

It took Peter a second to remember that Patrick was one of Rose Baldwin's rams. "Oh no. Coyotes again?"

Margaret and Emily, two of her yearling lambs, had been missing since late March and were presumed to have been taken by coyotes.

"No. That's why I called. Rose says it looks like his throat was cut. She's beside herself, she's so upset. Can you stop by on your way back to the clinic?"

"OK. It probably just got sliced on a wire or sharp branch. I should have enough time. By the way, I'm supposed to stop at the RCMP station after work. Kevin wants to see the Mjölnir."

"Yes, I told him about it. He said he was going to call you. Something about an investigation, but he was very vague about it."

"Maybe the Mjölnir is stolen. It might be quite valuable if it's as old as Grim says it is." Peter didn't like to talk while driving, so he was still in the university parking lot. "But I've got to go if I'm going to have time to look at Patrick."

"See you later tonight. Don't forget I've got a Craft Guild meeting, so I'm eating early and will be gone by the time you get home."

"Right, OK. Have fun. Bye."

The Baldwin farm was on the way back to New Selfoss, just off Highway 59, south of town, so it wasn't a detour. Peter put on his favourite Bach cello concertos and looked forward to the drive back up Main Street and then out of the city into the freshly greening April countryside.

Rose must have been watching for him because she greeted him outside as he pulled up. She was an older woman with a grey ponytail and a weathered but pleasant and friendly looking face. She wore an oversized green sweater. A row of small dragons was subtly picked out in the texture. To the practised eye it was obviously Laura's handiwork. Rose reached out to shake Peter's hand. She had been crying but was forcing a smile now.

"Thank you for coming, Peter. Laura told me you think it could have been a wire or branch. I hope you're right."

"Those were just guesses with minimal information, but I hope I'm right too."

"He's out in the far paddock. I left him where I found him." Rose turned around and opened a gate in the fence. She pointed to the northeast corner of the field against an aspen bluff. "Can you go yourself, Peter? I don't want to see him like that again."

"Of course. I understand."

Peter pulled on his rubber boots as he knew the field would be very muddy. There were still patches of old grey snow on the north sides of buildings and in dense clumps of trees, but everywhere else the strengthening April sun had melted it away. Sometimes this happened in a matter of days. And sometimes the big melt would be followed by one final blizzard when winter felt the need to have the last word. In 1997 almost half a metre of snow fell in a monster April storm, leading directly to the "Flood of the Century" in the Red River Valley. This year, the long-range forecasts were for nothing but warmth and sun, but weather forecasting for anything further than 48 hours ahead seemed to Peter to be little more than a dart-throwing exercise.

He zig-zagged across the field, avoiding the larger puddles and the obvious quagmires. He aimed for the dense bunches of grass, which were usually safe to step on. When he reached the far end there was another gate leading into the paddock where he expected to find Patrick. Rose obviously kept the sheep here because it was slightly higher and better drained. There was no more than a faint green fuzz of fresh grass, but there were several hay cribs, a water trough, and a three-sided shelter facing away from the prevailing northwest wind. Peter saw Patrick right away. The rest of the flock was in another paddock to the far west of Rose's property, looking like so many cotton balls flung across the field. Patrick was near the fence, beside the aspens. The gash on his neck was obvious from a distance, a dark red smear against the ivory white of his recently shorn coat. Peter strode over to the body and bent down to inspect the wound. It was deep, clean, straight, and smooth.

The word that immediately came to his mind was "surgical."

How odd.

He looked over the rest of the body. The penis had been cut off and the scrotum had also been cut open and the testicles removed. This was less bloody than the neck, so it wasn't obvious unless you lifted his hind leg and looked.

Peter sucked his breath in sharply and took a step backwards. This wasn't merely odd. It was insane.

Then he noticed something else. Though there was some blood staining in the fur and on the ground, it was not nearly as much as he would have expected given the fact that the jugular and carotid had been severed.

Peter pursed his lips while he patted Patrick's head absent-mindedly. This was definitely not an accident or a weird predator attack. A person did this. But how? And why? The when was clearer. According to Rose this would have happened overnight. That made sense. Patrick was just starting to stiffen up from rigor mortis. The process was a little slower in sheep than in humans, and the cool weather overnight and in the morning would have delayed it as well.

Peter's eyes drifted to the aspen bluff. The fence was a simple three-string barbed wire affair. It would not have represented a barrier to the sheep killer. He wasn't sure how big the aspen bluff was or what was behind it. He thought it was probably just Crown Land and couldn't think of any nearby roads in that direction. Perhaps the perpetrator came across the big field from the main road? It wouldn't be hard to do in the middle of the night. Sheep don't make enough noise to wake anyone up.

Peter was about to leave Patrick's body when a thought occurred to him. He rummaged in his jacket pocket for his Swiss Army knife.

It would be a good idea to take a small sample of skin, he thought. *Who knows, perhaps scent training Pippin to it might prove to be useful?*

As Peter crossed the field again, he kept a careful watch for footprints in the mud. Unfortunately, it was far too churned up from the sheep having been moved through in the morning for any other impressions to be visible.

Rose was waiting for Peter when he returned. Her face was tight with anxiety.

"I'm sorry, Rose, but I'm afraid your first instinct was correct."

Rose nodded and wiped her face with the sleeve of her sweater. "But why?" she asked quietly.

"I don't know. I really don't know. Have you called the police yet?"

"I'll call them right now. I wanted to wait for you to confirm that it was a deliberate killing by a human."

"Sadly, yes." Peter paused while gathering his courage to tell her about the other injuries too. He briefly considered not telling her as it would serve no purpose and would just upset her more, but he felt he was duty bound to. "Look, Rose," he went on, "Patrick was castrated too, and it looks like they drained and collected most of his blood."

"Oh my god!" She clamped her hand over mouth. Patch looked up at her. "You mean, they cut his testicles off and took them?"

"His penis too," he said quietly.

"Who would do such a thing? And his blood, that's just . . ." Rose began to sob. Patch, her sheepdog, looked concerned.

Peter just shook his head and looked down at his feet. There was nothing he could say that would be helpful. He wondered whether a hug was called for, but he was not a hugger and he was always terrified of misreading the situation. Human emotion was not something he excelled in understanding.

Rose wiped her face again with her sleeve. "Could it be like those cattle mutilator type people we used to hear about?"

"Maybe. Most of those were urban legends, or, should I say, rural legends, that ended up having reasonable explanations. Also, it's never been reported around here, but I guess we have to consider the possibility."

"Crazy people. There's crazy, sick people everywhere." Rose shook her head.

Peter considered Patch for moment. The black and white border collie–cross was intent on his master and was right up against her leg, staring up at her.

"Was Patch out with the flock last night?"

"Yes, but Patrick was separate. He's only with the ewes during breeding season. Coyotes generally won't go after a big ram, so I wasn't worried about that."

"But it's interesting that Patch didn't alert you to anything, even from the other paddock."

"I suppose it is." Rose blew her nose and reached down to pat the dog. "I guess that means that the killer or mutilator or whatever we want to call the bastard was very quiet."

"And knew what he was doing," Peter added, almost more to himself.

"That's a scary thought — someone slinking unheard and unseen across my property at night to do that horrible thing to Patrick. What if they come back?" Rose hugged her arms around herself. "I should let you go, Peter. Do you need Patrick's body for any tests or anything? Do you think the police will?"

"I don't. The cause of death is all too clear. The police will probably want to come out and see the body and the scene, but I doubt they'll need anything else. You can call Doug after they've gone." Doug had a small Bobcat excavator. He helped with most of the large animal burials in the district. Usually it was horses, as other farm animals could be sent for rendering, but special sheep, cattle, and pigs were given this more dignified end as well. And Patrick was special.

CHAPTER
Six

Peter only had three appointments at the clinic after his stop at Rose's, and all of them were routine, so he was finished on time. This was a rarity in the busy season, but that was just getting started. On the dog side of things, April was usually pretty busy, but May and June were the peak months because of heartworm and ticks. The preventatives for both of those needed to be started in the spring, so in the spirit of one-stop-shopping, people usually arranged to have all their dog's annual health needs taken care of then.

The RCMP station wasn't far away, so he was there shortly after six. The desk sergeant recognized Peter and waved him on through to Kevin's office. As always, the sight of the disorder on Kevin's desk gave Peter an inward shudder. It was impossible to imagine any constructive work getting done in here, but, by all accounts, his brother-in-law was a highly respected officer. *He must have some sort of weird, complex filing system*, Peter thought.

Kevin stood up to greet him. He looked like a latter-day Viking in a Mountie uniform. His happiest day on the force was when they finally permitted him to grow out his facial hair. The lavish red beard, full head of red hair, and large beer-keg-shaped torso never failed to make an impression. Kevin's loud, deep voice and crushing handshake confirmed that impression. You didn't mess with this guy. Laura shared her brother's red hair, but otherwise they were opposites in most respects.

"Sit down, Pete!" Kevin gestured to a plastic chair piled with papers. "Just sweep that shit off. Don't worry about it." Weird, complex filing system indeed.

Peter gingerly picked up the papers and set them down on a bare patch of floor beside the chair. "Busy day?"

"Nah, not really. It sounds like you've had one though. U of M, Baldwin farm, work —"

Peter cut him off. "You know about Rose's situation?"

"Yeah, she called a few minutes ago. Said his balls and dick were cut off. Is that right?"

Peter would bet the Mjölnir that those weren't Rose's words for the situation. "That's right, unfortunately. And most of the blood was drained. Very strange."

"Christ. The cutting up of animals being your department, have you got any theories?"

"None, really, other than a mentally ill person I guess, though it's a bit too precise and surgical for that. I'd have to wonder if someone is trying to scare Rose. A graphic warning. But that sort of thing is *your* department." Peter doffed an invisible cap to his brother-in-law.

Kevin smiled. "I'll head out there after we're done. Ask her whether she has any enemies, etcetera. She and her ex don't get along, right?"

"I'm not sure. I could ask Laura."

Kevin grunted and shrugged. "Long shot. We're not in *The Godfather* here. Anyway, I feel bad for Rose, but at the end of the day it's just a sheep."

"Don't animal mutilators often eventually graduate to people?"

"I suppose you've got a point there, Pete. But anyway, I didn't ask you to come down here to talk about wackos with sheep dick fetishes. Can I see the . . . the whatever it is that you found?"

Peter nodded and pulled out the still-wrapped pendant. He was going to set it on Kevin's desk, but nowhere looked safe, let alone clean. He stood up and reached across the desk to hand it directly to Kevin.

"Impressive, eh?" he said when he sat back down and Kevin had unwrapped it.

"If you say so. Kind of small and kind of weird. Laura said it's a Thor's hammer? Like a Norse religious symbol or good luck charm or something like that?"

"Yes, and Dr. Sturluson confirmed it. He even thinks that it's an original from the Viking age, not a replica."

"Seriously?" Kevin turned the Mjölnir over several times in his large, meaty hands. He looked skeptical. He handed it back to Peter and then reached into a desk drawer to pull out a coil-bound notebook. He looked at his desk, apparently trying to find a clear spot to set the notebook down, and then shrugged and pushed back from the desk so that he could write on his lap. "Tell me in detail where, when, and how you found this."

For the second time that day, Peter laid out the whole story, starting from Dan Favel's call about Big Bird. When he finished, he asked, "Are you going to give me any hints as to why you're interested in this?"

Kevin tossed his notebook onto one of the piles on his desk, sat back, folded his arms behind his head and regarded Peter for a moment. "Maybe. Are you going to promise me not to find some reason to get involved?"

"There would be no reason. I hardly know the Thorkelsons and haven't talked to Jim Junior in over 20 years, and even then I didn't know him that well. So yes, that's an easy promise." Peter smiled to himself. He knew that Kevin would eventually tell him. He always did. But his promise was real. He couldn't imagine what they'd be investigating there that would interest him.

"OK, it's not a big deal anyway. You know the Dukovskys up Humboldt Road?"

"Sure. Old couple. They've got a Shih Tzu or Lhasa Apso or something like that that I see from time to time."

"Yeah, them. So, they've been making complaints about unusual activity on the old Thorkelson property, which is just behind them up there."

"Unusual activity?"

"Strange lights, strange noises. That kind of thing."

"But the Favels haven't reported that too, have they?"

"No, but this would be up on the west side of the property, much closer to the Dukovskys' than the Favels'. But Kristine knows them and says the old couple are a pair of cranks." Kevin paused. "And then they called about finding a mutilated deer in the yard."

"A mutilated deer?" Peter sat up straight and leaned forward. *Maybe this is interesting after all*, he thought.

"Yeah. Weird, eh?"

"Mutilated in what way?"

"Don't know, but it was a false alarm anyway. Kristine checked it out and said that it had been hit by a car and had obviously just staggered into their yard. People burn up Humboldt pretty fast sometimes."

Peter sat back again. "So why are you bothering? Slow day at the cop shop?"

"Ha, hardly. No, but Dukovskys' son-in-law is the local MP."

"Didn't know that. Blaine Tanner's in-laws?"

"Yeah, and he's the justice critic in Ottawa. There's no pressure filtering through to me, but, you know, it doesn't hurt to take it seriously either."

"But little Viking hammers are probably not related."

"Nope. Probably not. The noise is it's likely kids having bush parties. Kristine says there's a clearing in there that looks like it might have been used for that."

"What if the little Viking hammer were valuable? Would that change the bush party theory?"

"Probably not." Kevin looked down at the Mjölnir, which was still in Peter's hands. "That aside, do you know how valuable?"

"No idea. I'll talk to Dan Favel and see what he thinks we should do. He gave it to me, but after what Grim said I don't feel right keeping it, especially if it is worth a lot."

Kevin sat up straight, adjusted his collar, cleared his throat, and adopted a mock-serious tone. "You know, Pete, technically if it's an archeological find it belongs to the Crown. You can keep it in perpetuity in trust, but you can't sell it."

Peter chuckled. "But how do you define an archeological find? There's no way Vikings were here, so this came from somewhere else much more recently."

Kevin slouched again and scratched his beard. "You got me there. That's a government lawyer question, not a cop question. But anyway, I gotta go. I was supposed to be off at six, and I'm meeting someone at seven."

"Meeting someone? Like a Grindr date?"

"Nah, I don't use Grindr anymore. Stuart's a friend of a friend."

"An old-fashioned blind date!"

"You bet. Hopefully I'll have better luck this way."

"Where's he from?"

"Gimli, but we're meeting at Kenzo's."

"A Veni!" Venis were West New Icelanders (Vestur Nyr Islendingur), in other words Icelanders who settled on the west side of Lake Winnipeg, whereas Aunis (Austur Nyr Islendingur) split away and founded a new colony on the east side of the lake. The terminology was a little confusing, because both groups were for a time referred to as West Icelanders by the actual Icelanders, who called themselves East Icelanders when speaking to a West Icelander. The rivalry between Venis and Aunis had once been quite bitter and intense, especially during the "Pickerel Fishing War" of 1922, when opposing groups of fishermen sabotaged each other's nets and hurled curses and cow dung at each other across the water, but now it was mostly good-natured, with junior hockey and darts leagues being the notable exceptions.

"No, he's Nigerian originally. But he says he identifies with the Venis." They both laughed.

"Tall?" Peter grinned.

"Of course. And dark and handsome, obviously." Kevin grinned back. His taste in men was an ongoing source of teasing.

"Good luck!"

CHAPTER
Seven

With Laura out of the house for her meeting, Peter decided to pour his tea into a thermos and take Pippin up to Snaefell before sunset. He wasn't that hungry, so he could eat later. This part of Manitoba was otherwise very flat, so the gentle Snaefell hills were an important geographic feature. As they marked the western edge of the East New Iceland colony, they were originally named Snæfellsjökull after the volcano at the western extremity of Iceland, but the name was too difficult for non-Icelanders to pronounce, so it was officially shortened to Snaefell. Snaefell means "snow *mountain*," but nobody was bothered by the exaggeration of what barely qualified as a hill. After all, the Venis had named a pancake-flat island after mighty mount Hecla!

Pippin was overjoyed. A midweek outing was a rarity. Normally they would just walk around the neighbourhood after supper, rather than get in the truck and go somewhere. Occasionally they would go to the Jarvinen Forest, or on a section of the New Selfoss Heritage Trail, but Snaefell was a special treat. It occurred to Peter that they hadn't been up here since the horrible events on the frozen lake during the winter. Pippin had saved his life then, so the spectacular view of the lake from Snaefell should be a positive thing, a celebration of their bond. But Peter realized that he had been avoiding looking out over the lake again, where he might see the location of that ice fishing hut. He wasn't always as logical as he aspired to be, and he couldn't shake a vague sense of dread.

The parking lot was empty. It was after ski season and before mountain biking season, so the trails were usually quiet. Only a few people appreciated what Peter loved about this area at this time of year. These hills were formed from giant sand dunes that had been at the edge of the ancient glacial Lake Agassiz. This meant that the soil drained much faster than the muddy lowlands, so it was always one of the first places where it was pleasant and dry to walk. But the real attraction was that it was still winter out on the lake until early May. Consequently, you could walk up through the warm springtime woods to the viewpoint and then look out over a frozen expanse to the far horizon. Peter normally loved strong contrasts like that. Sometimes in the summer you'd be treated to a view of a spectacular thunderstorm out over the lake, lightning forking down, a grey wall of rain slicing the lake in half. Or in the fall you could see winter approaching as snow squalls raced across the water toward you out of the north.

Peter sat on the bench at the viewpoint. The ice on the lake was taking on a greyish hue in patches as it began to soften. To his relief, seeing it didn't provoke any unwanted feelings. It was just a frozen lake where his dog had saved his life. Simple facts.

He smiled and gave Pippin a liver treat, and he opened his thermos of tea. It was a decaffeinated Earl Grey. Something about the oil of bergamot said "spring" to Peter. A chickadee landed on the closest branch and looked at Peter. Peter supposed that people often fed them here, but he had nothing to offer the bird. Only tea and liver. The sun was low in the west, and there was no wind. It was perfect. As he sat, he began to turn over the events of the day in his mind. He had learned three unusual things. First, the pendant Big Bird had eaten was likely a Viking artefact. Second, Rose Baldwin's ram's genitals had been cut off. And third, the Dukovskys had been hearing noises and seeing lights in the forest near where the Mjölnir was found. They had also reported a mutilated deer, which would make this even more unusual and added another thread binding these events, but it had been determined to be a simple accident. It was a good example of how what appear to be patterns can be misleading.

"Poisson clumping?" Peter asked Pippin. Pippin continued to look straight ahead. He had learned to distinguish when Peter was actually talking to him versus when he was really just talking to himself aloud but directing it at Pippin.

"Three unrelated events clump together, making the foolish human brain want to look for a pattern. That brain always confuses correlation with causation. Unrelated events are just as likely to clump together as they are to spread out from each other. Because they're unrelated there's no way for one event to attract or repel another event. No causation. That's Poisson clumping. Just look at the old leaves on the ground. Not evenly spread out. That's for lots of reasons, but it doesn't mean that one leaf caused the next one to fall beside it. When there's no clumping, when the events are evenly distributed, that's when you should look for a relationship. Imagine all these leaves perfectly spaced! That's when you should sit up and take notice. Right, Pippin?"

Pippin raised his eyebrows slightly at the mention of his name, but Peter's tone was still that of a man having a conversation with himself, rather than with his dog.

"And why do I include Patrick's death and castration in this clump and not, say, Mr. Meow's bladder infection or poor Duke's euthanasia today? The connection between the Mjölnir and Dukovskys is clear as both relate to that piece of land, but what about Patrick? Well, it occurred to me that some Icelanders eat both ram's testicles and penises."

Pippin raised his eyebrows again but kept looking resolutely ahead.

"I bet I could even calculate the odds of this being a Poisson clump versus . . ." Peter trailed off because Pippin had stood up and raised his tail. He was looking down the path that led back to the parking lot. "What do you see, boy?"

Pippin let out a soft woof, which was his noncommittal sound — neither positive nor negative, just alert.

Then Peter saw what Pippin had seen, a tall figure in a dark green coat moving toward them. The figure stepped into a shaft of low slanting sunlight in a gap in the trees. It was Ken Finnbogason.

"Hi Peter! And Pippin!" Ken called as he approached. "Lovely evening, eh?"

"Yes, it is! I didn't expect to see you up here." Peter stood up and took a couple steps forward to shake Ken's hand. Ken was always easy to recognize from a distance because of his bushy black soup-strainer moustache. He was otherwise mostly bald. Unlike their mutual friend Chris Olson, who was proud of his baldness and kept his head polished to a shine, Ken always wore a hat, indoors or outdoors. Today, despite the warmth, he wore a black wool watch cap with a grey lightning bolt stitched on it.

"I haven't been in some time, but Eva says I need more exercise, so I'm making a project of trying all the trails in the area this year."

"Good plan. But the sun's going to be down soon." Peter inclined his head toward the lake, which was glowing pearly white in the early evening sun. In half an hour or so it would tinge pink and then gradually darken to navy. Dusk was long and slow at this latitude, so there was little danger of getting caught in the dark in the woods, but it was late to be starting a long walk.

"Yeah, I'm only doing three k to start with. God, Eva's right, it's only been one k since the parking lot, and I feel like I need to sit down. Mind?"

"No, please go ahead." Peter motioned to the bench but remained standing. "Pippin and I have got to get going anyway. I haven't had dinner yet."

"Thanks. I guess I'll see you Saturday at the Beaver, birthday boy!" Peter's birthday was coming up, and Laura had arranged a party at the local pub, The Flying Beaver. Peter didn't have very many friends, so even acquaintances and friends of friends had been invited.

"You bet!"

Ken reached out to pat Pippin. As he did so his jacket sleeve rode up, exposing a very small tattoo on the side of his left lower arm. It looked like three snakes spooning. The top ends were similar to the dragon heads on Viking longboats, and the bodies of these snakes, or dragons, or even what could be a triple "S" he supposed, had intricate criss-crossing designs in them. Ken pulled his sleeve down before Peter could make out any more details. He wanted to ask Ken about the tattoo but felt awkward about it. He didn't know Ken all that well, and it somehow seemed like too personal a question. Peter was never too sure about these social norms and had been burned a few times before by misjudging them, like the time he asked Alice Richter what surgery she was getting. He thought it was an expression of polite concern when she mentioned that she had to postpone the dental procedure for her chihuahua, Mr. Miller, because her own surgery had been rescheduled to the same day. She looked him dead in the eye, smiled, and said, "Breast enhancement."

They said goodbye to each other and as Peter and Pippin started down the path Ken called after them, "By the way, Chris and I are going to gang up on you on Saturday and get you to join the Pointsmen! Fair warning!"

The New Selfoss Pointsmen was the local darts team. Its membership had been cut in half by the events of the previous winter. Peter hated group activities, especially if there was a hint of sports or competition about them, but he knew it was best to wave a cheery "OK!" back at Ken. He could think of excuses not to join later.

On the drive back home, Peter thought about Ken's tattoo. It definitely looked Norse. That made it a Poisson clump of four unrelated events. Probably unrelated.

CHAPTER
Eight

Peter loved his birthday. Although he was at an age where many people stopped truly celebrating, or perhaps only marked decade milestones, Peter looked forward to every birthday with the glee of a child. It wasn't the gifts, although he did look forward to those, it was the fact that it was a special day demarcated by traditions that no other day of the year shared. He hated the fact that modern society had flattened the calendar, making all days more or less the same. You could eat mandarin oranges in July. You could buy Halloween candy in February. You could watch Saturday morning cartoons on Tuesday afternoon. And you could shop for underwear on Sunday (even though Peter was an agnostic, he thought that Sunday should be different than Saturday or the weekdays).

The specialness of his birthday began right after he woke up. Peter was an early riser, usually at six, but sometimes as early as five thirty. In April it was still dark then. Peter prided himself on having good night vision, so he padded out of the bedroom, Pippin at his heels, and into the kitchen without turning on any lights. Today he was going to treat himself to a double espresso! Normally he had tea, most often an Irish breakfast blend, first thing in the morning. He might sometimes feel like an espresso, but the force of the tea habit was strong. Moreover, the espresso machine was loud, and he didn't want to disturb Laura. But today was his birthday. Laura wouldn't mind.

After he made the espresso and fed Pippin his breakfast, he made his way over to the armchair that faced the large windows on the east side of the house. They lived at the northeastern edge of New Selfoss and the windows looked out across the yard to a forest. They were on a slight rise, so the distant horizon was visible beyond the trees. Manitoba was generally a sunny place, and sunrise was an event worth making time for, but as no stars were visible, Peter assumed it was overcast. The sunrise would be a matter of "the lighter grey breaking through the darker one," as John K. Samson so evocatively put it. He patted Pippin absentmindedly as he stared out into the dark, making out the sawtooth line defining the top of the forest.

A darker black against the lighter one, he thought, and smiled to himself.

"Forty-two," he said to Pippin, shaking his head. "Hard to believe, eh?"

Pippin looked up at him.

"That makes me 14 times as old as you!"

Peter finished his double espresso and was weighing the pros and cons of having a second one when he heard Laura enter the room.

"Happy birthday!" she said as she hugged him from behind and kissed him on the top of his head. "I see you're done your espresso. Are you ready for your present yet?"

"Thanks! You didn't have to get up so early. I could have had a second espresso."

"Oh, it's fine. I was awake anyway and I know you'd regret it if you had two double espressos!"

"You're right. I probably hit my caffeine quota three-quarters of the way through the first one."

"Well, turn around. Your present is on the coffee table!"

In fact, the present covered the entire coffee table. It was a long package, wrapped in repurposed newspaper comic strips and tied with a big blue bow.

"Wow, it's a big one this year!" Peter got out of the chair and walked over to the package. He picked it up and shook it slightly. "I've got no idea what it is," he declared, grinning with the pleasure of anticipation for a big surprise.

"And I had no idea what to get you this year. I was getting desperate, and then it came to me in a flash on Thursday. It's a bit of a risk. I hope you like it." Laura sat down on the couch and pulled her housecoat tighter around herself. She looked a little anxious as Peter unwrapped the gift.

"Hmm, whatever it is, it's apparently called a Fisher F22," he said as a label was unveiled at one end of the box. "Still no idea! Fishing rod?"

Laura shook her head vigorously, biting her lower lip. Merry jumped onto her lap and began to purr loudly.

After the remaining paper came off Peter stared at the box for a second and then shouted, "It's a metal detector! You got me a metal detector!"

He had the face of a child at the carnival. Pure unselfconscious joy.

"So, you like it? I got the idea after you seemed so excited by that Mjölnir. I know there might not be anything more like that out there, but there are probably all kinds of other cool artefacts around New Selfoss."

"I love it! Thank you! This must have been expensive. Where did you get it?"

"It wasn't too bad. It's an entry level model. You can trade up if you really enjoy the hobby. I got it at a place called Basement Boyz in the city."

"Basement Boyzzz? With a zed?"

"Yeah, with a zed." Laura rolled her eyes. She hated deliberate misspellings as much as Peter did. "I hadn't heard of it either until I found it on a search. It's a new hobby store just off Main. They have all kinds of fun gadgets. And do you know who runs it?"

Peter shook his head as he worked on opening the box.

"Dwayne Lautermilch!"

Peter looked up. "Lautermilch? *The* Dwayne Lautermilch? You're kidding me."

"I'm serious. He seems really nice now though."

Peter snorted. His high school years were plagued by bullying, and the chief bully was Dwayne Lautermilch. Peter was shocked that he was not either dead or in prison. He was pretty sure Darryl Faucher was doing time in Stony, and he had heard that Darren Brodsky overdosed in Vancouver years ago. He just assumed something similar had happened to Dwayne. They were the "D-Krew" back in the day.

"I know, I know," Laura went on. "But seriously, I barely recognized him. He still has the rock and roll mullet, but it's mostly grey, and he sounds softer and quieter."

"Remember his ridiculous laugh? Like a walrus in labour?"

"Ha, yeah, but no, he didn't do that yesterday. He was very polite, and he asked a lot of questions about you. Said that he always knew you were going to be a success."

Peter snorted again. "Well, be that as it may, I'm glad I'm not the one that had to run into him like that."

Laura looked at the floor for a moment and then looked back up at Peter. "Please don't be mad," she said in a soft voice. "The metal detector comes with a free how-to lesson. Dwayne is coming tomorrow at ten."

Peter stared at her, his brain going in several directions at once. Fortunately, the winning direction was the one that realized that high school was an extremely long time ago and that since Peter himself had changed, why not Dwayne — shudder — Lautermilch.

"That's OK, thanks. I was joking. It'll be fun to see how much Dwayne has changed." He hadn't been joking, but Laura didn't need to know that, although he suspected she probably did anyway. Really, what had she been thinking? First of all, free or not, why would he need a lesson? How complicated could it possibly be? And second, Dwayne Lautermilch . . . *Dwayne "let's see if you fit in this locker, Petey-boy" Lautermilch*! She should know better. But there was no point in making her feel bad, and he didn't want to start an argument on his birthday. But still . . .

After Peter's favourite breakfast of Laura's fresh-baked buns with black currant jam and Seville orange marmalade, plus one soft boiled egg and one half of a large pink grapefruit, Peter was ready for the next fun part of his birthday, a long walk with Pippin. Now, to be sure, a long walk with Pippin was not particularly special as that happened most days, but on his birthday, he made a point of finding a new place to walk. Peter admired the explorers of old and often lamented the dearth of true opportunities to explore in the modern world (neither the deep sea nor outer space appealed to him). By this point he had exhausted all the trails in East New Iceland many times over. To compensate he developed a concept he called "micro-geography," wherein exploration was focused on the smaller details along the laneways, alleys, and small roads in his immediate area. This way he came to notice particular trees, gardens, mailboxes, or birdhouses that he had just zipped by before. And there were enough permutations of routes he could take that he was able to devise something new each year for his birthday. Pippin seemed to prefer this as the concentration of interesting smells was higher in the neighbour-hood than out in the woods.

Peter was getting his coat on when he felt his phone vibrate. He resisted the temptation to look at it. Personal callers, such as well-wishers for his birthday, had a different vibration pattern assigned to them. This was the vibration pattern associated with clients. This was odd as the system shouldn't be forwarding to his cell today as he was not on call. He shared on-call duty with Sheila Thiessen in Lac du Bonnet and made sure that the rotation put her on for his birthday. He put it out of his mind for the moment while he looked forward to the next part of his birthday after the walk — driving to McNally Robinson Booksellers in the city. He would allow himself the luxury of unlimited guilt-free browsing and then buy himself two books, one fiction and one non-fiction. He didn't plan either purchase in advance. He would leave himself open to pure serendipity. This departure from his carefully plotted norm felt transgressive and made him a little giddy with excitement. Birthdays were special.

But, try as he might, he couldn't resist looking at his phone. Dan Favel had called. Peter had given him his direct personal number even though Sheila had been on call the night of the surgery because he was nervous about Big Bird's recovery. What could happen this long after? Did the incision open up? Shit. Peter stared at his phone for several seconds and then, with a heavy sigh, tapped the green call icon. Pippin looked up at him, clearly wondering what the hold-up was.

"Hi, Dan? You called just now? Is Big Bird OK?"

"Thanks for calling back, Peter." Dan's voice was strained. "No, Big Bird is fine. It's Misty, our Shetland pony." The Favels had three ponies: Misty, Mandy, and Maple.

Peter was relieved. Whatever was going on he could refer to Sheila. "What's up with her?"

There was a long pause on the other end of the line. Then, choking back sobs, Dan said, "She's dead! And her head, it's . . . I . . . oh god. Something's eaten it or someone's cut it off. Can you come right away?"

Pippin seemed to sense that the walk was off, or at least post-poned, so his tail wag slowed down. But a truck ride was still better than hanging around the house. He jumped in beside his pensive master, and his tail began to wag a little faster again. Peter envied that the dog could be so upbeat.

CHAPTER
Nine

There was no way Peter could say no to Dan, even though it disrupted his birthday plans, and even though it wasn't at all clear how he was going to be of any use given that Misty was dead. Maybe other ponies had been injured? Dan had hung up before Peter could ask if the rest were OK.

Backing out of the drive, Peter considered how terrible this must be for Dan and Kim, let alone what Misty must have gone through. Hopefully he'd be able to find that her death had been quick and painless. But regardless, the decapitation sent a chill through him. Rose's image of someone slinking unseen and unheard across the land at night came to mind. He pictured a dark spectral shape hovering over the pony, similar to a Ringwraith or a Dementor. An absurd image, but he was unable to shake it.

As he came up the rutted gravel road toward the Favels' farm, he saw that an RCMP cruiser was there already. Four people were standing in a clump around a small blue tarp beside the pony pen, which was just past the larger ostrich paddock. The fence around the pony pen looked brand new with three bright strands of wire catching the sun, which had just started to poke through the thinning clouds. The ostriches were confined by a more serious looking six-foot fence. Both fences were electric. All six ostriches, including

Big Bird, were clustered in the corner nearest the people, watching them. The two remaining ponies were similarly intent on what was happening and stood side by side along their fence, opposite the blue tarp. As he stepped out the truck, Peter quickly made out Dan and Kim, his brother-in-law, Kevin, and another RCMP officer, Kristine. Where Kevin was red and wide, Kristine was blond and tall. They made a striking pair — a Viking and an Amazon. Peter had always found Kristine intimidating and wondered whether she had something against him. He was disappointed to see her there.

"Pete!" Kevin bellowed. "Glad you came. Happy birthday, by the way."

"It's your birthday?" Dan asked. His eyes were red-rimmed, and his voice was subdued. "I'm really sorry. I shouldn't have called you, but I didn't know what to do." Kim put her arm around her husband's shoulder. She looked distraught as well. Kristine was taking notes when Peter arrived and hadn't looked up from her notebook yet.

"It's a good thing that you called him, Dan. Pete can help confirm what I think."

"What's that, Kevin?" Peter looked up. He had been staring at the blue tarp, picturing a headless pony under it.

"I'm sure this wasn't a coyote, bear, or wolf attack — the cut's too clean, and a predator would never take just the head." Kevin bent down and pulled back the blue tarp they had been standing around. Misty lay there on a patch of last year's dead yellow grass, headless, but otherwise oddly normal and peaceful looking, as if her head had just been deleted in Photoshop. It was a shocking sight. Despite himself Peter let out a small gasp. It was not only a grisly scene, but there was something strange about it that Peter couldn't immediately put his finger on.

He slowly knelt beside the body. Kevin was right, the cut was clean. There were no other marks anywhere on the body. He looked closer at the severed neck. Then he realized what was strange. There was hardly any blood on the ground.

Peter adjusted his legs into a crouch and looked up at the other four. "Yes, I agree. This was done by a person. There are two cuts. This short one here is where they cut the jugular to kill her. It's smooth and clean. That was with a sharp knife. She wouldn't have suffered." Peter glanced at Dan and Kim when he said that. "The rest of the way around the neck is rougher, maybe done with a saw. But look at this." He waved his hand over the grass under the stump of Misty's neck. "There's almost no blood."

"Jesus," Kevin said just loud enough to hear. Kristine looked up, her brows furrowed.

Kim covered her face and began sobbing behind her hands. "Misty, my poor Misty." Dan hugged her and quietly turned her to face away from the dead pony.

Peter stood up and brushed off his knees. "First Patrick at Rose's place and now Misty. They took other parts from Patrick, but it's hard to believe that it's a coincidence given the proximity in time. What do you think, Kev?"

"I think there's a sick clown out there who's got it in for farm animals."

"But why? What motivation could there be to take the head here and the penis and testicles there? And where did the blood go? That's not just random slashing, but something more deliberate and premeditated."

Dan and Kim listened mutely as Peter and Kevin talked. Kristine put her notebook away and listened too.

"I said 'sick clown,' Pete. Sick clowns don't need reasons."

"But that seems too lazy and easy. How many crackpots who have no reason at all to be mutilating animals can there be in the area?"

"It only takes one."

"You're missing my point, Kev. Even if it is a twisted reason, there is going to be a *reason*. Nobody does something like this on a random whim. They are telling themselves some sort of story, or they're following some sort of plan. If you can figure out that story, that plan, that twisted reason, then you're several steps closer to identifying the crackpot."

Kevin rolled his eyes and was about to respond when Kristine cut him off. "Your brother-in-law is right, Gudmundurson. One mutilation we could shrug off, but two looks like the start of a pattern. Find the pattern, find the perp."

"Yeah, well, with this effing pattern we're looking for someone who's trying to assemble a Franken-sheep-pony one bit at a time," Kevin muttered. Dan and Kim had stepped away to rub Mandy's and Maple's noses, and Peter hoped they didn't hear that.

"Not funny, Gudmundurson," Kristine said, fixing him with a hard stare. Her eyes were a remarkably bright blue, like a desert sky.

"I thought it was," Kevin said quietly as he broke away from her gaze and looked down at his boots. "But yeah, I'll do some checking in the databases for animal mutilators and ask around at slaughterhouses about odd requests."

Despite the horrifying circumstances, Peter was amused by this exchange. He was used to his Norse warrior of a brother-in-law being assertive and domineering, but although they were of equal rank, Kristine clearly called the shots when she needed to. He walked over to where the Favels were and asked, "How are these two doing?"

"OK, it seems," Kim answered. "But do you mind checking them over anyway?"

Peter followed Kim through the gate into the pen. The gate had a wooden sign with a series of alternating black Shetland ponies and red hearts painted on it. He gave Mandy and Maple a brief examination while Kim held them. He declared them to be fine.

"If you don't mind, can I ask you where you found Misty?" he asked when he was done.

"Right where she is lying," Kim said.

"Outside the pen?"

"Yeah, the cops thought that was odd too. Whoever murdered her took the trouble to close the gate behind them as well."

"Maybe it isn't so odd. Maybe it was easier to do that outside the pen with the gate closed away from the other ponies crowding around. They might have made noise regardless though. Did you hear anything?"

"No, nothing, but we're both deep sleepers. And we don't have a dog to warn us about coyotes because these are supposed to be predator-proof fences and ponies and ostriches can usually look after themselves. But Dan and I were talking . . . we're going to get a dog now. Where did you get yours?" She smiled at Pippin, who was sitting quietly and attentively beside Peter.

"He's from the Dragonfly Lake First Nation up north." Peter gave Pippin a scratch behind the ears.

"A rescue?"

"No, he didn't need to be rescued. He would have had a good life with the family who had his mom, but Laura and I had been talking about getting a dog just before I went up there to do a vaccination clinic, so he came along at the right time." Peter laughed, "Actually, it's more like he rescued me."

"Well, he's lovely and he's so well-behaved, so if you know of any more like him, give Dan and me a call!"

"I will, for sure."

Peter and Kim were quiet for a moment, watching the ponies. Dan had gone over to discuss something with Kevin and Kristine, who were preparing to leave.

As Peter continued to scratch Pippin's ears, an idea came to him. "Kim, please tell me if this makes you uncomfortable, but can I take a little bit of Misty's body, just a small piece of fur and skin? Pippin is an excellent scent tracker, so I was thinking that if I could train him to Misty's scent, it might be useful."

"Please, yes, anything. It doesn't bother me, but I don't want you to go to any extra trouble."

"No, it's no trouble at all. Pippin and I really enjoy scent tracking."

After Peter gathered the samples he needed, gave his condolences again, and said his goodbyes, he and Pippin walked back to the truck. Peter considered himself to be hardened and tough, but the thought of someone killing and decapitating that pony made him feel sick. He knew it was unfair and irrational to feel more strongly about a pony, even an ill-tempered one like Misty, than a sheep, but it was automatic. He vowed to give Patrick equal mental and emotional time, but for now it was still his birthday, so he pushed both unfortunate animals out of his mind.

To cheer himself up, he turned to Pippin and said, "So, still up for a walk, boy?" This was a rhetorical question.

CHAPTER
Ten

The stop at the Favels' farm was brief enough that Peter and Pippin were still able to enjoy a pleasant walk, rambling around the little lanes along the northern edge of New Selfoss. This did not take long as it was a small area, even with a detail-oriented micro-geography approach to the walk. But if Peter had been honest with himself, he would have admitted that he had hurried the walk just a little because he was excited to set aside some time for scent training.

At the end of the walk, he swung by the house to pick up the necessary supplies — liverwurst, paper towel, and tape. Laura was out, which was fine as Peter would have felt awkward answering questions about why he was scent training Pippin on Misty's remains. She would wonder why he was going anywhere near a police investigation again. He would say that he was just trying to help his grieving clients, but Laura would be suspicious that his intellectual pride as a problem-solver had been activated again. He wouldn't necessarily have to be specific about Misty, he could just say that he was doing general scent training with Pippin, but that would also be awkward because Laura knew that hadn't been part of his plan. Since his special day had already been shortened as it was by Dan's call this would seem suspicious to her. No, it was better that she was out.

Peter drove to his favourite place to train, which was the old cemetery on the New Selfoss Heritage Trail. There was rarely anybody there, especially on a Saturday, and it was near the Jarvinen Forest, which was ideal for more advanced training. He had no specific idea where this training was going to lead. He couldn't very well walk up and down all the roads and paths in the district in the hope that Pippin would chance upon Misty's scent somewhere, pointing out the location of the missing head or even of the decapitator, or decapitators. But he also knew that sometimes it was useful to take a practical step down a path even when the direction of the rest of the path was unclear. Who knew what data would come along that might clarify the next steps? So long as it wasn't dangerous or unpleasant, why not be ready? And it was certainly neither dangerous nor unpleasant to do nosework on a quiet Saturday morning. In fact, it was a lot of fun for both Peter and Pippin, and Peter had learned to become very alert to potential dangers since the events of the previous winter. He was more careful now.

Pippin sat perfectly still, watching Peter while he rolled the paper towel into tubes and sealed the ends with tape. One tube had been rubbed on the inside with the chunk of Misty's skin. He let Pippin sniff the tainted tube. Pippin's nose twitched and his nostrils and upper lips flared as he deeply inhaled essence of Misty. As he did this, Peter wondered whether he should have planned to train him on Patrick's scent as well, but it was better to focus on one at a time, and Misty was more of a priority. When this was done, Peter said "Good seek!" and gave Pippin a dime-sized piece of liverwurst. Liverwurst was the brightest star in Pippin's gastronomic heavens. Sometimes when Pippin slept, he made little chewing motions with his mouth and flicked his tongue. Peter was sure he was dreaming of a liverwurst world where he lay in fields of liverwurst and noshed to his heart's deep content all day long. Stomach capacity and tolerance were not issues in this dreamworld. Peter himself was sometimes a lucid dreamer and could become objective about the contents of his dream while still in it, but he reasoned that Pippin, as smart as he was, likely did not have that ability. Moreover, it seemed unlikely that he formed memories based on dreams because he never looked disappointed when he woke up to a decidedly non-liverwurst world.

The cemetery was ideal for nosework because the old headstones leaning this way and that made for good hiding places, and there was always a lot of squirrel and rabbit activity to provide distracting smells. Not that Pippin was ever distracted, but in theory it made for a better test. It went marvellously well. Within twenty minutes they were able to move into the Jarvinen Forest where Peter hid a small piece of scented paper towel partly under a rock while Pippin waited obediently out of sight. Peter took his time walking back and forth and in circles with plenty of stops before and after hiding the target. Pippin began by sniffing in a rough, ever-expanding spiral, but within a few minutes he stopped and walked straight off toward the hiding spot, nose down, tail up. As Peter was out of sight Pippin declared his victory with a short sharp bark. It was liverwurst time.

On the drive back home, Peter spoke aloud to Pippin, as he often did when he was trying to work out something in his mind. "There are several odd things about this situation."

Pippin turned to look at Peter.

"Yes, several. The first is, why would this mutilator not take the whole animal after killing it, rather than taking the time to cut off the head, or penis, on site? He risked the other animals making noise while he was doing his gruesome work. It's not logical. And draining all the blood from Misty would have taken some time too."

Pippin hadn't heard any important words, so he turned back to look at the road. This did not deter Peter.

"The other odd thing is that I can't think of a connection between penises and heads and blood. Usually, mutilators specialize in doing one particular horrible thing. This guy's approach seems random, but what do I say about random, Pippin?"

Pippin looked back at Peter.

"Everything comes from somewhere! Everything has a cause, however obscure and difficult to identify. With enough data and a careful analysis of that data, you can usually find a more satisfying and useful explanation than 'random.'"

Pippin was back to looking out the windshield. A deer was grazing in the ditch. This was much more interesting than whatever Peter was talking about.

"Anyway, it's also good to not think too hard about these things until there is more data. Sometimes the best insights come from the subconscious mind, so we'll just let those questions percolate in the background for now."

Peter's birthday afternoon at McNally Robinson Booksellers in Winnipeg was close to perfect. He quickly found a non-fiction book he wanted to buy — Robert Macfarlane's *Underland* — and was trying to decide between Ann Patchett's *The Dutch House* and Muriel Barbery's *The Elegance of the Hedgehog* for his fiction read when he heard a familiar voice over his right shoulder.

"I've never thought of hedgehogs as particularly elegant, have you?"

Peter turned around. It was Peggy Dinsdale. Peggy was a client with a small hobby farm and, according to Peter's staff, a crush on Peter. She was an attractive brunette who paid a lot of attention to her appearance. The only time Peter could recall seeing her without tastefully done makeup and a flattering outfit was when he had come to perform that late-night c-section on Martha, one of her goats. Mostly he saw her with Emma, her basset hound, though. Sometimes it seemed like she was at the clinic weekly with that dog. Maybe the staff were right.

"Oh, hi, Peggy. Ah no, they're not, but that's why the title caught my eye." Peter hated small talk and hoped that this concluded the exchange.

"I bet a clever editor proposed that. I hope the writer is just as clever!" She flashed a bright toothy smile at him. "But funny running into you here because I left a message for you at the clinic this morning. Nothing urgent."

"Is Emma OK?"

"She's fine. It's Stinky. I found him dead on Friday morning."

"Stinky?"

"My billy goat. He was old. It's sad of course, but I wasn't too surprised. But then when Doug came to collect him Friday night, he noticed something weird."

Peter felt his stomach contract.

Peggy went on, "He said there was a gouge in poor Stinky's neck. He was lying with his right side down and it was on that side, so I didn't see it."

"A gouge?" Peter repeated, his voice slightly shaky.

"Doug figured he fell on something sharp. There are a few old nails here and there on the wall of his pen where I hang ropes and stuff when I'm working in there. I suppose if he was sick and was staggering, he could fall into one. But here's the weird bit."

She paused for Peter's reaction, but he just stared at her, so she went on, "Doug says the gouge went right through Stinky's jugular vein, but there was hardly any blood anywhere. Just a few small patches under where he lay."

"Just a few small patches?" Peter felt his stomach lurch. *Not again*, he thought, *what on Earth is happening in New Selfoss?* He glanced around for a chair.

"Yes. What do you think? Did he have some kind of anemia disease where he had less blood? Or maybe he was just really good at clotting his blood quickly?"

Peter struggled to regain his composure but managed to reply in his calm and detached doctor mode. "Maybe, but I doubt it. The pressure in a big vessel is usually too high to allow clots to form. And with anemia they have less actual blood cells, but just as much liquid in their veins. This doesn't sound like accident or disease."

Now it was Peggy's turn to stare at Peter.

"What kind of security system do you have? Any cameras?"

"What are you saying? That somebody broke in to kill my goat and steal his blood?" Peggy was half laughing as she said this, but the shock and fear was unmistakable in her voice.

"Yes, exactly."

The first thing Peter did when he got home was check on his and Laura's own goat, Gandalf, but the white Saanen goat with his long whiskery beard was perfectly fine, munching on the spring's first dandelion sprouts, looking up with surprise at Peter because he was usually left alone to do his goat things during the day. Peter and Laura spent time with him in the early morning and checked in on him again in the evening, but otherwise he seemed happy to be the goat introvert king of his little domain on the north side of the house. There he had a large fenced meadow to himself, dotted with various "habitat enrichments," such as a large wooden barrel, a battered picnic table, a small shallow pond, and numerous boulders for him to clamber on and thus feel more kingly. He had been found tied to the back of Peter's clinic two years prior. No tags, no note, nothing. Inquiries with the local goat community turned up no clues, nor did several Facebook posts and a small ad in the *New Selfoss Tribune*. So he and Laura decided to keep him and name him Gandalf the White.

Peter scratched Gandalf behind the ears, which the goat loved, longer than he might usually and looked out at the woods that surrounded their property. It was a quiet afternoon. Only a light breeze ruffling the few early leaves made any sound at all.

It was time to get ready for his birthday party, so Peter gave Gandalf one more vigorous scratch, whispered "Stay safe" and went into the house.

CHAPTER
Eleven

I t felt like a dozen small gnomes were mining behind Peter's forehead. At least it wasn't a dozen large trolls hurling boulders. That's what it had felt like the morning after the time Peter and his classmate Ross McLean had finished an entire bottle of 20-year-old Macallan scotch. That must have been 20 years ago. Ross had bought the bottle with his first paycheque. And then, feeling exuberant and carefree, they also killed a half bottle of Johnnie Walker Red Label that Ross had squirreled away in the back of a cupboard. At his birthday party last night, it had only been three pints of Manipogo Pale Ale and two generous drams of Laphroaig 10-year-old. But he still felt it.

He usually restricted himself to two pints maximum, or, if he was having scotch, one whisky and one pint, so his system wasn't used to even mild excess. Peter did the math to distract himself from his hangover. A pint was actually 1.4 standard drink units, so three of those was 4.2 drinks, and the Laphroaig pours were pretty close to doubles, but not quite, so that pushed the night's total to 8 standard units. A half-bottle of Macallan and a quarter of Johnny Red, like that infamous night with Ross, was around 20 standard units. No wonder he had gotten sick all over the futon that night, whereas this time his stomach only felt slightly queasy. He could handle his usual breakfast of muesli, but he hoped Laura wouldn't suggest a

Sunday morning breakfast of cheese omelet in Hollandaise sauce, as she sometimes did. Cheese omelet in Hollandaise sauce. The words themselves were enough to intensify the queasiness.

But it had been worth it, hadn't it? It's not every day one turns 42 after all. Laura had gone all out organizing the party at The Flying Beaver. There must have been two dozen people there. Lloyd, the owner, had allowed Laura to decorate the main room in a *Hitchhiker's Guide to the Galaxy* theme, with the 2005 movie adaptation playing on the big screen TVs, rather than the usual Premier League and Bundesliga. It was widely acknowledged that the BBC radio series was far superior, but nobody would have been able to hear that over the din of the birthday celebrants talking. Peter's friend Chris Olson even came dressed as Zaphod Beeblebrox, with an extra head stuck to his right shoulder. A large Marvin the Paranoid Android, made of cardboard and tinfoil, stood in the centre of the room and was featured in many selfies. Laura had considered paying extra to rent out the whole pub, but in the end thought it would be more fitting to allow the uninitiated to wander in off the street for a pint and wonder what the heck was going on.

A group of three 20-something guys in assorted hoodies and backwards ballcaps had come in and one of them asked, "Hey, what's the big deal with 42?" A large red and white bath towel hung above the bar with "Happy 42, Peter!" stitched on it.

Peter happened to be standing there, chatting with Lloyd. "You don't know? It's the answer to life, the universe and everything!"

The young man cautiously said, "Uh huh . . ."

Peter went on to explain that in *The Hitchhiker's Guide to the Galaxy*, the hilarious revelation was that "42" represented all meaning — the answer to the ultimate question of life, the universe, and everything — and this was especially hilarious after everything the hero went through to find this answer. It's postmodern humour, he explained. Peter couldn't remember clearly, but he thinks they went on to stay a while and watch some of the movie. But maybe they didn't. It was all a bit hazy.

Also, emboldened by the beer and scotch, he had asked Ken Finnbogason about that odd snake tattoo. At least, he was sure he had, but he couldn't remember the answer. Or maybe he hadn't asked at all and only formulated the question in his head. Hazy again. Much too hazy.

In fact, this was the worst thing about the hangover. Normally Peter's thoughts were like bricks — solid, defined shape, stackable, one set on top of the next until a useful structure emerged. Today his thoughts were like vapour — interesting, but amorphous and ephemeral, gone before he could commit the shape to memory. This was especially bad because one of the tendrils of vapour had started to assume a shape somehow related to the animal mutilations and bloodletting, but he had made the mistake of reaching for it quickly and it vanished, poof, like in a magic trick. He knew if he were patient it would come back, hopefully next time in the form of a brick. Taking a long walk around the Favels' new property, where the Mjölnir had been found, with Pippin and the metal detector would help a lot. Walking and fresh air always helped a lot.

Then he remembered that Dwayne Lautermilch was supposed to come along to give him that free lesson. It was originally planned for an hour around the house, but then in his happy birthday mood last night he had agreed to Laura's suggestion that Dwayne just come along to the Favels'. Dwayne had told her that he was free all morning, so it made perfect sense to her. She had even phoned Dan on his behalf to make sure that it was OK that Dwayne came onto their property as well. Ugh. Making small talk with his high school arch-nemesis was not going to help his hangover.

At breakfast (muesli all round, not a drop of Hollandaise sauce in sight, thank goodness) Laura asked him how he was feeling. She was visibly trying to suppress a smile as she did so.

"Oh, fine. Touch of a headache, but fine all things considered."

"Not like that night with Ross then." She was no longer trying to suppress her smile.

"Nope. That will never happen again. Never. But changing the subject, I don't think I mentioned that I ran into Peggy Dinsdale at the bookstore yesterday."

Laura's smile evaporated. She arched her eyebrows. She was well aware of the rumours. "No, you didn't mention that. So" — she paused and forced a smile back on her face — "what's new with her?"

"It's crazy, but it sounds like her billy goat was killed right in the barn and had all his blood drained out."

"What? That's nuts, and creepy. Like you said happened to that poor pony?"

"Similar, but they didn't take Stinky's head off. That was his name — Stinky."

"And then Rose's ram a few days ago. What's going on? Does Kevin know about the goat?"

"I told Peggy to call him. She had assumed it was some weird old goat disease, so hadn't thought to call."

"The blood missing disease?" Laura harrumphed.

"She didn't know that he had bled out. There was no blood to see and just this wound that Doug found when he came to pick Stinky up."

Laura gave Peter the "these people are idiots" look.

"But anyway, the point is that there is a clear pattern now. Each one — Patrick, Misty, and Stinky — has been different in the details, but it's still a pattern."

"Of craziness."

"Yes, of craziness, but what kind of craziness? It's horrible, of course, but it's so strange and unexpected that it's interesting too. People are going to be more careful with their animals as word gets out, but you can't guard all of them all night long, so there's a danger until this gets resolved."

Laura had been about to take a sip of coffee, but she set her cup down and sighed, "Don't get any ideas about getting involved, Peter, please. This has obviously become a police matter."

"Like I said, I told Peggy to call Kevin. But they were my patients, so I'm already involved."

"Just don't go trying to track down an animal mutilator." She said this quietly, but then brightened her voice and added, "If you're in an investigating mood, your new metal detector should give you an outlet for that. Go do some detecting for more Viking artefacts!"

"You're right, of course. And I am super pumped about the metal detecting!"

"Speaking of which, I think that might be Dwayne," Laura said, peering past Peter to the kitchen window.

Peter, who had started to feel better, felt worse again.

Dwayne Lautermilch was much as Laura had described him. He was still unmistakably the Dwayne Peter knew and loathed, but his brown mullet was heavily flecked with grey and he was generally softer looking. He was almost as tall as Peter, which was saying something, but where Dwayne had once been angular and hard, the intervening couple of decades had filled his cheeks, rounded his middle, and sagged his shoulders. His voice was the biggest change though. Dwayne had once been infamous for his loudness. At first Peter thought that he was drugged, his words were so now so slow and quiet. This was a vastly preferable iteration of Dwayne, but Peter was still wary.

On the drive to the Favel farm Peter was relieved to discover that small talk was not going to be required. He had a few polite questions prepared in case Dwayne was chatty, but his passenger just gazed out the window and hummed. He only spoke once when a red fox ran across the road, and even then, that remark was directed at Pippin, who sat behind them.

The Favels' drive was busy that morning. There was a white University of Manitoba van and a blue Chevy pickup pulling a small trailer. Peter recognized the truck as belonging to Doug Heikkinen. The trailer was empty, so Peter assumed Doug was out on the property somewhere, digging a hole for Misty. Dan was in the pen with the ostriches, doing something with their water trough. When he noticed Peter pull up, Dan stood, wiped his hands, and walked over.

Peter introduced Dwayne to Dan and inquired about the U of M van.

"It's that professor Sturluson," Dan said. "The one you showed the Thor's hammer to. He called Friday to ask if he could come up with a couple grad students and have a look around. This was before what happened with Misty. I totally forgot, otherwise I would have cancelled on him and asked him to come another time. Doug's here now."

"I saw."

"Kim's showing him a place behind the house. When he's done with the hole, we'll have a small ceremony. I'll burn some sweetgrass. Kim has prepared a few words."

"I'm so sorry, Dan. Is it OK that we're here today? I can come next weekend instead."

"Yes! I'm sorry, I didn't mean to imply otherwise with what I said about Sturluson. It's fine to have you and your friend here." He nodded at Dwayne. Peter winced inwardly at the "friend." "I was just worried that university crew would be loud. You know, students. But they've actually been very respectful too. Maybe you'll run into them out there."

"Yes, maybe. I'm curious what they think about the Mjölnir being there, and of course if they find anything else!"

"Not if we find it first!" Dwayne said loudly, startling Peter because up until that point he had been so quiet. Dwayne grinned at him. Dan laughed.

CHAPTER
Twelve

As they walked, Peter noticed the morning sunlight was low and strong, picking out the brilliant green of the first few aspen buds — a thousand small emerald speckles among the white and grey of the bare trunks and branches. To the untrained eye, aspen poplars look similar to birch, but their bark doesn't peel and the white of their trunks has the faintest greenish tint to it, whereas birch are a pure snowy white. Peter loved the smell of aspen in all seasons. Fall was, of course, the best for this, but even now in the spring an aspen bluff had a distinctive sharp, vaguely medicinal aroma, blended with a loamy, earthy note. *If a mere human like me can smell this, what is Pippin smelling?* Peter wondered. *Is it like walking into a Jackson Pollock exhibit with strobe lights flashing?* He glanced at his dog. Pippin had his nose low and was slowly swivelling it back and forth in a narrow arc as they walked. Peter looked back at Dwayne, who was several paces behind them, carrying the Fisher F22. He seemed intent on adjusting something rather than watching the path, and he consequently tripped several times over roots. Even then he didn't look up.

"Dan said that we'd reach a marshy meadow in a couple hundred metres down this path. That's where he thinks Big Bird found the Mjölnir." The ostriches had direct access to this meadow from their enclosure, at least until Dan closed the fence, but Peter and Dwayne had approached it from a trail that began near the house.

Dwayne looked up and said, "OK," before fiddling some more with the metal detector.

As they approached the meadow, they could hear an ever louder rhythmic trilling sound, or rather hundreds of rhythmic trilling sounds layered one on top of the other, creating a considerable din.

Dwayne looked up again. Peter smiled because his companion looked alarmed.

"What is that?" Dwayne asked quietly, as if not wanting to draw attention to himself from whatever was making that racket.

"Boreal chorus frogs! Here, let me point one out to you. They're amazingly small for something that makes such a big sound, and very tricky to see."

Peter crouched down and scanned the grassy water to the side of the path. He had a sharp eye for little details. He could miss a semi-trailer truck bearing down on him if he was lost in thought, but he was usually the first to spot a cool little bug or an odd plant in amongst the jumbled green of a forest floor.

It didn't take more than a minute. "There! Look. Immediately to the right of that taller cattail. See it?"

Dwayne stared hard. "I think so . . ."

Peter was sure he didn't see it, but he let it drop. "OK, let's see how this gizmo works." Peter gestured to the metal detector.

"Right!" Dwayne said, brightening. "It's really pretty simple, but there are some tricks to it." He handed the device to Peter. "Now hold it at a comfortable angle. You can use either arm, but if you're right-handed, I recommend your left so that your right hand is free to operate the controls. Now adjust your grip and the arm rest. Got it?"

"Yes. It's not too heavy."

"No, and the ergonomics are really good on this unit. Now have a look at the screen. The older ones have dials and analog signal strength indicators, but this baby has waterproof LCD with an extensive menu. The top-end models are all touch screen with Bluetooth to your phone, but for the money, this is the very best." Dwayne was really warming to his subject, and while he was still quiet, the pace of his speech was picking up.

"OK, cool." Peter pecked at the menu. "So, I presume I should set it to 'artefact'?"

"You bet. That picks up everything. When you set it to 'jewellery' or 'coin' it excludes high-iron-content items. Then you want to set your sensitivity. In a place where you expect a lot of trash, or where things are near the surface, like the beach, you'll set it low, but here I would set it high."

"Got it."

"Finally, turn it on and begin to sweep. Keep the search coils parallel to the ground as you do, about an even inch above the surface. This is the tricky bit."

Peter did as he was told. He didn't think it would be tricky, but as he was tall, he had to stoop a little. He was gangly and awkward at the best of times, so, to his frustration, the sweeps were jerky and uneven.

"Don't worry, you'll get the hang of it with practice. It's all about the rhythm." Dwayne swayed back and forth as if to music only he could hear. Peter thought he looked ridiculous but was surprised by his grace given his paunchy frame and absurd mullet.

Peter tried harder, but that only made it worse. Pippin looked at him, evidently concerned because his master was so tense.

Then there was a ping from the machine.

"Hey! There's something here! Just to the left of the path!" Peter shouted at Dwayne, who was doing something on his phone a dozen metres farther back.

"Excellent! Hang on, I've got a trowel. What does it say for depth?"

"Three inches." Peter's excitement quashed his annoyance at imperial measurements. Canada had been metric for 50 years and it was a much more rational system of measurement, but the detector was made in the irrational US.

Dwayne trotted over and pulled a small hand-spade out of his backpack. "OK, now move the search coils in a small circle around the area where you heard the ping. The machine has a pinpoint feature that will alert you to where the signal is the strongest."

"Right here," Peter said after a moment, and pointed at a damp patch of ground.

"Do you want to dig?" Dwayne asked.

"No, you do the honours. Besides, you're the expert."

Dwayne dropped to his knees and in one deft movement dug a perfect three-inch-deep hole where Peter had indicated. He reached in with his fingers and pulled out a completely rusted bent nail.

"Bingo." Dwayne said, clearly elated, as he stood up.

"A nail?"

"Looks like it. Not that exciting, but it shows the unit works perfectly."

"Not that exciting? Maybe it's a Viking nail," Peter said with a grin.

"Maybe. Who knows? We should ask that university dude if we see him."

Dwayne brushed the dirt off the nail, held it up to the sun, and peered at it.

"It's a nail all right," he said. "So where exactly was that Viking artefact found?"

"See those willows near the fence line? Just to the left of them, maybe 20 metres this side of the fence. You can actually see a couple of the ostriches in the field beyond." Peter pointed to a couple of small heads on long grey necks bobbing above a shrub in the distance.

"Yeah, OK," Dwayne said, squinting. "How deep is the water? Can we go over there?"

"It's really shallow, maybe a couple centimetres at the most, and we've got rubber boots. It's a good idea to bring a stick though and probe for deep holes or soft spots ahead of you. Don't want to get a booter!"

They were just turning around to go back into the aspen bluff to find sticks when Pippin's ears went erect and he made a low growling sound.

"What's wrong, Pippin?" Peter asked.

Pippin was staring directly down the path to where it disappeared in a stand of tamarack on the far side of the meadow. Then Peter saw what he was looking at. Four figures emerged, three of them carrying plastic totes. It took only a second to recognize Grimur Sturluson with his square glasses catching the light. The other three, carrying the totes, were variations on a theme of Nordic flawlessness. All were young, blond, tall, and athletic looking — one young woman and two men who could have been twins except for the fact that one of them had even broader shoulders and a more chiseled jaw. Grimur looked like a dwarf among these three, an effect that was accentuated when Peter and Dwayne walked up to meet them as they were both over six feet tall as well.

"Hi, Peter — I see we have a little amateur competition," Grimur said, looking at the metal detector. He was smiling and his tone indicated that he thought the concept of "amateur competition" was quite funny.

"Ha, yes, I suppose you could say that. Can't fault a guy for curiosity, can you?"

"No, not at all. But I'm being rude. I should introduce you to my grad students. This is Bjorn from Reykjavik, Jon from Trondheim, and Jessica from Minneapolis. And who is your friend?"

"Oh sorry, this is Dwayne." And then with a grin he added, "From Winnipeg."

They all chuckled and exchanged a round of handshakes and pleased-to-meet-yous.

"It looks like you've found something?" Peter asked, pointing at the tote nearest him.

"Yes, we certainly did," Grimur said, positively beaming. "I mean nothing like that beautiful pendant, but something remarkable, nonetheless. I do owe you for pointing me this way, but I can't say anything about what we've found yet. Due diligence, proper scientific process, and all that, you know."

"Sure, understood."

"Well, good luck with your own search. You'll let me know if you find something!" Grimur laughed a little as he said this. "We had best get back to the lab. There's a lot to analyze!"

Jon, the broad-shouldered one, nodded and repeated, "Ja, a lot to analyze." Peter couldn't help but think he sounded a bit like Arnold Schwarzenegger, although he had a much warmer smile.

After the foursome left, Dwayne turned to Peter and asked, "Find some sticks now and head across the marsh?"

"Yes, find some sticks and head across the marsh."

Peter and Dwayne had a pleasant time poking around the marsh in the warm April sun while Pippin splashed about, sniffing at every larger solid object protruding above the shallow water. The metal detector didn't ping once, but Peter couldn't help but notice how relaxed he felt and how much fun he was having. Spending time with Dwayne was the opposite of what he expected. He had anticipated either awkwardness and tension or some sort of cathartic apology from Dwayne for past sins. But there was neither. Whether Dwayne simply didn't remember what had happened back then, or whether he remembered but considered it to be irrelevant bygones, either way it was a revelation. It was clear that the past was in some ways no more than a set of stories that Peter could choose to pay attention to and allow to influence the present, or not. It was a choice. He was going to try harder next time to let the present speak for itself.

They arrived back in the parking area just as Doug was preparing to leave. Doug Heikkinen was short and round, almost to the point of being spherical. Peter couldn't recall ever seeing him without a cigarette protruding from the corner of his mouth, or without his trademark stained white T-shirt, regardless of the weather. He also had a reputation for being grumpy, so despite the fact that their paths crossed frequently, Peter didn't know him all that well. Word was that Doug was some kind of a weapons nut with a large collection of antique firearms, samurai swords, and various kinds of bows and crossbows, so that didn't endear him to Peter either.

Doug nodded at Peter and Dwayne.

"All done I guess?" Peter said, instantly regretting the inanity of the question.

"Yup."

"Sad about that poor pony, eh?" *Oof, inane. Again.*

"Yeah, I guess." Doug was looking down, counting his fee with dirt-blackened fingers as he said this, putting one 20-dollar bill after another slowly into his old brown leather wallet.

"OK then . . . well, have good day," Peter said as he and Dwayne climbed into the truck, with Pippin hopping in behind Dwayne.

Doug raised his hand in response as he got into his own truck.

CHAPTER
Thirteen

Monday was going to be a good day. Work looked like it would be relatively low stress, and Peter and Dwayne had made plans to head back out to the Favel property and have a look up the trail where Grimur and his students had come from, just for fun, of course. Or so Peter told himself repeatedly.

The morning began with four kitten neuters from the local shelter. Peter liked how they named all the individuals in a litter after a theme, like superheroes, or provincial capitals, or snacks, or, as in this case, vegetables. Pumpkin was even orange, but Zucchini, Radish, and Turnip did not resemble their names. Of all the routine surgeries in a small animal clinic, cat neuters were by far the easiest. Although he was otherwise an indifferent surgeon, Peter found he could neuter cats relying almost solely on muscle memory, much like riding a bike or skating. With some quick math Peter calculated that he had probably done about 1,800 cat neuters in his career so far, and not a single one had developed complications. That's how easy it was.

This morning in particular he appreciated being able to turn his thoughts elsewhere as he was still trying to puzzle out the recent spate of animal mutilations. In addition, he couldn't help but speculate to himself about what Grimur might have found out there among the tamaracks. *Wouldn't it be funny if old man Thorkelson had been a secret collector and had stashed the goods across the property? Wasn't there a story about him developing dementia near the end? That would explain a few things.* Peter still liked the magpie or raven theory though. *And could you still call it archeology when you're finding things that have already been found once before and then lost? Maybe call it re-archeology instead? Or lost-and-found-eology?* Peter chuckled out loud at his joke.

Kat, his tech, looked up from her anaesthetic chart, "What's so funny, Peter?"

"Oh, just a word I made up."

"Ah, OK." He knew Kat had learned not to ask for more details because they never made sense to her and then she'd just feel awkward. Like usual, she changed the subject. "Theresa told me what happened with Misty on the weekend. That's really terrible. Sick and terrible. I liked that pony, and I don't normally like ponies."

"Yes, it was awful. Dan and Kim are devastated. And you're right, she had character. I liked her too." Most veterinarians and their staff agreed that it was best to assume that ponies, while cute, were going to be ill-tempered. Like chihuahuas. That way they would be prepared if they were right and pleasantly surprised if they were wrong. Win-win.

Peter stopped for a moment while he checked Radish's incision. "But do you know what's really strange? Whoever cut her head off drained most of her blood out too, and did it cleanly."

"Wow, really?" Kat listened to a lot of emo bands, almost exclusively wore black, and was a devotee of the Twilight series of vampire novels. According to Theresa, the receptionist, Kat had Edward Cullen's face tattooed above her left breast. Inexplicable blood loss immediately got her attention.

"Yes. It's hard to explain. It's out of tune with what animal mutilation normally involves. And it would be time-consuming, increasing the risks of getting caught."

"I know what it is," Kat said in a casual tone as she clicked her pen and marked Radish's temperature on the chart.

Uh oh, here it comes, thought Peter. *A band of vampires with hacksaws roving around East New Iceland. But didn't vampires need human blood? The stories would be far less dramatic otherwise.*

"A cult. It's got to be a cult. Just look up which cults demand animal sacrifice and which of those use the blood."

"A cult in New Selfoss?" Peter asked. He had to admit to himself, though, that she might be on to something. He had assumed a lone maniac with some dark purpose, but a group, especially a religious one, made more sense. This would be much easier to pull off with a couple of people or more.

"Sure, why not?" Kat shrugged. "I mean we have that bondage cellar under Krafts 'n' Things and that nutty Northern Lights Pentecostal church. That's pretty much a cult, isn't it?"

Peter laughed. "Yeah, but I think the Christians left animal sacrifice behind somewhere in the Old Testament."

"I don't know about these 'Christians,'" Kat put her pen down to make air quotes. "But the point is, this town has its share of oddballs."

Peter smiled behind his surgical mask when he considered who was saying this, and then it occurred to him that he was perhaps not one to judge oddness.

Kat continued, "Weren't we even named 'Quirkiest Town in Canada' once? So, what's one more group, even if they're extra-quirky in an evil kind of way."

"Good point."

It turned out that Dwayne lived close to Peter and Laura's place. He commuted into the city to run Basement Boyz but preferred to stay in his hometown. His mother apparently still lived two doors down from him. He walked over to Peter's after supper, and the two of them drove out to the Favel farm together, with Pippin.

Peter felt more talkative now that he was comfortable with Dwayne. "We should have a good couple hours daylight still, so I'm hoping there'll be time to do a little scent work with Pippin too."

"Scent work?"

"Pippin's a champion scent dog. It's an organized international sport, getting dogs to find small hidden objects by smell alone."

"Like small hidden Viking objects?"

Before Peter answered he craned his head forward to look for traffic coming from the left as they were turning right onto the main road out of town. "Well, maybe, although I haven't figured out how to go about training him for that yet because metal doesn't have a smell and old wood and leather are too common. But no, specifically this time I want to see if he can track anything related to Misty."

"The dead pony. You think the head could be out there in the woods somewhere?" Dwayne asked.

"Maybe. It's as good a place to start as any."

"I heard a rumour that all the blood was drained, and also from a goat a few days ago."

"Boy, word does get around."

"My mom plays bridge with Doug Heikkinen's mom."

"Ah. Well, yes . . . Both those animals were bled dry and a ram had his penis and testicles cut off the day before."

"Oh my gosh."

Peter glanced at Dwayne. "Gosh" was an odd-sounding word coming out of a big tough guy like Dwayne Lautermilch, even if he had gotten softer with age. He accelerated to pass a tractor, waving at its driver as he went by. He was pretty sure it was crazy Art Blankenship. It never hurt to be friendly regardless.

"My theory now is that we're dealing with a cult of some kind," Peter said when he resumed his lane. "My staff even thinks it might be those Northern Lights Pentecostals, but I don't think so. They may speak in tongues, but they don't make blood sacrifices!" Peter laughed.

"No, we don't," Dwayne said. He sounded odd in a way Peter

hadn't heard before. "I haven't been for a month, but no, we never hurt animals."

Peter hoped that his jaw didn't physically drop. Dwayne Lautermilch, a Pentecostal Christian? His mind whirled. *Jailhouse conversion? Was that why he was so different? Shit.* In two days from enemy to friend to . . . what . . . he didn't know. Peter didn't necessarily dislike evangelical Christians, but in his experience, they were all far too conservative and narrow-minded for his taste. *Shit.*

Peter suddenly realized that he hadn't said anything in response to Dwayne, and that an uncomfortable silence was developing.

"Oh, right. Good. I mean, I'm sorry that my staff would think something ridiculous like that. No offense, I hope?"

"No, it's cool. Don't worry about it. I know what most people around here think."

"But you didn't go to church yesterday? Or, you said, for a month even?"

Dwayne smiled, "God doesn't smite us with a cartoon lightning bolt if we miss a few weeks. Pastor Phillips has been sick, and I don't like his replacement, Pastor Ragnarsson. A lot of shouting about us being God's shining elect and the rest of town being wicked idolators and Satanists. 'A war between us is coming,' he said. He's the kind of fire-and-brimstone preacher who gives Christians a bad name."

Peter nodded. "Right, OK." He glanced at Dwayne and took a chance on a joke. "Fire and brimstone, but not sheep and pony blood, eh?"

Dwayne laughed. "Not that I know of!"

And with that, the tension that Peter had felt building dissipated like a puff of smoke in the wind. He could still be friends with Dwayne. It would be narrow-minded not to, and it would be hypocritical of Peter to behave the same way he had accused the evangelicals of behaving. In fact, it would be interesting to observe a believer up close. And weird cultish behaviour at Northern Lights still had to be on the list, just lower down.

CHAPTER
Fourteen

Dan was expecting them and waved to them from the ostrich paddock where he was working on the water trough again, like he had been the other day. The easiest way to get to where they wanted to explore was directly across the paddock, toward the marshy area. Peter opened the gate and then he, Pippin, and Dwayne made a large detour around where the six ostriches were standing in a clump. Peter swore that Big Bird was staring directly at him, and he quickened his pace. He didn't think that ostriches were smart enough to remember and carry grudges, but there was no point in taking any chances. He doubted Dan would be able to stop an ostrich attack, and even Pippin would be no match. Perhaps Dwayne had hidden powers though? In any case, this was all pointless brain chatter, and soon they were over the far fence without Big Bird having budged.

The three of them moved quickly across the corner of the marshy meadow to the edge of the stand of tamarack where the ground was drier. Peter had always loved tamaracks. He felt an odd kinship with a tree that did not properly fit in its category. It was technically a conifer with needles, but they turned golden in the fall and fell off like a deciduous tree's leaves. Also, tamarack wood was his favourite for the fireplace. It didn't catch instantly, like well-seasoned birch, but once aflame it crackled merrily like a storybook fire. Sometimes the tamarack crackled so loudly it made Pippin jump up and bark, but mostly it just made for the perfect atmosphere to read and sip tea.

They followed the tamaracks north until they intersected with the path they had seen Grimur and his students come out of. The property wasn't large, so Peter didn't think it would take long to find the dig site. As it probably wasn't going to be directly on the trail, Peter asked Pippin to "seek person," a command he used when he wanted him to find the scent of any human, rather than a specific one. It was very unlikely that anyone other than the archeologists had been up here in weeks.

Pippin trotted along ahead of Peter and Dwayne, nose to ground, swinging his head from side to side. Dwayne fiddled with the metal detector as they walked. The sun was low in the west already, casting a gauzy yellowed light through the trees, but because sunset at this latitude and this time of year was a slow-motion affair, there'd be enough light for some time yet. A chickadee chirped somewhere nearby, but otherwise it was quiet. Even their footsteps made no sounds on the springy moist earth of the path.

Peter felt an unexpected prickle of fear run through him but dismissed it as silly.

Then Pippin stopped and, without looking back at Peter, turned off the trail to the right, winding between what was now a mix of tamarack and birch. There was a light understory of brick red dogwood. Peter and Dwayne fell behind Pippin as they thrashed through it. Dwayne turned on the metal detector, but quickly gave up trying to sweep as the brush kept getting in the way. Pippin was now out of sight.

"Should you call him back?" Dwayne asked.

"No, he's fine. He'll stop and bark if he finds something, or just stop and wait if he knows he's gotten too far ahead."

"Smart dog."

"Yes, he is."

Then they heard the bark. Another 20 metres along there was a small clearing. Pippin sat at the centre of it, surrounded by a circle of logs. Peter counted quickly. There were enough for about a dozen people to sit around. It was like a boy scout campfire circle, but there was no sign of there having been a campfire in it. Instead, right beside where Pippin sat, there was a deep, round hole, about the width of the thickness of Peter's arm. He knelt on the ground next to the hole and shone his phone's flashlight in. It was about 40 or 50 centimetres deep, and it was empty. He stood up and dusted off his knees. Dwayne was walking slowly around the circle with the detector.

"Nothing in there. And anyway, there's no way the archeologists just dug this one round hole and found something in it," Peter said.

"Yeah, seems weird. So far nothing metallic here either. Maybe this is something else? Maybe their dig is farther down the path, and Pippin picked up some other scent here?"

"Maybe. I'll ask Dan, but it seems like a stretch."

Dwayne didn't say anything in response. He was leaning over to look at something at the edge of the clearing.

"Did it ping? Find something?" Peter asked.

"No, it didn't ping, but I just about tripped on this." Dwayne lifted up a two-metre-long wooden pole, sharpened at one end. "Check this out," he said as he carried it to the hole and set the dull end into it so that it stood up, looking like a giant pencil. "Perfect fit."

"Now, that is interesting." Peter looked at the pole carefully. It was fashioned from a straight tree trunk, probably pine, and had been roughly sanded down. Knot holes were visible all along. "Check this out," Peter said, pointing at faint reddish stains around the tip.

"Pine beetle markings?"

"Maybe, but I don't think so."

And then, like a blurry photograph suddenly snapping into sharp focus, Peter knew. He pulled the pole out of the hole and laid it on the ground. Then he called Pippin over and pulled the baggy containing Misty's skin sample out of his pocket.

"Seek!"

Pippin needed less than a minute. He sniffed along the pole and the adjacent ground until he came to the tip. Then he stood rigidly at attention, staring at Peter.

"Good seek!"

Kat had been right. And it was not Poisson clumping.

Dwayne's eyes widened. "That pony's head . . . was impaled on this stick?" he stammered. He sounded truly shocked.

"I think so."

"But why? Is this the cult you were talking about?"

"Probably. Sort of. It depends what you mean by cult. I think this" — he indicated the pole with his foot — "is a nithing pole."

"Nithing pole?"

"Among ancient Norse and Germanic pagans, poles with animal's heads, usually horses, but sometimes sheep or calves, were erected to curse enemies. The poor animal's face would be oriented to look in the direction of the person to be cursed."

"That's horrible," Dwayne said quietly, shaking his head and staring at the pole. "But pagans, in modern times, and here in Canada?"

"Apparently there are neo-pagans, but they're more of the peaceful nature-loving flavour, so it is strange for sure. I'll ask Laura. She's Icelandic and knows a lot more about this stuff. She's been researching the neo-pagans and she's the one who told me about nithing poles."

"And where would they point it? The Favels' place?"

"No idea."

"I guess you'll have to call the police."

"I guess so."

Just then there was the sharp sound of a branch snapping behind them, back toward the path. Peter and Dwayne looked up, but it was directly into the low sun shining between the trees like a spotlight. Peter made a shushing motion with his finger to his lips and squinted. Was there movement? Possibly. The forest was hushed. Even the chickadees were quiet.

Then there was another sound, like a rustle.

Pippin stood still, staring at the direction the noise came from, growling quietly.

For a split second, Peter caught sight of a flash of hair or fur in a narrow beam of light. Blond possibly or light tan.

"Did you see that?" he whispered to Dwayne.

"Yes. Deer?" Dwayne asked softly.

"Maybe." *But Pippin wouldn't growl at a deer*, Peter thought.

CHAPTER
Fifteen

"A nithing pole?" Laura repeated. She and Peter were in the living room, drinking tea. She had set aside the Dungeon Master's vest she was working on. It was black, with the image of a grey 20-sided die on each of the pockets.

"I'm sure of it." He pulled out his phone and showed her the pictures. He had debated about telling her that he had trained Pippin on Misty's scent but decided that on balance it was better for her to know. As he had hoped, her passion for Icelandic lore overcame her annoyance at Peter dabbling in investigation.

"Looks like it. I mean, it's just a pointy pole, and there are lots of other kinds of pointy poles in the world, but if it had poor Misty's blood on it . . . That's so sad and gruesome. Have you told Dan and Kim?"

"No, I don't see the point."

"And Kevin? You have to phone him. This is police business, not vet business." Laura made eye contact with Peter and glared at him hard.

"Of course. Right away, but first, what do you think? Is it even plausible now? I mean, didn't this die out a thousand years ago? When you told me about nithing poles before, it was in one of the sagas. Have we got Viking ghosts roaming the land here, dropping mjolnirs and decapitating ponies?"

"Sure, it's plausible. No ghosts necessary." Laura softened her tone, warming up to a subject she enjoyed. She woke her phone, quickly finding what she was looking for. "There have been recent uses in both Iceland and Norway. In 2006 a farmer in the Westfjords in Iceland erected one against his neighbour. Claimed the neighbour had run over his puppy. The police took it very seriously, saying a nithing pole is a death threat."

"Crazy." Peter shook his head and then took a long sip of tea. Pippin was at his feet, and Merry had taken advantage of the cessation of knitting to climb onto Laura's lap.

Laura picked up her phone and tapped at it for a few seconds, "And they've been used for protest — in 2016 with cods' heads against government fishing policy in Iceland and in 2020 with svith to protest poor treatment of nurses during the pandemic."

"Svith?"

"That boiled sheep's head dish."

"Yum."

Laura was quiet for a moment as she continued to tap and scroll, and then she quickly shifted forward in her chair. "Whoa. Grab your phone. I was searching Icelandic news, and this popped up. Grimur's about to give a press conference in front of his lab. The headline is 'Prof Says Dramatic New Selfoss Discovery Overturns History.'"

Peter picked up his phone. "Where did you find that?"

"CBC national feed. There's a live video. Come over here."

Peter stood up and jogged the three steps to Laura's armchair. He crouched to see the screen of her phone.

"That's right where I was on Thursday!" Grimur Sturluson stood behind a portable lectern on the lawn in front of the archeology building.

"Shh . . . it's starting."

Grimur wore a dark grey suit and a tie patterned like the Icelandic flag. His three graduate students stood off to the side. Grimur smiled and waved at someone off camera and then began to speak.

"Thank you for coming here today. This is a very special day. It is a very special day because what I'm going to tell you will overturn your understanding of history. I have devoted my career to researching the settlement patterns of the Nordic peoples. In particular, my focus has been on their exploration of Greenland and North America. You are all no doubt familiar with the L'Anse aux Meadows archeological site, discovered in Newfoundland in 1960 by Anne Ingstad. The world was astonished when she proved that the Norse had settled there around the year 1000. Many did not want to believe it, but they had to. The narrative before had always been 'in 1492 Columbus sailed the ocean blue.' And indeed, he did, but many preceded him, and the evidence is that he made use of their knowledge. Yes, I said 'many.' Not just Leif Erikson in 1000, but others. Historical documents and archaeological evidence are so fragile that their absence proved nothing. How can anyone believe that L'Anse aux Meadows was a single, isolated case? The Polynesians explored much larger areas of the ocean in smaller craft, and the Norse were in every way their equal as navigators and sailors. No, I never believed L'Anse aux Meadows was unique, and today I am gratified to be able to announce that there is no longer that absence of archeological evidence."

Grimur paused, adjusted his glasses, and smiled before going on.

"Today I am able to announce that my team and I have found conclusive proof that Norse peoples, originally from Iceland, settled in the New Selfoss area of Manitoba around the year 1050."

Grimur paused again, smiling and nodding in apparent appreciation of the gasps and murmurs in the crowd.

He held his hand up and continued. "We know that the Medieval Warm Period from roughly 950 to 1250 permitted relatively easy travel in arctic and subarctic regions around the globe. Greenland was settled as a result, and contact with Baffin Island, only 400 kilometres farther west, is well known too. From there, travel onward around the southern end of Baffin Island and into Hudson Bay would be a relatively simple matter. Well-established Indigenous trade routes lead from the shores of the bay into the interior of the continent. Travel to and settlement of the southern Lake Winnipeg basin region would not have been a challenge for these people. We believe that the New Selfoss Norse settlement lasted for several generations, possibly past when the Little Ice Age of roughly 1300 onwards made travel much more difficult and likely cut off trade and communication with Greenland, much as Greenland itself was cut off from Iceland at that time."

Grimur smiled and looked around again. The crowd was silent now.

"I know that you have many questions, and I will be delighted to answer them at another time, but this is all the information I am prepared to release at the moment. Allow the scientific process to move forward, and then I will be able to confirm more details and provide the world with a fuller portrait of this astonishing discovery."

Reporters shouted questions at him anyway. You could hear, "Dr. Sturluson, what specifically did you find?" and "Where exactly is this settlement?" and "Dr. Sturluson, how large was the settlement?" But Grimur held up his hand, smiling continuously, and then turned around and walked into the building. The camera turned to the reporter, who made some brief remarks, but Peter was no longer listening.

"Holy crap," Peter said.

Laura just shook her head, staring vacantly at her phone through to the end of the clip before stopping it from auto-playing the next story about auto insurance rates going up.

"Holy crap," she echoed. "So, the Mjölnir ties to this?"

"I guess, but they must have found other evidence because there are lots of other ways to explain a single artefact like that. It must have been what they were carrying out in those totes on Saturday."

"A day is enough time to analyze whatever they found?"

"You wouldn't think so, but maybe it was just icing on the cake. Maybe he's slowly been accumulating other evidence."

Peter went back to his own chair and absentmindedly took a sip of his tea. It wasn't hot anymore, so he made a face and set it down again.

"But you and Dwayne didn't see the dig, only this clearing with a nithing pole in it."

"I assume the dig was off the trail somewhere else. But it is odd that something else related to the Norse was located so close by."

"And something in current use, not just ancient archeology. Do you think Grimur has something to do with the nithing pole?"

"The thought occurred to me. One thing I didn't mention to you last week was that he was adamant that the pendant should be called a Thor's hammer, not a "mjolnir," because that word only refers to *the* Mjölnir, capital 'M.' This seemed quite important to him. At the time I thought he was just being a typical picky academic, but now I wonder."

"Wonder what?" Laura asked.

"Maybe he's also some kind of historical reenactor, like those SCA guys we knew at university in Saskatoon."

"The Society of Creative Anachronists bashing each other with foam swords in Kinsmen Park? Maybe, but I don't see that crowd butchering ponies."

"No, that part doesn't make sense. They go for as much realism as possible without actually spilling blood."

Laura nodded and both of them fell quiet for a minute. Then Laura said, "What's odd though, if this is supposed be a real nithing pole, is that it has to be seen by the target to be effective as a curse. You say this was in a secluded clearing."

"So, more evidence maybe that they were just playing at it, not seriously trying to curse anyone? Or maybe they were serious, but didn't do their homework?"

"Maybe. Or maybe it's someone trying to make people think that Icelandic traditionalist wackos are behind it. Throw the scent off the real culprit."

"Wouldn't they try to make it a little more obvious then? Like leave the head there too, and not count on someone accidentally stumbling on the pole and figuring out what the blood stains meant?"

"A work in progress perhaps that you interrupted? Regardless, call Kevin. Now."

CHAPTER
Sixteen

Peter arranged to meet his brother-in-law the next morning at the clinic because while he had an 8:00 a.m. appointment, there was a free half hour after that. The rest of the day was going to be busy. Mondays usually were.

"Sorry, Kev, Duchess wouldn't sit still for her eye exam, so that took a lot longer than expected," Peter said as he walked into the office and saw Kevin waiting for him. He was in Peter's chair, swivelling back and forth, twirling his RCMP cap on his finger in an affectation of boredom clearly put on for Peter's benefit.

"Eye exam?" Kevin stopped swivelling, tossed his cap in the air, caught it, and set it on his unruly nest of red hair. He seemed to take pride in pushing his grooming right up to the tolerance limit of his superiors. "You're a vet optometrist now, Pete? She was having trouble reading, or maybe driving at night? High-fashion eyewear for stylish pooches?" Kevin grinned as he said this.

"Ha, no. Just trying to save the eye and keep her comfortable. She's got glaucoma. High eye pressure."

Kevin stifled a stagey yawn. "Right. Enough shoptalk. *Your* shoptalk anyway. Let's move on to my shoptalk. It's usually much more interesting." Kevin grinned again. "You said on the phone that you had more information about the pony decapitation?"

"Yes. As you know Laura got me a metal detector for my birthday, so I decided to go check out the area where that little amulet was found. Dwayne Lautermilch was with me. He sold her the detector."

"OK, so far, so good." Kevin was scribbling in a little coil-bound notebook, his large pink right hand engulfing the pen.

"While we were searching for more artefacts, we found a sharpened pole with blood on the tip."

"Uh-huh." Kevin didn't look up.

"And, well . . ." Peter paused.

"Go on."

"You see, I had trained Pippin to Misty's scent, you, know, just in case."

"Misty . . ." Kevin flipped back through his notebook. "The pony?"

"Yes."

"Just in case? Just in case of what?" Kevin looked up at Peter as he said this, his eyes narrowing ever so slightly.

"Just in case of something just like this. It never hurts to be prepared. I thought there was a chance that the head hadn't been taken very far. And Misty was my patient, so I think I have legitimate interest."

"That's a stretch, Pete. Is an animal still your patient when it's dead? Technically speaking, I mean . . ."

"Sure, I do autopsies on my patients all the time, and obviously they're dead then."

"OK, OK." Kevin sighed. "I should know by now not to argue with you. For the record, I'm just going to say that you shouldn't be looking for evidence in cases that are under active investigation. I've said that before. Maybe, oh, 50 times. But probably you forgot. You've got a lot on your mind. If we want your help — *if we do* — we know where to find you." He yawned and stretched his arms out. "Sorry, late night. Anyway, no harm done, I suppose, and ultimately, so what? We already know a sick clown was involved, and now we know that said sick clown not only cuts heads and balls and stuff off but then also spears the heads. Don't want to know what he did with those balls."

"It's a nithing pole, Kev."

"A what?"

"Call yourself an Icelander?" Peter laughed.

"No, I don't. Not really. A Canadian of Icelandic extraction is more like it. And this Canadian of Icelandic extraction does not know what a nithing pole is. Sue me."

"It's used in a Norse religious ritual where an animal's head is put on a pole and pointed toward a person to curse them."

Kevin rubbed his beard and then made a few notes. "OK, fine. It's not unusual for the aforementioned sick clowns to have religious delusions. But it might be helpful, the Norse angle, so thank you."

There was a long pause while Kevin wrote some more in his notebook. When it looked like he was done, Peter said, "Did you see the news last night?"

"Yeah, Stuart and I watched them. Second date by the way — always a big one." Kevin winked. "Crazy story about that archeologist! Vikings here in New Selfoss! That's what you're referring to? The Vikings supposedly being here?"

"Yes. They want the location kept quiet for obvious reasons, but the dig site is also on that old Thorkelson property."

"Also?"

"Are you paying attention? We found the nithing pole in the same general area where Grimur claims to have found this ancient settlement, but the pole is new."

Kevin looked up. "Hmm, any idea if they dig at night? Maybe that's what the Dukovskys were hearing."

"I doubt it. But what about whoever used the pole? That sounds like a nighttime activity to me."

"Yeah, could be. Guess I should talk to this —" Kevin flipped a couple pages in his notebook "— Dr. Sturluson guy. But I don't see profs crawling around at night beheading ponies and castrating sheep. Besides, the honourable Blaine Tanner notwithstanding, there's only so much time and energy I'm going to put into this. Honestly, I'm up to the eyeballs." Kevin put his right hand flat and level with his eyes as he said this. "For one frigging headache of an example, Leonard Alexander's family is holding a press conference at noon today."

"The missing kid from last year?" Peter interrupted. Leonard had been considered when unidentified human remains turned up in the swine barn case last winter.

"The same. A hand, burnt to a blackened crisp, was sent to them in the mail, with a note claiming it was Leonard's. The note was full of racist garbage. Totally sick. Anyway, the family doesn't think we're moving fast enough on this. Christ on a stick, I don't know what else we can do."

Peter had just opened his mouth to reply when Theresa screamed from the waiting room.

"Peter! Emergency!"

Peter sprinted out of the office and down the short hall to the reception area. It took him a full, long second to process what he was seeing.

Laura was carrying Pippin through the front door. Pippin was limp in her arms. Both of them were soaked in blood.

CHAPTER

Seventeen

The world fell away. Suddenly there was only Pippin's injury and Peter's training. Afterwards he would look back on this as something akin to an out-of-body experience. Dr. Bannerman, DVM, the seasoned veterinarian, stepped in and took command, while Peter, Pippin's best friend, stepped back and watched, struck dumb.

"Kat, get a catheter in! Theresa, take his vitals! Laura, put him on the induction table and grab the clippers!"

Kat, Theresa, and Laura moved quickly without talking. Laura had obviously just come from the shower as her bright red hair hung wet around her shoulders. Red and white. Red hair and white skin. Red blood and white blouse. Fortunately, she knew her way around the clinic as she had briefly worked as an assistant after giving up on paleobiology and before setting up her Etsy online knitwear shop. Both of them knew that husband-and-wife teams rarely worked well in vet clinics, so it was always meant to be temporary. Taking office politics home was a bad idea, and the staff usually resented the non-veterinarian half of the couple. But Peter had needed the free help after taking over the practice.

Pippin was unconscious and his gums were extremely pale. Peter examined him quickly while Laura shaved a front leg for Kat to put in an IV catheter. His vital signs were alarming. He was as close to death as any trauma patient Peter had ever seen.

"He's in shock. Chest is clear. Kat, bolus the LRS. Theresa, grab the heating blanket. Let's get ready to intubate."

Peter then concentrated on locating the source of the blood loss. The thick fur on both sides of Pippin's abdomen was soaked in it. He found the wound quickly. A round hole just behind the last rib on the left. And then he found a second hole on the right side. Neither seemed to be actively bleeding at the moment.

"Full penetration wound. Probably ballistic," came a quiet voice from behind Peter. He hadn't seen Kevin follow them into the treatment area.

"You mean he's been shot?" Peter asked, not looking back at Kevin as he shaved the wounds.

"Yes. But who the hell shoots a dog? Did you hear the shot, Laura?"

"No, but I was in the shower. Pippin was in the yard. After I got dressed, I went downstairs to let him in, but he wasn't near the door. I called, but he didn't come. Then I saw him lying off to the left, in the middle of the yard . . ." Laura began to cry. Theresa put her arm around Laura's shoulder.

"Gandalf?" Peter asked in reference to their goat.

"He's fine, thank god," Laura answered through her sobs.

Peter didn't say anything else. His jaw was set like cement as he worked to clean the wound.

"IV's going well," Kat said. "I'm going to call Pam and get her to bring Tank for a possible transfusion." Pam was Kat's sister. She only lived a block from the clinic and Tank was an amiable Rottweiler who had served as an emergency blood donor before when they didn't have time to get blood products from the city.

"Thanks, Kat," Peter said quietly.

"No scorch marks. Very clean exit wound," Kevin said as he watched Peter work. The room was quiet otherwise, except for the beeping of the monitoring equipment. "Compound bow, I bet. I'm going to call Kristine and have her check your yard out. Maybe the arrow's sticking in a tree. When you're ready, Laura, we'll need more details on exactly where you found Pippin, his position and stuff."

"I'm ready now, but I don't want to leave Pippin until I know he's going to be OK. Can I talk to Kristine about it over the phone?"

"Sure."

There was a light tinkle of bells as the front door opened.

"Hello!" called a voice from reception.

"Shit, it's Mrs. Dunlop and Freckles for their nine o'clock," Theresa said. "I'll explain and rebook. If you guys are OK here for the moment, I'll try to rebook the rest of the morning."

"Rebook the whole day. I may have to go into surgery with him if there's active bleeding."

"What do you think, Peter? Did it go through the liver?" Kat asked.

"Possibly, yes. It's too low for the aorta and kidneys. Could have hit the liver, stomach, or pancreas though. I'll get the ultrasound on him as soon as he's stable."

Time became rubbery. Moments were hours and hours were moments. And then somehow it was midday and Peter was prepping for surgery. Tank had been generous with his donation, and Pippin was looking better but was still losing blood somewhere internally. The ultrasound was unable to pinpoint the exact source, but Peter could see that blood was slowly accumulating in there. Not a gusher, it seemed, but something was oozing — oozing enough that Pippin would need another transfusion by evening if it continued.

Kat managed the anaesthetic, while Theresa assisted in surgery. Normally in an emergency situation when Peter needed both staff members, the phones were set to play a pre-recorded message and a sign was put up on the door, but as Laura was there and insisted on being given something to do lest she go crazy, she looked after the front desk, selling the odd bag of food and fielding the usual array of both strange and mundane phone calls that come into a vet's office. She willed herself not to go back to the operating room every two minutes to ask how Pippin was doing. She went back once and was waved away with a terse "Don't know yet." Peter didn't enjoy surgery and became very tense while in big procedures. She would find out soon enough. One way or another.

After what felt like at least an hour, she couldn't stand it anymore and started to get up from her chair. Just then Mabel Heikkinen walked in. Laura sighed and sat back down. Mrs. Heikkinen was widely accepted to be New Selfoss's most prolific gossip. And that was a hard-fought title. She was a tiny woman, dressed all in black, with enormous round glasses that magnified her eyes, and she had to be at least 80 years old, albeit with the energy of a woman half her age. She owned an incontinent chihuahua who was even older in dog years. Ruby's incontinence, chronic cough, weepy eyes, and a host of other mild ailments had Mrs. Heikkinen in the clinic on a weekly basis, especially as she didn't follow any of Peter's directions. Laura recalled Peter reporting that typical conversations went like this:

"How are Ruby's new pills working?"

"Oh, I decided not to give them."

"Really? Why did you do that?"

"I didn't like them. My hairdresser said that the same pills made her dog act strange."

Mrs. Heikkinen was also the leading elder in the local Finnish-Canadian community, in part because of the force of her personality and in part because the famous Paavo Jarvinen, New Selfoss's eccentric first millionaire, was her great-uncle. Icelanders may be in the majority in New Selfoss, but the Finns were prominent as well.

At least conversations with her were never dull, so Laura settled back in her chair, thankful for the distraction. Mrs. Heikkinen did not, however, get the opportunity to say much more than hello and comment on the weather when Theresa trotted up to the front. Laura swivelled away from Mrs. Heikkinen while the old woman was in mid-sentence.

"How is he?"

"Good. He's good. He'll live. Peter's just starting to close up."

Laura felt everything in her that was hard and solid instantly become soft and formless as all the tension left her, like air escaping a tire that had been filled to near-bursting.

"Oh, thank god, that's wonderful!" Laura sighed. Mrs. Heikkinen looked ready to interrupt, but Laura ignored her. "What did he find?"

"Torn liver lobe, so he had to do a lobectomy. A bit touch and go for a while, but it'll be fine now. I would have come sooner to update you, but it was all-hands-on-deck back there."

"No, that's cool. I understand. Thank god, thank god, thank god. I don't believe in him, but I'll thank him anyway! And you! And Kat! And Peter! And lucky stars! And . . ."

Mrs. Heikkinen was staring at the two younger women, her mouth partway open, clearly bursting to ask what was going on.

"It's my own dog, Mabel," Laura explained. "Someone shot him, but he's going to live. He's going to live!"

CHAPTER
Eighteen

Kevin returned to the clinic around three in the afternoon and found Peter and Laura in the office drinking coffee. Both of them looked haggard and exhausted. Peter normally didn't drink anything caffeinated after ten in the morning, but he was so drained from the events of the day, and was in such a deep post-adrenaline slump, that caffeine felt like a medical necessity if he was going to be able to navigate the rest of the day. So, with a great deal of reluctance, he suspended his caffeine rule. Laura had no qualms about drinking whatever she wanted, whenever she wanted. She was on her third cup.

"Hey guys, how's the pup?"

"Better, much better. Thanks," Peter said, motioning to a low stool that was the only remaining place to sit. "He's awake now, and other then being tired, having two holes in him and a quarter of his liver gone, he doesn't actually seem that much worse for wear."

"Pippin's a tough one," Kevin said as he manoeuvred himself onto the stool. Given his considerable size, he looked absurd perched there. Like an adult sent back to playschool.

"Kristine find anything?" Laura asked, smiling at her brother's discomfort.

"Yeah, an arrow embedded in a tree on the west side of your yard. It's already off to Winnipeg for analysis, but I doubt we'll learn much. It's a pretty standard carbon broadhead model used by bow hunters. Easy to buy at Cabela's."

"West side," Peter said, almost as if to himself. "So, the shooter would have been on the east, in the trees there. Neighbours see any unusual vehicles up our road?"

"No. Kristine says people were either not home or didn't notice anything."

"Tracks?"

"She had a good look, and, no, nothing useful. The ground's pretty firm already for April."

"OK, thanks, Kev," Peter said, and took a long sip from his coffee.

"How did the Alexanders' press conference go?" Laura asked. "Peter told me about it."

"Total shitshow. Makes us look like fools, or worse, foot soldiers of structural racism. Nobody gets how much time these investigations take or why we don't release a blow-by-blow of what we're thinking and doing." He sighed and shook his head before adding in an emphatic tone, "We are working our asses off on it."

Laura nodded and shifted the conversation to Kevin's new boyfriend. Peter tuned this out as he slipped deep into thought. Leonard Alexander's hand was burnt black. That reminded him of something. But what? The caffeine had made him more alert again, and his brain was moving quickly, but it felt more like a car doing doughnuts in the parking lot rather than one zooming down the highway toward a destination.

Peter interrupted Laura and Kevin, "So, are you going to take this seriously now, Kev? I know there're no dead humans yet, but even you have to admit that something serious is going on here." Tact wasn't Peter's strongest suit at the best of times, and this was not the best of times.

Kevin sounded cheerful while chatting with Laura about Stuart, but he looked tired and sad when he turned to look at Peter. "Of course, Pete. You're a smart guy, so I know you understand that we have to assign priorities based on the severity of the crime and the available evidence. We can't put a full investigative team on every case. One sheep, even if gruesomely mutilated, is honestly lower priority. Add a decapitated pony and a goat bled dry, it goes up the list a couple spots. And now with Pippin, assuming there's a connection, and I agree with your implication that there likely is, it goes up the list a few more spots. In fact, I'd say it's just below the Alexander case now." He rubbed his face in his hands and then looked at Peter again. "Make sense? Satisfied?"

Peter nodded.

"And now I have a question for you," Kevin said. "Why do you think Pippin was targeted, and why in a way that did not seem like it would lead to a mutilation?"

"I think I know why. There's one thing I didn't mention about finding the nithing pole. I didn't mention it to you either, Laura. Kind of slipped my mind. Didn't seem that important."

Laura cocked her head and gave Peter a half-smile that he read as somewhere between indulgent and annoyed.

Peter continued, "After we had found the pole and placed it upright in its hole, all three of us — me, Dwayne, and Pippin — heard something moving in the bush nearby. I told Dwayne that it was probably a deer, but I'm sure I saw a flash of blond hair. Human hair. And Pippin reacted the way he reacts to strange people, not wildlife."

"So, you think someone saw you or was watching you?" Kevin asked as he fished his notebook out of his jacket pocket.

"Yes. It was only a moment, but they may have been watching for a while, even before we were focused on the pole."

"And your theory is . . ." Kevin paused as he switched pens, the previous one having run dry, " . . . that this watcher saw Pippin sniff the pole and perhaps heard you discuss with Dwayne that this identified it as a nithing pole that had had Misty's head on it? And you believe that the watcher then became afraid that Pippin's skill represented a threat to them?"

"Very good, Kevin." Peter caught himself sounding condescending and adjusted his tone. "I mean, that's right on. As weird as it sounds, yes, that's what I think."

"Maybe it's not so weird. I mean the whole thing right from the start has been weird, so within the context of that weirdness, this theory is . . . whatever the opposite of weird is."

"Normal? Mundane? Ordinary?" Laura offered.

"Yeah, ordinary. I like that. Just an ordinary dog assassination. At least they're not killing humans yet, but I want you guys to be careful. I'm going to have to talk to Lautermilch too."

"And Sturluson," Peter said quietly, as an unsettling realization began to dawn on him. "But to question, not warn. Grim's blond, he knows those woods, and if anyone in Manitoba other than Laura knows what a nithing pole is, it's him."

"I said before I'd talk to him, and I will. I still think that's a long shot, and he certainly didn't look like the bow hunting type on TV, but then you never know." Kevin straightened his cap and stood up. "Anyway, I just came to check on Pippin. I'm glad he's pulling through. If you think of anything else that might be helpful, you know what to do." Turning to Laura he added, "And you'll make sure he does, right?"

"One hundred percent. No private investigating this time. Not with a lunatic armed with a hunting bow running around." Laura leaned forward, put her hand on Peter's knee and gave him a hard stare. "Understood?"

"Understood," Peter said.

"OK, bye guys. Now I've got to cancel tomorrow night with Stuart," Kevin muttered as he left the office. "Gonna be 18-hour days all week."

Laura left soon after as well to get the laundry room ready for Pippin. They used it from time to time as a makeshift hospital ward for patients Peter didn't want to leave in the clinic alone overnight. After she left, Peter texted a colleague in Winnipeg who was sometimes available for short-notice locum coverage while he took at the least the next two days off. He wanted to spend the time with Pippin, but he also planned to pursue a couple of hunches. He had told Kevin and Laura that he understood that they did not want him to investigate, but that was not the same thing as promising not to. Not anywhere near the same thing. And this had become personal, very personal.

Peter went to the back of the clinic to see Pippin. He was dozing under a thick blanket in an observation kennel on the side of the treatment room. An IV line ran into one of his forelegs. The IV pump made a faint whirring noise. Otherwise, it was quiet back there. Peter opened the kennel and sat down on the floor beside Pippin's head. He whispered his name quietly as he stroked him behind his ear. Pippin opened his eyes halfway and began to wag his tail with a quiet thump-thump.

CHAPTER
Nineteen

Peter had trouble sleeping that night. He knew in advance that he would. Generally, he was an excellent sleeper, especially since he was so careful with caffeine and always did all the right things in the evening — bedroom kept dark and cool, no electronics near the bed, plenty of sunshine and exercise during the day, no alcohol or heavy food right before bed, and so on. He had read the literature, and as was his habit with so much else in life, if there was a scientific consensus regarding the correct approach to something in life, then he abided by it. It was that simple. (a) Find out what the right thing to do is. (b) Do it. That others didn't follow this uncomplicated strategy continued to confuse him.

Even Laura, who was at least as smart as he was, followed her feelings and scientifically unfounded inclinations far more than seemed advisable. But curiously, she was at least as happy and satis-fied with her life as Peter was, so somehow her shambolic approach also seemed to work. Perhaps she had been lucky so far. But there was no getting around the fact that she was fast asleep, and Peter was staring at the ceiling. As he stared at the ceiling, he reasoned that because he normally was so successful at keeping his emotions at a distant clinical remove, when a sudden and especially strong emotion came along that could not be kept at bay, he was out of practice at coping with it. Consequently, while he was working to save Pippin's life that morning, it did flash across his mind that he might have trouble sleeping tonight. The emotions were going to be too strong and persistent.

Peter got out of bed and went to check on Pippin again. It was only 1:20 a.m., and the next check wasn't scheduled until 2:00 a.m., when it was Laura's turn, but he may as well. Perhaps it would settle his mind. Pippin was sleeping. The colour of his gums was good, and his breathing and heart rate were normal. But Peter still felt the buzz of emotion and disordered thoughts commandeering his brain. He rubbed his eyes and stretched. He knew what would help. He would write out his theories. The act of obliging unruly thought to become straight lines on a page always felt akin to running a comb through his tangled neurons.

The correct place for this was the antique desk in the living room. Peter turned the small ornate brass key and slid the rolltop open. His favourite notebook for this sort of thing was in a cubby on the left. It was a bison-hide book that had been given to him by a client in thanks for saving her bulldog, Bella, so he called it Bella's book. He pulled the book down and leafed quickly through the pages that detailed the winter's adventure with the exploding swine barn until he came to a fresh page. Then he retrieved his best fountain pen, a jet-black Lamy, and checked the nib to make sure it was clean. Peter adjusted the light, a green-glass banker's lamp, and adjusted his chair, knowing that as he did these things he was stalling. He didn't know what to write. Normally Pippin would be curled up beside him, and somehow that helped. Perhaps Merry would come? Merry was usually on the couch, but he didn't see her there. Maybe he should look for her? No, he was just stalling some more. She would have gone into the bedroom after Peter left. He had a "no pets in the bedroom" policy as part of his sleep hygiene regimen, but the cat was alert to any opportunity, day or night, to snuggle with Laura.

So, what were his thoughts?

Maybe the best way to start was to use the S.O.A.P. format he had been taught for problem-solving in veterinary school. Write out your subjective findings, objective findings, assessment, and plan. He began to write.

Subjective:

- *None of Patrick, Misty, or Stinky's owners reported having seen or heard anything. None of them could think of any enemies or conceivable motivations for what happened.*

Peter paused. There wasn't much to write here. Subjective findings were generally just the client's reporting of the history of the problem and their observations of the animal at home. That didn't really apply here. Perhaps the S.O.A.P. approach was not that helpful after all. But he decided to keep up with it, if only to try to clear his mind.

Objective:

- *Patrick Baldwin castrated, including penis, and bled out. Found in his field, near the edge of an aspen bluff.*
- *Misty Favel decapitated and bled out. Found outside her pen.*
- *Stinky Dinsdale bled out. Found in his barn.*
- *The Favels, Rose Baldwin, and Peggy Dinsdale have no other connection to each other.*
- *Pippin shot with an arrow in his yard.*
- *Pole with Misty's blood found in a clearing on Favels' new property. Clearing has a ring of 13 seats made of logs but is otherwise unremarkable.*
- *Someone saw us in the clearing and ran away.*
- *Dr. Grimur Sturluson and three graduate students*

claim to have found evidence of an 11th century Norse settlement in the same woods as the clearing. The exact site is unknown.

- Big Bird swallowed a mjolnir that appears to be from the same era on the same property.
- This property recently belonged to Jim Thorkelson, who died of a heart attack. Jim's son, who lives in Calgary, sold it to the Favels. Jim Sr. was interested in his Icelandic heritage. Don't know about Jim Jr.

Assessment:

- *Theory 1:* Everything is connected. The person or persons who mutilated Patrick and Misty, and who bled all three animals dry, is also the person (or persons) who shot Pippin with an arrow, and who set up the nithing pole, and who saw us investigating the clearing.
- *Theory 2:* Not everything is connected. Some of this is coincidence. Patrick, Misty, and Stinky must be connected, and the nithing pole must be connected, but Pippin could be a coincidence, and the possible watcher in the woods could be a coincidence.
- *Assessment of 1 v 2:* Given that violent crime against animals owned by other people is rare (although abuse of one's own animals is sadly too common), especially when it takes on unusual forms as it has here, it is very unlikely that Pippin is in a Poisson clump with the others. It must be connected.

Peter paused to recharge the ink in his pen.

But the watcher could be unconnected. Also unlikely, but not as unlikely. And Grimur's archeology could also be a true coincidence, ~~although less unlikely.~~

Should avoid double negatives, Peter thought.

> *and is more likely to be so than the watcher. Most likely to be a true coincidence is anything to do with the Thorkelsons.*

- > <u>*Assessment of Motives:*</u> *Regardless of whether Theory 1 or 2 is correct, both indicate that the perpetrator or perpetrators is collecting animal blood for some purpose. If Theory 2 is correct, it does not seem they intended to collect Pippin's blood. He had probably lain there for at least ten minutes before Laura found him, and there is no evidence that anyone entered the yard, and his throat certainly wasn't cut. Thank goodness! So there the motive would be to prevent him from sniffing out evidence, which puts suspicion on the watcher.*

> *But regarding the blood — why? The perpetrator is (a) truly insane or delusional, (b) using it in some sort of ritual, (c) trying to cause fear. The last one begs a further "why." Given that the three owners aren't connected, it's unclear.*

<u>*Plan:*</u>

1. *Research ritual uses of blood.*
2. *Return to the area around the clearing to look for evidence the watcher might have left behind and to look for Grimur's dig. Ask Dwayne to come along? Not sure.*
3. *Talk to Rose, Peggy, and Dan and make sure there's no other connection.*

Peter sat back and yawned. This had been useful. His mind felt more orderly again, like a bookshelf that had been straightened and alphabetized. He looked over his plan. None of this intruded on RCMP turf. The first item was just reading, the second was just a repeat of what he had already been doing with his birthday present, and the third was just talking to his clients. Perfectly innocent. Not at all "acting like a private investigator." Nonetheless he was careful to place Bella's book under some papers in a drawer rather than in the open cubby.

CHAPTER
Twenty

Raj, Peter's locum colleague, was able to come up to New Selfoss to cover the clinic Tuesday, but he was unavailable for the rest of the week. Peter had hoped to stay home Wednesday as well, but Pippin was so much better by Tuesday morning already that Peter felt OK about going back to work earlier than planned. Besides, Laura would be home, and even if Pippin took a turn for the worse, he could come with Peter to spend the day at the clinic. There was no logical reason to stay home. Even staying home Tuesday wasn't logical, but somehow Peter just did not feel like being in the clinic. Was this some sort of mild and transitory form of post-traumatic stress disorder? He wasn't sure what that was supposed to feel like, but whatever it was, it was distinctly odd to realize that he was obeying a "feeling."

Pippin's recovery really was astonishing. It didn't matter how often Peter saw this with his patients, he was still amazed by how quickly an animal could bounce back from a major surgery. Spay a dog, and you have to try to stop it from running around the next day. Not too many women even leave bed the day after an ovario-hysterectomy, let alone cause their doctors to worry about them "running around." And for the males, neutering a dog means you've removed his testicles, not just done a little vasectomy snip, yet those guys are ready to jump and play as soon as the anaesthetic wears off. Ask a man who's clutching a bag of frozen peas to his groin after a vasectomy how much jumping and playing he's planning to do! There was no doubt about it: civilization had degraded humans physically and psychologically. Peter had tried to increase his pain tolerance over the years, figuring it might be useful at some point, but he had failed to make much progress. The best he had managed was to always switch his hot shower to ice cold for a few seconds at the end. And he never took painkillers for headaches, although this meant putting up with Laura rolling her eyes at what she called "pointless masochism."

After his breakfast porridge and tea, Peter went into the laundry room to sit with Pippin. Laura had gone out to get some groceries. Pippin's IV was still running, and his wounds and surgical incision were obvious, but otherwise he was very much the same old Pippin. He looked at Peter with his head half-cocked as if to say, "OK, now what?"

Peter understood it to mean that and said, "You know what? I don't think you need to be in here anymore. We don't need all these supplies right at hand, and you're not going to have an accident, are you?"

Peter's tone was upbeat and singsong, so Pippin's tail began to wag slowly. Peter eased the dog to his feet and then took the IV bag off its hook in the wall. They walked slowly down the hall, through the kitchen, and into the living room. Peter glanced around and then took a painting of a puffin off the wall near his armchair. The picture hook was perfectly positioned for the IV bag. He then placed a loose throw blanket on the floor under the hook and settled Pippin in.

"How's that? Not bad, eh?"

Pippin placed his chin on one of his paws and raised his eyebrows at Peter.

"You just rest there while I do some research."

Pippin watched Peter for another minute and then closed his eyes.

Using a small laptop that he kept under the end table, Peter carried out a series of internet searches using various combinations of the words "animal," "blood," "sacrifice," "ritual," and "bloodletting." It was disappointing. It seemed just about every major religion had at some point in its history slaughtered animals and used their blood either to ritually fertilize the soil, or offer to their gods, or anoint themselves with. Some, like Hindu rituals, were plainly less likely in New Selfoss, but the range of options was still too wide. When he added the word "cult" to the search parameters, an even wider array of practitioners of animal sacrifice were presented, from Satanists to adherents of Santeria, which appeared to be an amalgam of voodoo and Catholic practices. Even ancient Greek religion was frequently mentioned in these articles, with reference to their castration of rams catching Peter's attention. Apparently, the Titan Cronus castrated his own father when he deposed him, and he is often depicted in art carrying a sickle, the instrument with which he carried out the bloody emasculation.

He saw that this could turn into a deep internet wormhole, but Peter was tired, and he was wary of wasting time. He stood up slowly so as not to wake Pippin, who was sleeping soundly, making little twitching motions with his paws as he dreamed. Peter stretched and glanced at his watch. *Time for a decaf tea? A bit early, but sure, why not.*

As he was waiting for the kettle to reach 93°C, the ideal steeping temperature for his beloved decaf lapsang souchong, Laura came in through the side door, several bags of groceries in each hand.

"How's the patient?" she asked as she set the bags on the counter.

"Splendid. Resting now. I'll let him sleep a little more and then I'll take him out in the yard. I'm sure his bladder must be full!"

"And what've you been up to?"

"Just researching."

"Researching? About a patient?" Laura asked this with a half-interested tone as she put the groceries away.

He paused. He decided to be honest. "Sort of. It's the blood-letting." Laura didn't say anything and kept stacking cans in the cupboard. "It won't interfere with Kevin's work, and I'm curious. They're my patients after all." This came off sounding more defensive than he had intended.

Laura turned around and sighed. She pushed a loose strand of red hair out of her eyes and then smiled. "It's OK. I get it. I'm curious too. And besides, nobody's going to shoot at you through the screen of your phone or laptop. What did you find out?"

"Not much. Or too much."

Peter's tea was ready, so they walked into the living room together, each to their respective favourite chairs. Pippin didn't stir.

"I mean, every religion does this, or did it at some time in the past, and most cults too. The only one that seems to have an edge is Hellenism because they also have a castration angle."

"Hellenism? Like worshipping Zeus and Apollo and them?"

"Yeah, it's been revived and has official status in Greece again. There's a couple thousand of them there, and then maybe a hundred in the US."

"But none in Canada?"

"Not that I could find. It's a bizarre idea anyway. Can you imagine? Some guy from around here with a wreath of laurel leaves on his head, dressed in white, wielding a sickle?"

"Ha! No, I can't imagine that. But what about blot and heathenism?"

"That didn't show up in my searches. *Blot*, like 'blood' in . . . what? Norwegian? And heathenism, like the religion of the non-Christian heathens?"

"Even though the word sounds like blood, and Icelandic for 'blood' is 'bloth,' the root seems to be Old English for 'sacrifice,' whether blood sacrifice or not." Laura, among her various talents, was also a bit of a linguist, with a particular flair for the old languages of the British Isles and Scandinavia. She could read *Beowulf* in the original Old English. One of her most popular sweaters was a heavy dark green one with the first line, "Hwæt! We Gardena in geardagum, þeodcyninga, þrym gefrunon" picked out in tan in a beautiful flowing font. Peter knew it translated as "Listen! We the spear-Danes in the years of yore."

Peter nodded as he sipped his tea. Laura went on, "Like I mentioned before when I started looking into this, Heathenry is definitely back. They've reclaimed the word 'heathen' and celebrate it as a positive thing. It's a rediscovery of the old Norse, Anglo-Saxon, and Germanic pagan religions. There are lots of different flavours, but one called Ásatrúarfélagið —"

Peter raised his eyebrows, so she stopped to explain.

"It means Asatru Fellowship. Ásatrúarfélagið has official religion status in Iceland now, so they can officiate at marriages and enjoy tax benefits. I think they've even built a temple there."

"So, they make blood sacrifices? Blot?"

"Blot, yes. Blood sacrifice, no. Blot has come to mean any religious festival associated with Asatru. They officially reject animal sacrifice. They're universalists, not folkists."

Peter raised his eyebrows again. When Laura hit her stride on a subject she was knowledgeable about she could be oblivious to how obscure that knowledge was. He supposed he might be similar that way.

"Heathenism is roughly divided into the universalists and the folkists. The universalists take a modern approach to their religion and welcome people of all ethnic backgrounds, whereas the folkists celebrate Heathenry as the true original religion of the northern white race and consider it reserved for them. Folkists still do blood sacrifice and try to adhere to the old ways as closely as possible."

"So, these universalists lean toward New Age paganism, while the folkists lean toward Neo-Nazism."

"Exactly. Some folkists call themselves Odinists, which has a distinctly fascist ring to it."

"Like the Soldiers of Odin far-right group?"

"I guess, although those guys seem more purely political than religious. But I'm sure some of their members are also Odinists."

Pippin stirred, briefly opening his eyes, stretched, rearranged himself, and then went back to sleep. Peter and Laura were quiet for a moment, Peter drinking his tea and Laura looking at something on her phone.

Peter set his tea mug down on the end table. "Remember when I told you that Grim was very quick to correct me when I called the hammer artefact a mjolnir? He said that there is only one Mjölnir, which is the original, wielded by Thor. He was dead serious."

Laura put her phone down and looked at Peter. "Yeah, I remember. I was just searching for Heathenry groups in Manitoba. There're a few, but most seem New Agey, and then there's a handful of plain-tiff posts on a message board from young guys looking for fellow folkists. Do you really think our good Dr. Sturluson could be a folkist or Odinist?"

"It fits." Peter stared at a distant point over Laura's shoulder — giving his brain the space to decode patterns and assemble logical sequences. He was aware that it made him look odd and intense, but he knew that Laura was used to it.

"You'll tell Kevin?" Although this had a rising inflection, it was clearly more a statement than a question.

Peter nodded, still staring. And then Pippin woke up with a noisy yawn and got to his feet. He looked at his IV line with an expression that could only be read as "What is this thing?"

CHAPTER
Twenty-One

Pippin still needed to be on IV, but he was doing so well that Peter felt comfortable leaving him. Laura would be home now regardless. She had an order of Game of Thrones mittens to complete. As always, she kept the designs subtle enough that it was little more than a wink to the in-the-know, as well as keeping the copyright lawyers at bay. Today it was House Stark's silvery grey wolf's head repeated in miniature in a ring around the cuffs of a pair of black mittens. The wool came from Rose Baldwin and had been spun and dyed during the winter. Mittens like these would not be cheap, but her buyers never seemed to care.

Part one of his plan done, he texted Dwayne to find out if he was available and interested to go out to the Favels' again and help with part two: combing the woods for more clues. *Not clues, artefacts*, he corrected himself. As he waited for a reply, a message came in from Dan Favel.

> Heard about Pippin. Really sorry.
> Hope he's doing OK! When you have a minute,
> there's something going on with Bert. No rush.

The coincidence unnerved him, but he quickly reasoned that as their lives had often intersected recently, it was not unusual for both him and Dan to be thinking about contacting each other at roughly the same time.

He texted back.

> No worries. Thanks for asking.
> Pippin's doing really well. So well that I was
> thinking of coming by your place
> to look around some more, if that's OK.
> I can look at Bert then.

That's great about Pippin!
Sure, come by. We're home all day.

Peter found himself hoping that whatever was going on with Bert would give him an excuse to call Alicia. He swatted this thought away as foolish, but it continued to hover in the deep background.

Peter was just about to let Laura know that he needed to go see the ostrich when a reply arrived from Dwayne.

Normally would love to, but the whole pagan thing
bothers me more than I thought it would.
Am working today anyway. But maybe sometime we can
go looking for old Paavo Jarvinen's gold. Good luck.

Peter wrote him that it was OK, he understood and that, yes, it would be fun to try to find that gold. According to the oft-repeated story, it had been lost or hidden somewhere north of town as Paavo had had some sort of mental breakdown and attempted to walk to Finland a century ago. Peter restrained himself from writing what he actually believed, which was that hundreds had tried and failed to find the gold because it either didn't exist or was lost much farther north. The probability of it being within easy access of New Selfoss struck him as exceedingly low. But he liked Dwayne now and didn't want to disappoint him. For someone who once always spoke his mind, heedless of the social consequences, this was still a novel feeling. Peter felt proud of himself at his restraint.

He bid Pippin goodbye, telling him that he wished he could take him along, and then double-checked the metal detector to make sure that he knew how to use it without Dwayne's help. Laura walked by him as he was doing this and remarked, "Checking for metal in that ostrich?"

"Ha, no! But I wonder if it would work. Dan didn't say what was up with Bert. Maybe he swallowed something like Big Bird did!"

Laura folded her arms across her chest and narrowed her eyes. "Do you think looking for artefacts out there is a good idea? Whoever shot Pippin seems to be connected to the woods there."

Peter looked sheepish and, without meeting Laura's steady gaze, said, "Yeah, maybe you're right. I thought Dwayne might come along, but he can't. I'll just see what's up with Bert and leave the metal detecting for another day when they've caught the guy."

This is not what he actually wanted to do, but he had been foolish fussing with the device in the house. He should have quietly loaded it into the truck and dealt with it at Dan's. But maybe Dan would also wonder about the wisdom of poking around the woods on his own. The actual risks could be calculated as very low, but the perceived risk was high, and sometimes one had to allow oneself to be governed by perception.

Laura looked at him skeptically. She knew Peter well enough to know that he was probably saying that just to please her. "And have you called Kevin yet?"

"No," he said, sounding even more sheepish. "But I'll do it right now." He pulled his phone out of his jacket pocket and tapped Kevin's name in recent calls and rang through.

"Voicemail," he said quietly to Laura.

"Hi Kev, it's Peter. Give me a call. Laura and I have been talking and we think there's even more reason to be interested in Grimur. There's something I forgot to tell you about the time I saw him at his office."

"Thanks," Laura said. "I hope the ostrich is OK." She smiled and pecked Peter on the cheek.

Dan was in the paddock with the two remaining ponies when Peter arrived. It was another glorious spring day with the sun making the puddles shine like quicksilver. There was a trace of a silky breeze, and a meadowlark sang in the distance, or at least what Peter thought was a meadowlark. He didn't like to admit this to people, but he didn't know his birds nearly as well as he felt he should.

Dan left the paddock and came over to meet Peter.

"Before I take you to see Bert, I want to show you something," Dan said, his face hard.

"Sure."

"Look at this." Dan pulled a folded piece of paper out of his pocket and handed it over. "It was in our mailbox this morning." He pointed to the silver-grey Canada Post community mailbox which was just visible down the road.

Peter unfolded it and sucked his breath in loudly as he read it.

Skraelings! Now that you have proof that you occupy the sacred Vesturvatnsland of our ancestors, you have no excuse to stay.

This will be your only <u>written</u> warning.

Muna Bjartur!

"Skraelings?" he asked as he handed it back to Dan.

"Yeah, I had to look it up. It's what the Norse called the Indigenous people they met in Labrador and Newfoundland." He paused and gave Peter a wry smile. "It's not a term of endearment. I had to figure out 'Vesturvatnsland' with an online Icelandic dictionary. It appears to mean 'west water country,' which I guess refers to the lands around the lake here. But when you search the word on Google you get one of those very rare zero-hit returns, so it doesn't seem to be a real thing. And 'muna' means 'remember.' Bjartur is a name, but who he is or was, I have no clue."

"But it's a threat regardless."

"After what happened to Misty? You bet it is. Kim is really freaked out."

"Have you called Kevin yet?"

"I called the station. Kevin was out, so they're sending Kristine." Dan read Peter's face. "Yeah, I know. But she's good. You know, solid and professional. Not saying anything bad about your brother-in-law, but she's maybe the better cop."

"But not necessarily the better human being."

"No, not necessarily. Let's go have a look at Bert while we're waiting." Dan jerked his head toward the paddock beyond where the ponies were.

"Aren't you going to put him in the stanchion?" Peter eyed the bird's massive legs and pictured the spike-like toenails. Fatalities were rare, but they were undeniably vivid, ranging from people having their jugular vein sliced open to being disembowelled like in some gruesome medieval execution.

"Nah, Bert's really gentle. It's Mr. Hooper you have to watch out for. He and the others are in the far pasture."

While Dan held the giant bird still, Peter carefully inspected her feathers and skin. Dan swore that he had seen "bugs." Sure enough, there they were — a half-dozen ticks, some crawling and some embedded in the pinkish skin. Dan had found them exceedingly horrifying. Peter explained that they were a nuisance rather than a health risk as there were no bird diseases in Manitoba transmitted by this type of tick. He was about to dive into deeper scientific detail when Dan was saved by the arrival of an RCMP cruiser.

As they walked over to meet Kristine, Peter quickly wrapped up by explaining that while ticks could cause significant blood loss in smaller animals, given Bert's size it would take hundreds more than the few ticks they found to do him any harm. Dan shuddered when Peter said "hundreds more." Nonetheless, Peter said he would prescribe a tick control product.

Dan took a couple of brisk steps ahead of Peter and extended his hand to Kristine. "Thank you for coming, Corporal Björnsdóttir."

"You're welcome." She shook Dan's hand and then turned to Peter with a smile that he felt could best be described as ambiguous. The corners of her mouth were up, but the rest of her face was as if stone carved. "Hello, Dr. Bannerman."

"Peter," he corrected, as he always did when she called him Dr. Bannerman.

She appeared to take no notice and turned back to Dan. "Have you got the threat letter with you? Is that it?" She indicated the paper he was still holding.

He nodded and handed it to her. She examined it silently for a couple of minutes, turned it over, and held it up to the sun before giving it back.

"No envelope? Nothing else?"

Dan shook his head.

"And this is the first time you've received something like this?"

"Yes."

"I'll have a look at your mailbox too before I leave, but this is kids thinking they're being funny. Be alert, but don't worry too much about it."

"That's it?" Peter asked, unable to stop himself from sounding incredulous.

Kristine looked Peter hard in the eye. She was almost as tall as he was. In her perfectly pressed uniform, and with her blond hair in a tight bun under her RCMP cap, she looked especially imposing, like a Nordic ice goddess about to wreak vengeance, perhaps by firing lasers from her unnaturally intense blue eyes.

"A report will be on file," she said crisply. "I will also ask if any of the other owners of mutilated animals or any of the neighbours around here received similar notes. And I will search the databases for 'Bjartur.' But other than that, yes, that's it."

CHAPTER
Twenty-Two

Laura called to Peter from the living room as soon as he stepped in the door. "I think I found something!"

"Great!" Peter called back as he took his boots off and hung up his jacket. "And wait until I tell you what happened at Dan's!"

Peter stepped into the living room. "But first, where's my boy?"

Pippin stood up from his dog bed near the fireplace and wagged his tail. He seemed to know that his IV line would prevent him from coming up to greet Peter, so he didn't try, although he clearly had the energy now to do so.

"Something crazy?" Laura asked while Peter gave Pippin a good ear scratch, murmuring, "Not yet, boy. A little longer on the fluids. Just a little."

"Yeah, they found a letter in their mailbox this morning accusing them of occupying sacred Norse land. They called it . . ." Peter paused as he tried to recall the compound Icelandic name, ". . . Vesturvatnsland. And the letter referred to Dan and Kim as Skraelings, which is apparently a racist term."

"It wasn't originally. It was a neutral way of referring to unfamiliar groups of people who weren't Norse. The Irish were called Skraelings too. But it's taken on a different meaning these days, which plugs in neatly with what I found."

Peter sat down in his armchair opposite Laura, wondering as he did so whether he should make some tea first, but deciding that he was curious enough to hear what she had to say that the tea could wait.

"I did a bit more digging online after you left," she continued. "Specifically, I decided to do a deep dive into the Canadian 8kun folkist message boards. And bingo, I started finding references to a Manitoba-based group called the Saga Study Society. They don't have any kind of internet footprint elsewhere, but on these message boards the members openly talk about how the Norse need to be considered among the original peoples of Canada and be accorded rights as such."

"Ha!" Peter laughed. "So, they wish they had had the 'right'" — Peter used air quotes — "to be sent to residential schools? The 'right' to have their culture considered inferior? The 'right' to be given crappy little parcels of land in the bush in exchange for their freedom?" He laughed again.

"Yeah, no. That doesn't come up. But the point is, that seems to be the same philosophy as whoever wrote that letter."

"For sure. I don't suppose any of the posts are signed 'nutty-archeologyprof101'?"

Laura smiled. "No. The main people seem to be 'valkyrie3939,' 'MBthorsbondsman,' and 'vesturvatnslander88.'"

"I get 88, but are there really 3,938 other valkyries out there?"

"Maybe, but three and nine are also sacred numbers in Norse mythology. What's 88?"

"Eighth letter of the alphabet is H, so 88 is H H, or Heil Hitler." Peter rolled his eyes as he said this.

"Oh, Jesus. It always goes back to Hitler, doesn't it? Who did these doorknobs worship before him? Genghis Khan? But it is starting to make sense now. In a twisted sort of way, I mean."

Peter nodded and said, "Yes, in a twisted sort of way. I'm going to make some tea. Want any?"

"No, thanks."

When Peter returned to the living room Laura was engrossed in her knitting, her needles making a rhythmic click-click-click sound he found soothing. Every so often she would stop and jot something down on a pad of paper she kept beside her. It was always numbers, but he didn't know what exactly they referred to. He had never thought to ask. He set his mug down and went over to pat Pippin again before returning to his chair to sip and think.

The reference to a "Saga Study Society" in particular kept looping through his mind. It resonated with something just beyond the grasp of his immediate conscious memory. Some people referred to clues like this as puzzle pieces, but he visualized them more as Lego pieces. Puzzle pieces can only be placed together in a specific way. But that's not the way these things worked. People were always putting pieces of information together incorrectly, creating a picture, but not the right one. You could never do that with a jigsaw puzzle; those pieces can only be made to fit together in a specific way. With Lego, on the other hand, every piece can be stuck to every other piece. But if you don't have the instructions, and you don't even know what the final product is supposed to look like, you could easily build the wrong thing and convince yourself that it was right. That pile of grey bricks could become the Starship *Enterprise*, or Hogwarts. Only by looking at the details do you start to get a notion as to which is more plausible. Sure, you could *try* to build the *Enterprise*, but it would be an odd looking one.

He held the Saga Study Society piece in his mind for a couple of minutes, trying it with various other pieces, but nothing looked right so he set it to the side. More data was needed, more pieces. And several of the existing pieces needed to be brought into clearer focus. Experience told him that this would just take time. There was no point in forcing the mind to do something it wasn't ready for yet. The Lego metaphor was still apt. Although he sometimes thought about joining an AFOL (adult fans of Lego) group, he hadn't built with Lego seriously in a few years. But back when he did, he'd sometimes get stuck, staring at a pile of bricks, unsure of what he wanted to build and therefore having no way of knowing what pieces he needed. Once he had decided what he was building, he'd know where the gaps were, but at this early stage, he had no idea how many pieces were missing, let alone where they might fit. And then when he did fill those gaps, had he even built the right thing?

Peter shook his head. Metaphors were always inexact descriptions of reality, and there was a danger in getting too caught up in them. In reality, Saga Study Society reminded him of something, and he wasn't sure what. He'd let that ferment in his subconscious for now.

When he snapped out of this reverie, he saw that Laura was still knitting but had looked up to smile at him, and Pippin had gone back to sleep. Merry had entered the room silently at some point in the last few minutes and was lying on the empty brown leather chesterfield, to Peter's right. The whole family was there. There was a time when Peter pitied clients who referred to their pets as children. It seemed an unnecessary comparison to make, and somehow undignified and a little overblown, overwrought, and too sentimental, besides being a misuse of the language. In his younger, more arrogant days, he would often smile inwardly at women who did this, wanting to ask them what it was like to give birth to a puppy or a kitten. Peter and Laura had decided not to have kids, so Peter couldn't make a fair comparison, but for many years he remained firm in his belief that pets were not children. It was a metaphor, like his clues as Lego pieces, but a metaphor of limited use.

Yet here he was now, thinking of the four of them as a family, with Pippin and Merry as dependent junior members of that family. In other words, children. The evolution of his feelings on this had occurred by stealth, without him even being aware that he was changing his mind. He still felt that it would be preferable if the language offered a different word for dependent junior family members who happened to be animals, but it didn't, and he realized that nobody else was confused by this. Everyone understood that there wasn't an implied biological connection. And what about adopted human children? Or blended families? Clearly the language was being bent and adapted in all sorts of other ways anyway.

And then there was Laura. His wife, his best friend, his partner in many ways, and the indisputable centre of his life, but also someone he was so comfortable with that he knew that he took her for granted. They had known each other since high school and been dating since they met by chance again at university in Saskatoon, which was now 20 years ago. She was so integrated into his life that she sometimes felt like just another component of his identity, like his height, or his profession, or his passion for geography, rather than being a whole independent person who was the self-referential centre of her own universe. Moreover, they had become so easy with each other that there was no friction at all, other than her annoyance at him dabbling in investigation, and even that had lessened it seemed. She was actually helping with this one. Where there was no friction, there was also no heat. A physics metaphor and thus, again, limited like every metaphor, but it stuck in his mind and it bothered him.

From Lego as clues, to pets as children, to lack of friction as . . . ? Peter couldn't quite find the word. And that was too many metaphors anyway. He sighed. He had let his tea go cold. Laura continued to knit, and the pets continued to sleep. He hadn't checked his phone in a while and the alerts were off, so he picked it up. In addition to a half-dozen Instagram likes of his arty black and white picture of Pippin sleeping earlier this morning, there was a text message from Kevin.

Been at a sweat for the Alexander kid.
Mending fences. It was good. You have info
on Sturluson? I'll call you when I'm done here.

And a message from Alicia Loewenstein.

In town tomorrow thru Fri. Dinner?

Funny, he had just been thinking about her earlier that day when he went to see Bert! If he were a superstitious man, he would make something of the timing of her text coming in and what he had just been thinking about regarding Laura. But Peter was not a superstitious man. Far from it. This was coincidence in its purest form. A little Poisson clump of women.

CHAPTER
Twenty-Three

K evin called just after lunch. Laura had gone to pick up some more wool from Rose and to drop that D&D vest off at the post office, and Peter was about to take Pippin on a short walk up and down the street.

"Back from the sweat now. Never done one before. It was pretty cool actually, and I think we're closer to being on the same page as the family. I'm going to put more time into that case and shift a few other things to Kristine, Ryan, and Mark."

"Including the mutilations and the attempt to kill Pippin?"

"I'll share that one with Kristine. She tells me she was out at the Favels' for another matter anyway."

"I think they might be connected. The threat's from a group that according to Laura's research could be involved in animal sacrifice." Peter hoped that by giving Laura credit, Kevin would take the theory more seriously.

"Oh? And this is also connected to what you wanted to tell me about the prof?" Kevin's voice was neutral but betrayed a suggestion of curiosity, which was unusual in his conversations with Peter. Normally his tone when discussing police work was more on the skeptical side of neutral.

Peter went on to relay what Laura had told him about Heathenry and the difference between its universalist and folkist branches, and what she had found out about the presence in Manitoba of a right-wing racist folkist group called the Saga Study Society. He then explained why he thought Grimur might be a practitioner of Heathenry.

When he was finished there was silence for a moment. He could practically hear his brother-in-law think.

"So, you are proposing that Dr. Sturluson, that scrawny little academic with the goatee and natty outfits, is some kind of a Norse cult leader and is draining the blood of farm animals" — Peter made a noise to interrupt, but Kevin went on — "and is also trying to scare Indigenous folk off their property because he wants to . . . what? Rebuild an ancient Viking settlement and get back to the good old ways?"

"I wouldn't put it exactly like that, but yes, other than the rebuild part, that's more or less it."

Kevin laughed. "You're out of your freaking tree, Pete, but I grant you that I do need to consider Sturluson a person of interest at the least. I'm supposed to meet him this afternoon anyway. Called him after the last time we spoke. Very polite guy. Seemed quite surprised I'd want to talk to him."

After he hung up, Peter looked at Alicia's text again. It would be fun to see her. Laura knew her from back when they were all in Saskatoon, so they could all have dinner together. Laura had her Craft Guild meeting Thursday, but Wednesday was free.

Great! How about dinner Wednesday?

The reply came almost immediately.

Shoot, sister just texted that
she got us ballet tix Wed. Thurs OK?

Peter considered a moment. Laura wouldn't mind — she had her meeting.

Sure. Thursday's good.
I'll make reservations and will let you know.

Dinner with Alicia Loewenstein. Peter was looking forward to it, but, at the same time, felt odd about it in a way he couldn't define.

Pippin continued to show astonishing improvement. When they got to the end of the block, he strained on the leash to go farther. Carrying an IV bag aloft would have made this impossible, but Peter had disconnected the IV for the walk and capped it.

"Really, boy? *More* walking? Are you sure?"

Pippin looked very sure, so they walked on, down the slight slope to where the road curved toward town.

"Damn it!" Peter suddenly said. Pippin looked up at him. "Sorry, Pip, nothing to do with you. I just remembered that I promised Chris and Ken to meet them tonight for a stupid darts club practice."

Not hearing any of the key words that interested him, and noting that the tone didn't suggest anything either, Pippin turned his attention to sniffing a lamppost.

"I didn't promise to join, I just promised to come try. But I can cancel because you're sick."

Pippin looked anything but sick as he pulled on the leash to check out the next pee spot, a prominent boulder at the bend up ahead.

When they returned home, Laura was back. Peter mentioned cancelling the Pointsmen meeting, but she insisted he go. Pippin was doing fine, and she'd be home anyway. Peter needed to get out and see friends more often. Laura had a busy social circle in her crafting community, as well as old high school friends she was still in touch with. It would be good for Peter to do more of that sort of thing. He reluctantly agreed, and then after Laura left the room he realized that he had forgotten to mention the dinner plans with Alicia.

As soon as he stepped into The Flying Beaver that evening, Peter was glad that Laura had talked him into it. Pippin was doing well, and it was good to get out, and he was looking forward to a fresh pint of Manipogo Pale Ale. The darts were secondary. Even so, he decided that he would make a reasonable effort in order to not disappoint Chris, who he supposed would count as his best friend, although they rarely saw each other outside of couples' games nights and dinner parties.

He loved The Flying Beaver. In his mind, there was no place he knew of west of Toronto that come as close to nailing that old British pub vibe he loved so much. He couldn't point to just one specific element. It was one of those situations where the whole was greater than the sum of its parts, with the parts being the slightly irregular dark wooden beams, the small seating nooks, the stone hearth, the eccentric bric-a-brac on the shelves, and the jumble of signs, posters, and photos on the wall. There were also the dried hops festooned like a garland over the bar; the mix of worn Persian carpets, flagstones, and beat-up hardwood on the floors; and, not least, Lloyd, the laconic but warm-hearted owner and chief barman. The eponymous Castoropteryx, the taxidermal beaver with goose wings, on the wall behind the bar was the chief element that would seem out of place in the English Lake District.

Chris and Ken were already standing by the dartboards, their pints half-drained. Ken spotted Peter first and waved him over.

"Horrible news about Pippin, but so glad he's doing well enough that you could make it," Ken said.

"How you holding up Peter?" Chris asked.

"I'm good, thanks. And yes, he's doing so much better than we feared."

"Crazy stuff. I hear it was an arrow?"

"Wow, word does get around. Yes, a hunting arrow through his liver. In one side and out the other, just missing major blood vessels."

Chris shook his head. "What an effed-up world."

Ken, who had been straightening the dartboards, shook his head as well. "Effed-up," he agreed. "But darts is where we leave the world behind!"

Peter nodded, keeping his doubts firmly to himself.

"Tonight's just a chance to see where you're at. We've got high hopes with you being a surgeon!" Ken laughed and clapped Peter on the shoulder as he said this, while Chris nodded and smiled broadly. "Season's done anyway. We had to drop out after, well, you know."

"Bullseye Gliders took the cup," Chris explained, guessing correctly that Peter hadn't followed the Manitoba Darts Federation season, or its finals.

"Effing Gimli. Those guys always swagger around wearing their effing Viking helmets and fur vests. Roaring, chanting, chest thumping," Ken muttered.

"Viking helmets?" Peter asked.

"Oh yeah. Authentic ones, they say. But it's that cartoon crap with horns on the sides. They even pray to Odin before the match. Or fake it to psych us out. Tried to bring a trained raven in here once, but Lloyd said no way." He took a swig from his beer. "Effing Gimli. Effing Venis." Then, brightening up, he went on, "Anyway, we've got till October to get in shape. Lots of time. Next season is the 50th anniversary of the MDF, so everyone will be gunning for the Golden Dartboard even more. The steering committee is going to get it re-gilded!"

"Re-gilded?"

"Yeah, just imagine!" Ken said, beaming.

Peter pictured this and was unmoved. Was he really going to sign up for weekly sessions with a bunch of goofy darts fanatics? Friendship was important, and as a geek of sorts himself, he had sympathy for anyone with a fanatical devotion to an unusual hobby, but darts? Really? He would do his best to aim badly, and they'd have to find someone else. He could come and watch some of their matches for the camaraderie, but it was dishonest to pretend to be excited about winning a trophy, even if it were being freshly painted gold. These guys deserved a true enthusiast, not a pretender. By throwing really badly tonight he would be doing them a favour. He was a true enough friend to swallow his pride and suck.

But he didn't suck. Try as he might, the darts flew true. Chris explained the arcana involving the dart weight (anything from 18 to 40 grams, with lighter flying in a more parabolic arc and being better for beginners) and metals (brass, nickel, or tungsten, with the latter being the most desirable and, naturally, also the most expensive) and shape (personal preference, but some interesting physics at play), and as he explained it something shifted inside Peter. A quiet voice deep within him whispered, *This is kind of cool.* The other factor was that it turned out that he could not swallow his pride as he had planned. The selected dart felt so perfectly balanced in his hand, and his vision narrowed on the bullseye like some kind of advanced laser targeting system, that he knew he could hit it. To not hit it would be a bigger lie than the lie about being interested in the game. Luckily, he never told them he wasn't interested, not in so many words, despite having felt disinterested when Ken enthused about the 50th anniversary cup. And now that he had more data, he saw that interest was possible and not incompatible with who he was.

Ken's and Chris's jaws both slackened as Peter hit three bullseyes in a row, before the fourth went just wide of its mark.

"Jesus H," Ken said, almost in a whisper.

"You just did an Alan Evans!" Chris exclaimed.

"A what?" Peter asked.

"An *Alan Evans*," Chris said, still looking like he had just witnessed the Second Coming. "That's what we call three bullseyes in a row. Kind of like a hat trick in a hockey game, although those goals don't need to be consecutive. Evans was world champ back in the '70s and '80s."

Ken was positively frothing with delight, "Ha! Look out, Selkirk, Morden-Winkler, Steinbach, Brandon, and effing Gimli! You're a goddamned natural! We won't even hold it against you that you're not an Icelander!"

Peter tried to stop himself from beaming. Although he denied it, he had always enjoyed praise. It probably stemmed from his parents only offering a benign but bland "That's fine, Peter" when he brought home straight-A report cards.

"Actually, I'm an Orkneyman on my dad's side, and that's probably as much Norse blood as it is Scottish, if not more."

"Well, that's perfect then! Welcome to the New Selfoss Pointsmen, Dr. Peter Bannerman!" Ken shot out his hand for a hearty shake, as did Chris.

"This calls for something a step up from beer. I'll grab us a round of whiskies, eh? Highland Park for our Orkneyman?" Ken pushed his shirtsleeves up past his elbows and crossed his arms in an emphatic way.

"Sounds great! Thanks," Peter said, and just as he said it, he caught sight of the tattoo he had seen up at Snaefell — the three spooning Nordic-looking serpents or dragons. What was it that Ken had said about it during his birthday party? Had he even asked? "Hey Ken, I might have asked this before, but what's the design of that tattoo mean? It's new, right?"

Ken glanced at his arm and then smiled at Peter, "Yeah, about six months or so. It's for the three dragons in Norse mythology: Jormungandr, Nidhogg, and Fafnir. But to be honest, I just thought it was a cool design."

That didn't sound even remotely familiar. Perhaps Peter hadn't asked after all? Or had he just completely destroyed that particular memory neuron?

The scotch was brought round, toasts were made, and a few more darts were thrown, with Peter continuing to score high. It could have turned into an uproarious evening, but Peter wanted to get home to check on Pippin.

As he was getting ready to go, a thought occurred to him.

"Don't we need a fourth?"

"It's not mandatory for MDF play, but ideally, yes," Chris answered. "But we haven't had any luck yet. Do you know anyone who might be interested?"

As a matter of fact, Peter thought he did.

CHAPTER
Twenty-Four

Peter wasn't tired when he got home. He'd had just enough to drink to give him the kind of buzz that made him feel more alert. One more would have made him sleepy, and any less wouldn't have given him this boost. Perhaps the buzz was heightened by his Alan Evans performance at the dartboard. It was the first time in his life he had been considered a natural at any sport, although he had to admit to himself that calling darts a "sport," as its practitioners tended to do, was allowing more semantic licence than he would normally be comfortable with. In his mind, darts occupied the borderlands between sport and game, along with bowling, curling, golf, croquet, and a few other unathletic "sports," although he had to admit that "sport" sounded cooler than "game."

Pippin was asleep on his blanket in the living room, and Laura had dozed off in her chair beside him with a book on her lap. This never failed to astonish Peter. If her body demanded it, Laura could sleep anywhere, anytime. Peter, on the other hand, needed the conditions to be just right, or he needed to be in a state of extreme exhaustion and sleep-deprivation, like that time after a sleepless flight from Toronto to London when he passed out at Heathrow and missed his connecting flight to Amsterdam.

He smiled at his dog and wife as he quietly snuck past to retrieve the laptop from the desk. He wouldn't even make tea. The kettle was too loud, and in any case, oddly enough, he didn't feel like it tonight. He would get some stuff done on the computer until he got tired. That wasn't a proper sleep strategy as it would be too much screen time before bed, but he was in a mood to throw caution to the wind.

The first order of business was to shoot Dwayne an email asking him whether he'd be interested in trying out for the Pointsmen. He wasn't sure how he'd mesh with Chris and Ken, but something about his quiet and unexpected poise made him think that he'd be good at darts. Now that Peter was on the team it became important to him that they win, so native skill trumped social dynamics.

Next, on a whim, he decided to Google the three Norse dragons, Jormungandr, Nidhogg, and Fafnir, that Ken had said his tattoo was based on. While it was interesting, it wasn't especially helpful. Jormungandr was apparently the mortal enemy of Thor, while Nidhogg was described as the "corpse gnawer," and Fafnir guarded a hoard of gold. Apparently, Fafnir had originally been a dwarf, but he decided to slowly turn himself into a dragon so as to better guard the gold. Collectively they represented chaos, death, and greed. He assumed that Ken was oblivious to this symbolism.

Peter sat back and stretched, arching his back, and reaching his arms up as far as they would go. A little stiff, but still not tired. He wasn't sure why he was checking up on Ken's tattoo. It was just an ill-defined feeling. Given that this was an irrational basis for any further searching, he let it go.

He glanced over at Laura and Pippin. Both were still fast asleep. Merry had appeared in the living room in the meantime though, but she was asleep too, on Laura's lap, wedged between her stomach and the book. That's how soundly Laura slept. Peter shook his head slowly in amazement and then turned back to the laptop.

There was one more thing he wanted to do, and then he would go to bed, tired or not. He wasn't sure how to access the 8kun message forums, and a Google search only brought up hits discussing it rather than any sort of link to it. Variations on 8kun.com or .net led nowhere as well. Then he noticed an unfamiliar icon on the desktop. He clicked it, and there he was. Apparently, these message boards ran off of their own software rather than through a standard browser. That made sense, he supposed.

The landing page was plain, like something from the early days of the internet in the 1990s — just a long list of what appeared to be individual forums. As it was alphabetical, it was easy to find the Saga Study Society. Peter clicked on the blue underlined link and was taken to a page dominated by a picture of a stone onto which were carved a series of runic letters. He guessed they were some banal celebration of Nordic excellence, but he left the decoding for later. For the moment, his attention was drawn to a chat box below buttons marked "login" and "new member." He clicked on the latter. This opened a box where he was invited to create a username. Peter thought for a moment and then typed "heimdall9." Heimdall was the lesser-known Norse god who guarded the Bifröst bridge between Asgard, where the gods lived, and Midgard, where people lived. And Laura had explained that nine was a sacred number to the Norse. It seemed like a good choice.

The username you have selected is taken.
Please select a different one.

Peter rubbed his chin and then tried, heimdall88.

Welcome heimdall88. A group administrator will contact you
with an access code to the forum. Please check back later.

Pleased to have gotten this far, but disappointed that he couldn't dive directly into the forums, Peter was about to shut the laptop down when typing appeared in the chat box. It was valkyrie3939.

Who sent you?

Peter thought hard for a few seconds and then took a chance.

Bjartur.

There was no response. *Shoot*, he thought, *I was wrong.*
Then suddenly the chat box came to life again.

What did he tell you?

Peter took another chance. He quickly opened a tab with Google
Translate.

Vesturvatnsland er fyrir íslendinga.

West Water Land is for Icelanders.
The cursor blinked in the box for two or three long minutes
before typing began again.

Icelandic. Nice touch. Access code: bhjg56acg

Thank you!

Chat soon. Góða nótt.

Peter was eager to start a chat but figured it would be wise to
take the "good night" at face value.

Góða nótt.

He couldn't resist having a peek though, so he clicked on the login
button and entered heimdall88 and bhjg56acg. This took him to a

page with a live chat that was not active at the moment. However, there was a sidebar listing links to files hosted on the group's fileserver.

One link immediately caught his eye: Bjartur Saga. It was a PDF. He clicked on it and what opened appeared to be a scan of an old document. It was tan coloured — antique vellum, Peter guessed. It was eight pages long and was written in a beautiful but, to Peter, unreadable script. He scanned this for a few minutes, trying to make out any words, but was unsuccessful. He backed out and looked again at the files. Nested under the Bjartur Saga file was another PDF titled BSEngTrans. He chuckled to himself at the abbreviation for Bjartur Saga before opening the document. It began with the words, "The Greenlander Bjartur, son of Ingolf, sailed west beyond Helluland before sailing south into a great new water into which flowed a mighty river that pointed the way farther south to a rich country."

Peter sucked his breath in. *I guess I'll make some tea after all*, he thought.

Peter deliberately avoided looking at the kitchen clock while he made his decaf green tea. He didn't want to know how late it was, but he couldn't stop his brain from automatically estimating. Probably shortly after midnight. It took an enormous force of will to stop himself from confirming that. He distracted himself by watching the kettle carefully so that he could take it off at 75°C, before it became noisy. He had picked green tea because it was ideal at this temperature. Not only did he not want to wake Laura out of kindness to her, but also because he didn't want her asking what he was doing up so late on the computer. It wasn't that he wanted to hide that he'd logged into the Saga Study Society — Laura had done that herself after all — it was more that he wanted to study and digest before discussing this with anyone. As he considered this, he realized that he didn't know what Laura's username was. He'd have to ask.

Peter sat back down with his tea and began to read the saga. It was much as he might have guessed. Bjartur and his doughty band of companions eventually found their way down what was obviously Lake Winnipeg and settled on the southeast shore, presumably where the archeology site near present day New Selfoss was. He grimaced at the coincidence of 19th-century Icelanders ending up exactly where their 11th-century predecessors had been. He didn't like this sort of coincidence. Real coincidences occurred, of course, but this one struck him as odd. As always, more data was needed. He read on.

The colony was described as thriving. It was claimed to be on land that was unoccupied neutral territory between the warring tribes. They weren't named, but Peter presumed these to be the Sioux to the south and west, and Anishinaabe to the north and east. It also struck him as excessively convenient that the Norsemen found "unoccupied land" to claim. But then the sagas generally were written in a self-serving retrospective voice. There followed a dull accounting of the toing and froing from Greenland of various settlers, as well as squabbles within the community. He kept alert for the mention of nithing poles or animal sacrifice, but there was none. Only people slaying each other with axes in dull-witted blood feuds over land or love or straying sheep. Peter wondered about sheep being transported that distance by sea. Viking ships were open and —

"Whatcha reading?" came a playful voice from directly behind him.

Peter let out a little yelp and whipped his head around, "Don't do that! Don't sneak up on me like that!"

Pippin jumped up from his napping blanket at the sudden noise, looking dazed and groggy.

Laura laughed, "I wasn't sneaking. I woke up and came over to say hi. You were just so focused on the computer."

"Well, you just about gave me a heart attack."

"Sure. So, what are you reading?" She craned her head closer and before Peter could answer continued, "Ah, I see you found Bjartur."

"Oh, you know about this?"

"Yeah, I dug around a bit while you were tossing darts." She yawned and stretched. "How'd that go, by the way?"

"Well. It went well. Turns out I have knack for it." Peter shrugged and made a "who would have guessed it" face.

"So, you're a, what, Pointer now?"

"Pointsman, yes."

"Points*man*, so no women?" Laura said this in a flat deadpan.

"Good" — Peter paused a fraction of a second — "point."

They both laughed. Any odd doubts he had had about their relationship dissipated like morning mist in the sun. What had that been about? And anyway, real Alicia would be nothing like fantasy Alicia.

"What did you think of the saga?" Peter asked.

"It's interesting for sure," Laura said as she slid a stool over to sit down beside Peter. Pippin had fallen back asleep, and Merry was nowhere to be seen. The house was silent, and the night was utterly black outside the windows, no streetlamps or neighbours' lights being visible from their angle. "There have always been rumours about lost sagas. My parents used to talk about them. In the early 1700s there was a massive fire in Copenhagen where all the sagas were kept. Arni Magnusson, an Icelandic scholar working there, managed to save most of them, but not all."

"All the sagas were in Denmark? That makes no sense."

"It was originally an oral tradition, and Iceland was an extremely poor place in the Middle Ages. They only started writing them down in the 1200s and 1300s, and then only a few copies on vellum. In the 1600s a bishop in Iceland gathered up all the copies he could find and sent them to Denmark — Iceland was ruled by Denmark then — because the storage conditions would be better there. Iceland had no libraries, archives, or anything like that. Magnusson carried on the work, trying to gather all the fragments of sagas, as well as the *Edda* —"

"*Edda*?" Peter interrupted.

"Those are shorter stories and poems, and more mythological than the sagas." Laura cleared her throat and continued, "He gathered everything he could, including from Sweden. But then there was this terrible fire which burned for four days and destroyed most of the city."

"That's terrible. Amazing to think what else might have been lost, given that there were so few copies of most books and documents in those days. Kind of like the burning of the Library of Alexandria in Caesar's time."

"Actually, there's some debate about what really happened in Alexandria, but you've got the right general idea," Laura said. "So, Magnusson is a hero."

"Absolutely. Most Icelanders to this day know his name and what he did. He single-handedly saved 90 percent of their cultural heritage. The sagas and *Edda*s are everything. It's Shakespeare, Dickens, and Austen all rolled into one for them."

"But not 100 percent."

"Not 100 percent."

"So, do we know anything about how or when Bjartur's saga surfaced?"

Laura pointed at the screen. "When you get to the end there is a note thanking an Ingvar Gustafsson for finding it in a forgotten private collection in Norway and providing it to the Saga Study Society. I searched for him. It's a pretty common name in Sweden, with ten on LinkedIn alone, plus a Wikipedia reference to an apparently well-known colonel in the Swedish military."

"But no one in Iceland, Denmark, or Norway, and no one with any connection to history, archeology, the antiquarian document trade, etcetera?"

"Nope. And searches for 'Bjartur's saga' only return hits for the main character in Halldor Laxness's *Independent People*."

"I love that book." Peter's gaze darted to their copy in the bookcase beside the fireplace.

"Me too." Laura smiled.

"But nobody anywhere outside of the Saga Study Society ever mentions an ancient saga by that name."

"Nope."

"Weird."

"Very. And I need to update Kevin on all this, but it's late. I'll call him tomorrow." Laura said this quietly as she leaned over to kiss Peter on the shoulder. "Coming to bed now?"

Peter had returned his attention to the screen. "Yeah, soon," he said, distracted.

CHAPTER
Twenty-Five

"So, how did Raj manage?" Peter asked Theresa at the clinic on Wednesday morning, after he detailed Pippin's remarkably good Tuesday.

"Really well. It was pretty busy, but he handled the pace fine and the clients seem to like him."

"Super! And how's it looking today?" he asked as he rifled through the mail.

"Busy. No surgery, but back-to-back appointments all morning, and then five farm calls this afternoon."

"Five?" Given the amount of driving and the variability in how long these calls could take, they tried to schedule no more than four in an afternoon. He smiled though to make sure that Theresa didn't think he was upset.

"Yeah, sorry, but Dan Favel called first thing. He apologized a dozen times because you had apparently just been there yesterday, but another one of the ostriches doesn't look right this morning. I squeezed him in at the end of your day. Thursday's really busy too."

"It's OK, no worries. Did he say which one?"

"I think he said Mr. Hooper. Does that sound right?"

"Yeah, they're all named after Sesame Street characters. Mr. Hooper's the mean one according to Dan. Great." Peter dragged out the "great" with a comic Scottish accent and sighed dramatically. He privately wondered whether Dan was becoming an ostrich hypochondriac. He had seen this sort of thing before with new pet owners. Their first puppy so much as hiccups and they're on the phone in a panic.

Peter's morning was as busy as Theresa said it would be, but everything was routine, so it flowed in a way that made it feel like three minutes had elapsed, not three hours. The afternoon was also routine and not only felt quick, but was quick, so he was able to get to the Favels' at four thirty, half an hour ahead of schedule. An RCMP cruiser was in the drive, but the only person Peter could see was Dan.

"Yeah, you just missed Kevin. He got here a few minutes ago. He's in the woods now, I think." Dan inclined his head toward the aspen and tamarack across the field.

"He say what he was looking for? Investigating that letter, or Misty?"

"Maybe, but he said that Dr. Sturluson didn't show up for a meeting they had scheduled and one of his students said he might be out here."

"But his van isn't here."

"Yeah, I pointed that out to Kevin, but it didn't seem to faze him. He looked pretty intense, even for a Mountie. He didn't say anything else, but just walked really quickly into the trees."

Peter's stomach tightened. He felt an irrational, almost magnetic, pull emanating from the woods. He knew that this was his ravening curiosity trying to take command of him again, but it would have to wait. There'd be no way to explain to Dan why he would choose to chase Kevin, rather than stay here and look at Mr. Hooper.

He pulled himself together, and said, "OK, so where's the patient?"

Mr. Hooper was the largest ostrich, and he had an undefinably different look on his face. The others always seemed disinterested or a bit dull, but Mr. Hooper had what Peter could only think of as a gleam in his eye. Perhaps this ostrich was unusually intelligent. Or perhaps it was evil. Or perhaps both. While Peter got his instruments ready, Kim came out to help Dan herd the bird into the squeeze chute and hood him, as she had done with Big Bird.

Dan's concern was that Mr. Hooper had suddenly developed a pronounced twitch. He wasn't twitching while Peter examined him, but Dan said that it was very intermittent. In order to perform a complete neurological exam, the hood would have to come off. Peter estimated the reach of Mr. Hooper's neck, in case he decided to peck, and tried to assess his pupillary light response from that distance. It was difficult, so he leaned in slightly, and then, in a split-second blur, Mr. Hooper pecked at him, coming within millimetres of Peter's right eye. He felt the peck — a sudden rush of compressed air — more than properly seeing it. Peter pulled his head back quickly and reached up to touch his eye and cheek. No blood, but that was close — far too close.

"Whoa!" Dan said. "Better back up, Doc!"

Peter nodded, shaking slightly. He finished the exam quickly.

"He looks perfectly normal, so I don't have an easy answer for you, but we're in luck because tomorrow I'm going to meet with the zoo vet who helped us with Big Bird. She just happens to be in town. I'll ask her what she thinks and will let you know. In the meantime, maybe try to catch an episode on video if you can."

"For sure. Good idea!"

"Just email it to me, and I'll call you after I talk to Dr. Loewenstein." Peter started putting his instruments away before adding, "I need to chat with Kevin about something, so I'm going to try to find him, if that's OK."

"Of course. And by the way, I think this will be the last of our birds you'll be seeing for a while."

"Oh, why's that?"

"Things come in threes, right?" Dan laughed.

"Right!" Peter replied and laughed too, restraining himself from pointing out the obvious logical flaw in that old superstition: bundling events in threes depended entirely on when you started and stopped counting. You could just as easily say that things "come in fours" and then draw mental circles around groups of similar events once the count hit four. Humans were silly. Ostriches were silly too, of course, but they didn't know any better not to be. Humans had no excuse.

It was the first overcast day in a while, and a low pearly layer of cloud lay across the sky like a cap on the world. A blue sky made the world feel infinite, almost coldly so, whereas this made it feel bounded and circumscribed, which felt cozy to Peter. It was warm enough that he removed his jacket before heading off across the field, but he knew how quickly things could change, so he brought it along, slung over his shoulder. The air was dense and still. The only sound was his own footfalls, squelching across the spring-damp grass. Even the red-winged blackbirds, who normally filled the April air with their insistent trilling, were quiet at the moment.

As he approached the marshy area across the old property line, he was pleased that his profession compelled him to wear rubber boots on farm calls, especially in the spring when some paddocks are shin-deep quagmires of sodden manure. He was also pleased that on his previous visit he thought to make note of the quickest way across to that path that he, Pippin, and Dwayne had been on a few days prior. He wished that Pippin were with him, or even Dwayne.

As he stepped onto the path and turned west, he heard something behind him. It was very distant.

He stopped and listened.

Sirens?

It was definitely sirens, probably police rather than volunteer fire or ambulance.

Were they coming this way? It was hard to tell. They were getting louder, but the police in the form of Kevin were here already, Peter reasoned, so the sirens were probably going somewhere else. He peered back across the marsh and field to the visible part of the road, but he couldn't see anything to explain what he was hearing.

He turned back and entered the tamarack forest, hoping that Kevin would be at the dig site so that, in finding him, he would also solve the mystery of its location for himself. Kevin was large and loud, even when he was by himself, so he would be easier to spot through the trees than an area of disturbed earth.

As he walked, he pondered excuses for his presence here. Kevin would be angry at what would automatically look to him like interference in police business. Peter had better be ready with something good quickly. He had an easy and unimpeachable excuse for being on the farm, but for following Kevin, nothing popped into mind. He stopped for a moment and thought hard, lest he run into him suddenly and only be able to stammer.

That's it! The thought came to him like a fast-swimming fish from a great depth. Out of the inky abyss it appeared, silver and flashing, rocketing to the surface.

The body.

That half of a charred-looking skeleton in Grim's lab.

He had completely forgotten to mention it to Kevin. It was the perfect excuse. Hearing from Dan that Kevin was looking for Grim here, Peter thought he'd try to catch him before he found the archeologist. That way Kevin could ask Grim about it when he found him. Brilliant.

Peter was pleased with himself. Not only did that sound plausible enough, but it was actually an interesting question. Given that he had a powerful feeling that Grim was behind all the mutilations and now also the racist threats, how much of a leap was it to suspect him of murder or, at the very least, mishandling human remains? Grim had only said that the bones were old and that they would be in the news. But how easy was it for the forensics to date human bones? Pretty easy, he assumed. Kevin's people would quickly sort out the lie. Academics were often arrogant. That would be Dr. Grimur Sturluson's downfall.

Peter's thoughts were running along down that speculative avenue when he suddenly realized that he was near the clearing where the nithing pole had been found. It made sense to check that out first before going farther up the path toward the presumed dig site.

No sign of Kevin yet.

How he wished that he had Pippin with him.

The clearing was beginning to come into view when he heard something moving ahead of him and slightly to his left. He looked in that direction, but the light was muted and dim. Whatever it was, it was large. Not a squirrel or rabbit. Maybe a deer, or, god forbid, "the watcher," or —

"Peter, what the hell are you doing out here?"

It was Kevin, of course. The big man pushed through the brush toward Peter. His face was crimson. A branch knocked his cap off, but he didn't seem to notice or care.

Peter began to babble, "Dan called me out to see an ostrich and I saw you were here, and I've got some information that —"

Kevin cut him off, "Save it! It's an effing crime scene! Get the hell back! Back on the path, Peter!" He waved both of his arms at Peter like a traffic cop ordering a car to back up. Peter saw that Kevin's right hand had blood on it.

Kevin had a look in his eyes that Peter had never seen before. It was more a look of horror and distress than one of anger. He looked wild and unhinged.

Just then the sun broke through a fissure in the cloud layer and a broad finger of light stabbed through the trees and illuminated the clearing behind Kevin, creating a cinematic backlight for his unruly red hair.

Then Peter saw it.

In the centre of the clearing, he could now clearly make out a pole with an object at the top. The pole was the same length as the nithing pole he and Dwayne had found, and the object was roughly the size and shape of a volleyball. For a fragment of a second Peter absurdly thought of a game of tetherball frozen at the moment where the ball passed the tip of the pole.

But it wasn't a volleyball or a tetherball. It wasn't a ball at all.

It had a nose and ears. A human nose and ears.

And a small goatee.

CHAPTER
Twenty–Six

When Peter thought back on that moment, what struck him was his own reaction. He had seen a murder victim before and had become paralytic with shock and revulsion, but this time, on seeing Grimur Sturluson's head, his reaction was calm and detached. His first thought had been, *Well, there goes that theory.*

He reasoned that this flat response was because the head was farther away and somehow far more abstract than the previous body had been. In fact, he never did see the entire body this time, just the head. And a head on a pole, regardless of how much he had read about nithing poles, was absurd and unreal. His eyes took the image in, but his brain was in charge of filing it, and had initially placed it in amongst movie scenes and newspaper photos. Perhaps the quality of light and Kevin's unexpected derangement further nudged it into that category.

Maybe a feeling of horror was still to come. It was possible. It was just hours after the event, and it could be that he was merely benumbed by the surprise of what appeared to have happened. The subconscious brain was probably busy processing the flood of new data, using resources that might otherwise be committed to having a stronger emotional reaction. Was this what it was like to "be in shock"? Or was something else going on?

Peter had just made a cup of tea and was planning to read while waiting for Laura to return from visiting her brother. Soon after he found Kevin, a swarm of officers appeared. It looked like the entire New Selfoss detachment. And within an hour, while Peter was being questioned by an icily businesslike Kristine, several more RCMP vehicles arrived, discharging unfamiliar officers, possibly from the city. Kevin waved off one officer who had approached him with a blanket and a concerned facial expression. Before he left, Peter told Kevin that he would get Laura to check in on him. Kevin nodded at this, his face a blank.

Tonight's tea was a decaf Earl Grey Peter had bought at a specialty shop on Academy Road in Winnipeg. In winter he gravitated to the dark smoky comfort of lapsang souchong, but with the air warming and the days lengthening, the bright, citrus-tinged Earl Grey was a better complement. *Perhaps it would be more logical to contrast rather than complement? The sunny oil of Bergamot oranges in counterpoint to the long darkness of winter?* But Peter liked the seasons, all of them, and felt drawn to try to deepen each one rather than to do something to dilute the season's power. This applied to his reading as well, at least the non-fiction part of it (he diligently alternated fiction and non). Winter was the time to read mountaineering and Polar exploration accounts, whereas spring, with its return of greenery and migratory birds, made him want to dive into natural history. He stood, tea mug in hand, before one of their dark cherrywood bookcases beside the fireplace and scanned the titles. He knew that there was at least one Christmas gift he hadn't read yet. Before he could find it, the front door opened and Pippin, who had been lying on the flagstones in front of the hearth, jerked awake, quickly assembled his legs, and bolted for the door.

"I'm home!" It was Laura.

"How's Kev?"

"Wait a sec . . ." Peter heard Laura talking quietly to Pippin and the sounds of Pippin's tail hitting the front hall closet door, thump thump thump, as he wagged in response.

A moment later she was settled in her favourite chair opposite Peter. She ran her fingers through her tussled red hair and smiled at her husband. "Earl Grey?" she asked.

"Yes, did you want some?"

"Not right now, thanks. So, Kevin. He'll be OK, but he's pretty shaken. Stuart was there, so I didn't stay long. It was good to meet him — he's really good with Kevin. Knows how to calm him down."

Peter nodded and looked at the surface of his tea for a moment before looking up. "Do you know if Kevin has any interest in Heathenry?" He paused, realizing how out of left field that sounded, and then added, "Just wondering."

"Um, no, not that I know of," Laura answered, speaking with the slow deliberation of someone who's signalling that they do not like the direction the conversation has taken. "Why do you ask?"

Peter smiled to try to defuse the rising tension. "It's just that when something so unexpected like this happens, you have to be open to every explanation and set aside personal feelings and preferences. Just because you don't like an explanation doesn't invalidate it."

"What are you getting at? That Kevin should be a suspect?" Laura's voice rose as she said this, and her face began to flush.

"Very improbable, I grant you, but not impossible, and —"

"Have you gone insane?" Laura was shouting now. The Gudmundursons were known for being able to go from zero to sixty in seconds. Pippin stood up and watched her with concern, but Merry, who had climbed onto her lap, kept purring, eyes closed.

"Laura," Peter said with deliberate care, like a man gingerly trying to place a lid on a boiling pot, "he had blood on him, and he had this look that I've never seen before. He —"

"He had that look because he had just seen a fucking decapitated head!" Laura very rarely swore, so it had all the more impact.

Peter looked down at his tea again and took a deep breath. "Look, I didn't mean to upset you. He's like a brother to me too." He paused, and then added quietly, "That makes it all the more important to strive for objectivity."

Laura shook her head, patted Merry for a long moment to calm herself, and then finally said, "Sometimes I don't understand you. Normally I think I do. Normally I think I get you and I think I get your concept of logic. But then . . . then you say something totally batshit like that."

Peter didn't respond and they both fell quiet, not meeting each other's eyes. Pippin lay down again between them and Merry appeared to be asleep now.

"Just leave Kevin alone, please. Don't ask him any weird questions. Don't ponder any weird theories. Don't mention this to me again. The Mounties have their own internal review process, and you can be sure that Kristine won't hold back if there's even a remote hint that something's not quite right."

"OK, and you're right. It is a totally batshit idea."

They both laughed, but in a tired, forced way. Laura picked up her knitting, a cardigan in Ravenclaw house colours, and Peter went back to the bookshelf and, after a few minutes' consideration, pulled down *Are We Smart Enough to Know How Smart Animals Are* by Frans de Waal.

Peter couldn't fall asleep that night. This was the second night in a week that he was having trouble sleeping, which was unprecedented. He had done everything correctly, including an hour's quiet before bed and then lights out at precisely ten, but he just lay there in the dark, unable to still his brain. He considered getting up and rewriting his theories because writing them out in the first place had helped the other night. He had followed through with most of the plan that he had written out. Only talking to Rose, Peggy, and Dan and Kim again was left on the list. And now he knew that the dig was connected, unless there were two independent parallel crimes underway, both connected to the ancient Norse. It would be like finding a large tumour in the chest of a dog and then several smaller but otherwise identical looking ones in the abdomen. Without a biopsy, two unrelated cancers could not be conclusively eliminated as an explanation, but it was several orders of magnitude less likely than the smaller ones representing spread from the larger one.

Probabilities.

It was all about probabilities.

He really should get up and write all of this down in Bella's book. It would help, but he felt oddly lethargic and unmotivated. This was not the pleasantly sleepy lethargy that follows a long day, but something else, an unfamiliar flavour of lethargy. It was an absence of a will to do anything, but at the same time it felt like something was buzzing or vibrating deep inside him. Was this anxiety? He wasn't sure. Maybe seeing that head had affected him more than he was able to consciously assess.

Peter got up and went to the bathroom, even though he didn't need to. He drank a little water and then padded into the living room and over to their large east-facing floor-to-ceiling windows. All the lights in the house were off. He stood and stared deeply into the moonless night. He thought about the person who had been watching the house at dawn back in the winter during the swine barn incident. And he thought about the more recent watcher at the clearing with the nithing pole. Peter considered that in this absolute dark he wouldn't be able to see if anyone were out there. But they wouldn't be able to see him either. This made him feel better.

And then he noticed a patch of dim light, high in the sky to his left, which was north. Faint and pale greenish, then suddenly brightening to acid green streaks, tipped in pink and arrayed side by side like a fence or a curtain, undulating as if blown by a celestial wind. It was the aurora. It brightened further, throwing the sawtooth tops of the forest into sharp black relief and casting faint opalescent shadows across the yard. Peter stood absolutely still, mesmerized. It didn't matter how often he saw the northern lights, every time it felt as profound as the first time. And it didn't matter how much he understood about charged electrons hurtling through the ionosphere, it still felt magical, in a primal way beyond words and science.

And then just as suddenly, it faded and stopped. It had been exactly what Peter needed.

Soon after returning to bed, he fell deeply asleep and dreamed of paths running through a vast forest, the paths spreading like rivulets of water seeking the route of least resistance between the densely spaced trees. He was there, but disembodied, floating above. Just a watchful presence. And then he was on the ground, running. Nobody and nothing behind or ahead, just Peter alone in the forest, running, finding ever more new paths sprouting ahead of him. Then, abruptly, he was aware that he was dreaming and began to expect something bad to happen. This was about to turn into a nightmare. Something was around the next corner. Or the next. Or the one after that. But there was nothing. Nothing happened other than that the trees suddenly were no longer there. It was just a field, and the paths were more sensed than seen. The dread dissipated leaving only the running. It was exhilarating.

CHAPTER
Twenty-Seven

When Peter woke up, he remembered wispy fragments of the dream, especially the running and how good that felt. He thought that was curious because he didn't actually like running. He had been told in high school that he had the long legs and lean build of a long-distance runner, but he didn't find it interesting enough to apply himself. Maybe he should try again?

He waited for his morning tea to steep and patted Pippin as he scrolled through the news headlines. There was an article about Sturluson's death, but it made no mention of the gruesome details, only stating that RCMP were treating it as a homicide investigation. A linked article quoted the Chief of the Yellowgrass First Nation as offering condolences to the professor's family while expressing hope that growing divisions between the Indigenous and Icelandic-Canadian communities could be healed. His tone was respectful, but he was obviously hinting at Sturluson's opinion that, based on his discoveries, the Norse should be regarded as "First Peoples."

There was a further link at the end of that article to a translation of an interview he had given to an Icelandic journalist. In it Sturluson laid out the case for sustained habitation over several generations of the southeast shore of Lake Winnipeg by the Norse. He went on to talk about the historical movements of various Indigenous tribes to make the point that who was settler and who was truly native to any given piece of land was fluid and murky. The journalist challenged him, pointing out that Indigenous people had been there for hundreds of generations, not just a handful, and that their culture was entirely based on that land, not imported from another continent. Sturluson retorted that we didn't yet know how the Manitoba Norse evolved their culture.

Theresa had warned Peter that it was going to be a busy day, so he planned to go in early to get a head start on some of the paperwork before appointments began. He wanted to finish on time because he was meeting Alicia in town at seven. He had debated about cancelling because Laura was going out too and Pippin would be alone, but other than the large shaved area and the line of staples like a curving railway track marking the incision, you would never know he had almost been killed by an arrow three days before. He would be fine alone, and Laura wasn't leaving until eight, so if Peter made sure he was home by ten, it would only be two hours.

Spring was busy in the practice for a variety of reasons, and today was going to be especially busy because tomorrow was Good Friday and they'd be closed. It was also Peter's habit to close on the Saturday between Good Friday and Easter Sunday in order to have a proper long weekend, although he'd have to be on call. Peter was fond of Easter. He had always felt bad for the B-list holidays that languished in the shadow of almighty Christmas. A springtime celebration of rebirth and renewal felt essential to him. Both the Christian story and the modern bunnies and chocolate eggs were tangential, peripheral. The heart of the thing felt pagan. He thought about this on the way to work and wondered whether this kind of thinking was a gateway into Odinism.

Puddles aside, it would have been a nice day to walk to work, as he almost always did, but since he was in a hurry, he drove. As he turned the corner from their street onto the main road, he reasoned it was just as likely to be a gateway to the more benign, New Agey flavours of Heathenry. Or, more likely yet, a gateway to a deeper appreciation of the power of nature, with no religious interpretative filter needed at all. As he parked behind the clinic, he affirmed for himself that ritual celebrations need not be religious in any way.

He also affirmed for himself that he was not going to discuss finding Grim's head. He expected that Kat and Theresa, and possibly some clients, would make concerned noises, saying that they hoped that he was OK and stuff like that, and they would possibly fish for more details as very little had been revealed in the press. He would reply that he was fine and that it was a police matter that he couldn't comment further on. Kevin and Laura would be proud of him.

His first appointment was with Dwayne Lautermilch's mother, Betty, a short, bony elderly woman with a faintly purple perm and oversized red-framed glasses. She had an old Siamese cat named Fiona who appeared to have developed an overactive thyroid gland. This was a common problem in old cats, and easily managed with medication. Betty was delighted that Peter would be able to do something about the yowling. And she was relieved that there was a simple medical explanation. For the last month, the cat had been stalking up and down the hallways of her bungalow all night long, wailing like a banshee. To Peter this was a clear sign of hyperthyroidism, but to Betty it had been evidence that Fiona was losing her mind or, she said in a lower voice while leaning forward, of demonic possession.

Peter wasn't always the best at reading people, so he wasn't absolutely certain whether she was joking or serious. He assumed the latter though, since Dwayne had mentioned that his mother always joined him at the Northern Lights Pentecostal Church. She had always been quietly religious. Dwayne's father had not been fond of churches, but he had been dead for many years now.

Fiona was sent out of the exam room for Theresa and Kat to collect a blood sample to confirm Peter's diagnosis. While they waited for her to be brought back, Betty began to talk about Dwayne, beaming as she told Peter how delighted she had been to find out that Dwayne and Peter had become friends.

"He's never had that many friends, and I worry that he's lonely. So, I just clapped my hands with happiness" — she made a little clapping motion as she said this — "when he mentioned that you and him were treasure hunting together! 'He's my vet,' I said!"

"Small world," Peter said, instantly regretting the cliché.

"Exactly! That's exactly what I said! You must have been such pals back in high school and then drifted apart when he fell in with the wrong crowd."

Peter smiled. He didn't like telling lies, even when they were white lies. Usually, it was better just to set people straight with the truth, but he had learned that sometimes this caused more problems than it solved. In those cases, no response was often the best idea. The worst response for him was insincere agreement. He was sure that he was not good at it and that most people would see through it.

"I thought he and Doug might have something in common. You know, Doug Heikkinen?"

"Yes, I do."

"Well, his mom, Mabel, and I are bridge partners, and she was always saying how she was worried that her boy Doug spent so much time alone, so I thought I'd invite them both for dinner."

Peter marvelled at the notion of these elderly ladies arranging "play dates" for their forty-something-year-old sons. "That's nice of you," he said, hoping it didn't sound as inane coming out of his mouth as it did inside his head.

Betty beamed, "I thought so! Well anyway, it turns out that those two are like oil and water. Nothing in common at all. Dwayne has been so mild mannered since he got out, and I've never heard him say anything bad about anyone, but after they left, he told me, 'Mabel's nice, but I don't like Doug.' Didn't want to explain." Betty shook her head at the memory.

"Since he got out" — so Dwayne was in Stony or Headingly after all, thought Peter. But "That's too bad" was all he said to Betty.

"Well, anyway," Betty went on, "I'm just so happy that you and Dwayne *do* have something in common!"

"I'm happy too." Peter smiled at her but wondered why it was taking so long to get Fiona's blood. This conversation was straining his social skill set. Small talk always made him feel awkward and false.

Betty seemed fully at ease though. She leaned forward and lowered her voice, "You know, Darlene's been gone almost two years now."

"Darlene?"

"You didn't know?" Betty chuckled. "I guess men don't talk about these sorts of things, especially when they're out treasure hunting! Darlene was his pen pal while he was at Stony Mountain, and —"

Betty was interrupted by a knock on the door followed by Kat coming in with Fiona.

"She was so good!" Kat said as she handed the disgruntled looking cat to Betty, who had stretched her arms out toward her, cooing. Kat's sidewise glance to Peter told him that Fiona had not in fact been so good, but what was the point in telling her owner? Another white lie. Kat and Theresa were experts at it.

"And Dr. Bannerman, Theresa needs you right away. Mr. Petursson is waiting and is in a hurry."

"I'll call you with Fiona's results later," Peter said as he stepped toward the door, following Kat. "It was great to catch up with you!" he added, proud of himself that he had remembered a standard nicety.

Earl Petursson was a big man in every respect — tall, wide, loud. He always wore some article of clothing with a camo pattern, whether it was a shirt, pants, vest, jacket, hat, or, like today, all five. His dog, a German shepherd named General Brock (never just General or just Brock), sat beside him, prim as a calendar model. But Peter knew that if he took one step too close, General Brock would bare his teeth. One more step after that, and he would lunge and take a piece out of Peter's thigh. That is, if Earl didn't give the signal to stay put. General Brock was Pippin's chief competition in the local scent dog trials, but it was a friendly rivalry. Despite the aggressive vibe he gave off to the casual observer, Earl was friendly and was happy to give Pippin his due when he won, which was most of the time.

"How's Pippin?" he asked.

"Good, really good. Dogs are amazing at healing. And how's General Brock?"

"Pretty good, but there's this one thing," Earl lowered his voice as he saw Betty Lautermilch come out of the exam room. "He keeps licking his ass."

"Ah, well let's have a look at that. Theresa will set you up right away."

"Do you think it's worms?"

"No, probably not. It's probably his anal sacs."

Earl looked surprised and lowered his voice further. "His anal what?"

"Sacs," Peter enunciated the vowel carefully. "Little glands either side of a dog's anus. Sometimes they get plugged up."

"Oh, OK, I thought you said something else." Earl blushed.

A few minutes later in the exam room, while Peter was squatting behind General Brock, he caught a glimpse of something on Earl's left arm. Earl had the dog in a bear hug and was whispering, "Good boy. It'll be OK. It'll be over soon." Peter adjusted his position to have a closer look.

It was a tiny tattoo of three S-shaped Norse serpents side by side.

After Earl and General Brock left, Peter asked Theresa, "Do you know if Earl is related or connected to Ken Finnbogason?" Like all good receptionists, she had a freakish level of knowledge about their clients and how everyone knew each other.

"I doubt it. Earl's originally a Veni and the Finnbogasons are Aunis going back to the beginning, so they're not related. Could be friends though, but I don't think so because they move in different circles. Earl's more the huntin' and fishin' type while Ken's into golf, curling, and, as you know, darts. Why'd you ask?"

"Don't know. Just thought I saw a resemblance."

Theresa raised her eyebrows briefly but didn't say anything. Peter was glad she didn't quiz him further. His reputation for saying odd things that weren't worth pursuing came in handy sometimes.

CHAPTER
Twenty-Eight

For his dinner with Alicia, Peter had selected a small Spanish tapas bar, El Caballo Blanco, in Winnipeg's Exchange District. He loved the Exchange, but then so did most people. It had the most intact streetscape of late-19th century architecture anywhere in North America and was consequently a favourite site for movie shoots. Real estate at the time was briefly more expensive than in Manhattan, when Winnipeg boomed as the Hub of the British Empire. "Chicago North" they called it. Then the boom went bust, and like a fly caught in amber, the Exchange remained intact during the following century when nobody in Winnipeg had enough money to knock down the old buildings and replace them with something newer and snazzier. This Snow-White sleep lasted long enough for the old to become fashionable again. *How could anyone have seen this as anything other than beautiful?* Peter thought as he walked down Bannatyne from where he parked his truck. And then he considered the modern buildings that most people now thought were ugly. *Was that the same thing? Would they be viewed as ugly for a hundred years before being rediscovered?* This line of thought was cut short when he saw a tall woman elegantly dressed in a long black coat approaching from the opposite direction. It was Alicia. They arrived at the restaurant door simultaneously, each grinning broadly.

"We always had the same precise internal clock! Good to see you, Peter, you look great!"

"You do too!" And she did. There was a dusting of grey in her otherwise jet-black hair, but that made her look even more striking. And her blue eyes had the same jewel-like brightness he remembered.

They ordered drinks — a Spanish beer for him, and a whisky for her — and caught up on life events while they examined the adjective-studded menu. Alicia had been married and divorced twice. With her first husband she'd had a daughter, who was now a teenager and was with her father this week. Alicia currently lived alone in a condo in downtown Toronto and was loving the urban single life. Peter hoped that El Caballo Blanco was hip enough for her, but she had paid it several genuine-seeming compliments already. Was she also a good white-lie teller? He couldn't recall but guessed that she probably was. He was mostly focused on not looking at her cleavage. She had worn a deep-cut dark red cocktail dress. Looking at those eyes was dangerous too, but not as inappropriately dangerous.

By the time Alicia was done and said that it was his turn to tell all, they had ordered and eaten the first course, a selection of briny olives. Peter didn't have much to say. Same wife as always. No kids. He could have said quite a bit about the practice, but she hadn't mentioned work, so he presumed that was not cool.

"But what about that crazy story with the pig barn? Tell me all about that!"

So Peter did, and that took them through the next three courses. By then he had switched to whisky as well, self-consciously ordering the same one as Alicia, and mentally taking note of alcohol units consumed and time elapsed, given that he had to drive home. He would sip this one slowly, and he would be fine.

"And New Selfoss is in the news again! Murder capital of rural Manitoba, it seems. An archeology prof this time?"

"Yeah, and I'm kind of involved this time too." Peter knew it was shallow to enjoy her attention based on his connection to big events, but he didn't care. One beer and one whisky were enough to loosen him. Besides, Alicia had always been a really incisive and rational thinker. She won numerous academic awards in vet school. His own thinking on the recent events was muddy. Perhaps she would bring some clarity.

Peter explained everything that happened since finding the Mjölnir in Big Bird through the attack on Pippin to yesterday's events in the woods. Alicia listened, rapt, occasionally interrupting Peter to ask for clarification on a detail. When he was done, she ordered another whisky for herself. Her fourth or fifth? Peter declined, albeit reluctantly.

Alicia placed her hands flat on the table on either side of her plate and leaned forward. "Do you know what I think is going on?" she said. Peter noticed for the first time how red her lips were. Fire engine. Candy apple. Lamborghini.

"No, but I'd love to know, because I'm stuck. Grimur's murder in particular makes no sense."

"That's where you, Dr. Peter Bannerman, as brilliant as you are, are wrong. You are wrong because his murder is actually what makes the most sense."

"Oh? OK, now I'm really curious."

Alicia took a dramatic swallow from her whisky and licked her lips. They were very shiny now, catching the light from the funky blown-glass lamp dangling low over the table. "Two words, my friend: 'internecine strife.'"

"Internecine strife? A group fighting amongst itself?"

"Yes, precisely. My take is that this Grimur Sturrr . . ." She smiled as she stretched out the "r," waiting for Peter to remind her.

"Sturluson. Grimur Sturluson."

"This Grimur Sturluson was part of an Odinist group. Agreed?"

"I think it's probable, yes."

The waiter came by again and inclined his head at Peter's empty glass. Peter shook his head no, but Alicia knocked back the remainder of her glass and held it out, flashing a toothy smile. She had exceptionally white teeth, Peter noted. Artificially so, he assumed.

"Odinists are extremists and extremists always eat their own. Always. Agreed also?"

"I'm sure there must be exceptions, but broadly speaking, yes, agreed."

Alicia held up her hand and began counting off on her fingers: "Nazi SS versus SA. French Revolution Jacobins versus Dantonists. Stalinists versus Trotskyites. Maoist hardliners versus everyone else in the Chinese Communist Party. There is always this drive for greater purity and greater control to achieve that greater purity. And there are always some people who eventually think it's going too far or the wrong way, so they split."

"Disagreeable people by definition have trouble agreeing with other disagreeable people," he said.

"Exactly. And splitting means people will die. It's telling that these groups often refer to such killings as a kind of cleansing."

The whisky arrived, and the waiter asked whether they would like to see the dessert menu. Alicia looked mildly interested, but Peter realized that it was getting late, and he wanted to be home for Pippin soon.

"I'd better drink fast then," Alicia laughed, and downed the remainder of her whisky in one gulp. "To wrap up, I'll say that it's always the less extreme extremists who die first. Find out who Grimur hangs out with in secret — sorry, *hung* out with — and you'll find your animal mutilators, as well as your murderers, of course. The *in secret* part is important because this kind of violent extremism is mostly secret in a democracy. He belonged to something. Some radical Odinist outfit. Dig through the deeper, darker layers of the internet or remind the cops to."

"I'm pretty sure he belonged to something called the Saga Study Society."

"Sounds promising . . ."

"I found them on the 8kun Odinist forums." Peter felt briefly guilty for not mentioning that it was actually Laura who had found them.

"You're ahead of the game then! That is the place to look for sure, but there are other forums like Neinchan and Endchan. You also want to look for the dog-whistle coding on more open and accessible forums."

"You know a lot about extremist ideology for a zoo vet," Peter remarked as he signalled for the cheque.

She nodded and said quietly, "My grandparents died in the Holocaust."

Peter and Alicia stood for a moment on the sidewalk outside of El Caballo Blanco making the kind of small talk people do just before wrapping up to say goodbye.

Then Alicia smiled at him and said, "Have you even been in the Fairmont? You should come up for a few minutes. The nighttime view is amazing if you've never seen it."

Somehow Peter heard himself saying "Sure. Why not?" even though he could easily list a dozen reasons why not.

CHAPTER
Twenty-Nine

Later Peter would remember what followed as a kind of out-of-body experience, where he was watching himself gliding down the street as if guided by an invisible hand, and then around the corner, down another street, past the red uniformed doorman into the hotel lobby, up the mirrored elevators, down the empty hall, and into Alicia's suite.

The view was amazing, just as promised. The intersection of Portage and Main far below was the hub of a vast wheel of diamonds. Peter stared out the window, unable to generate a clear thought, while he sensed Alicia standing beside and slightly behind him. He didn't dare look at her.

Then she touched his shoulder. "It's quite something, isn't it?"

"It is."

"Can I get you something? A drink?"

Peter turned around. "No, thank you. I'm fine, thanks."

There was something in the way Alicia smiled at him in response that made his stomach lurch.

"Nothing at all?"

Peter felt his mouth go dry and his heart begin to race. *Oh my god*, was the only thought he could generate.

Alicia smiled again and stepped forward, her eyes catching the light from the lamp in the corner.

Without thinking about it, Peter fumbled in his pocket for his phone. Pulling it out he stammered, "Oh wow, it's later than I thought. I really need to check on Pippin!"

Alicia chuckled and Peter was out the door after a hasty goodbye and thank-you.

Peter's thoughts were in turmoil as he drove home. It was dark and the traffic on 59 was light since it was a weeknight and not cottage or beach season. He could give his mind full rein to churn as it pleased as he set the cruise control on the long straight highway into the black.

Had Alicia been flirting? He wasn't sure. Laura was his first and only girlfriend. What Peter knew about such things mostly came from what he had read in novels and seen in movies. His courtship, if you could call it that, with Laura had been unconventional. They started by meeting for coffee after they had run into each other on campus in Saskatoon. Neither had known that the other was studying there. It was just coffee and catching up on old times at New Selfoss High School, where they had first met at the Dungeons & Dragons club. It was not really a date, and there was no flirting on either side that he could remember. It was a friendship that gradually evolved into something more.

Alicia had dressed nicely, but maybe that was just the way she dressed whenever she went out. Some people liked to look attractive even when they weren't actively trying to attract anyone. Irrational, but apparently normal. She hadn't touched him, other than that light tap on the shoulder (which oddly he could still feel now as he drove), and she hadn't said anything obvious. Was the "Nothing at all?" question meant to be suggestive? It probably was, but he couldn't be certain.

Those eyes, they shone and had slightly crinkled when she smiled at him.

Get a grip on yourself, Bannerman! That's just Alicia. That's the way she always was, and that's the way she is around everyone. And you love Laura. She's the love of your life even! Things had gone through a dull patch, maybe even strained, but they were better now, right?

Peter slowed down as the highway went from twinned to single lane. He would have to pay closer attention to the occasional oncoming vehicle (*Turn down your high beams!*), but otherwise he could keep his focus inwards.

Enough about Alicia. Think about Grimur.

Turning on the radio might help.

It didn't. He was out of range of the better FM stations in the city, so the choices were either agitated chatter about hockey or irritating auto-tuned pop music. He tapped the Bluetooth icon. He had most recently listened to Glenn Gould's *Bach: The Goldberg Variations,* so that popped up on the screen. Perfect. This was clear thinking music. Logic converted into a pleasing sequence of notes.

Grimur. Alicia was right. He must have been tied into something like the Saga Study Society and then run afoul of their more extreme intentions. But who else was in this group? That was obviously the key question. New Selfoss was full of odd characters and people who were keen on their Nordic heritage, but right-wing extremists? It was a pretty liberal and progressive town. Gimli always voted conservative, whereas New Selfoss had the highest percentage of Green voters in rural Manitoba. But there were more than a few exceptions. There had been a smattering of lawn signs for the fringe Nation of Canada Party during the last election campaign, and he'd noticed that Doug Heikkinen had one of their bumper stickers on his truck. Finns were geographically Scandinavian, but not ethnically. He was fairly sure their pagan ancestors worshipped a different set of gods than the Norse. He'd have to double-check. *And what about the rivalry with the Venis in Gimli? Was this rivalry more earnest among the Odinists? Were there Veni and Auni factions in the Saga Study Society? Hadn't Ken mentioned that the Gimli dart team wore Viking gear and prayed to Odin?*

If he was honest with himself, Kevin wasn't a serious consideration. The way he acted that evening was much more easily explained by the horror of stumbling on a head impaled on a spike. Not an everyday occurrence, even for an RCMP officer. The blood on Kevin's hand had an easy explanation too. He shouldn't be handling evidence but given the amount of blood that comes out when someone's head has been sliced off, it might be difficult to avoid touching some of it. Ockham's razor again. It was a much cleaner and simpler explanation than Kevin somehow concealing being an Odinist fanatic. Peter chuckled to himself.

Then there was that new Northern Lights Pentecostalist pastor, Ragnarsson. He had been on the radio recently spouting something about Canada's threatened Christian heritage. That would put him in opposition to pagans. Maybe in violent opposition? *This isn't Alicia's theory of extremists eating their own, but it's a valid theory too,* Peter thought. In the same general category of violent opposition to Norse pagans were the rumours that some of the young men on the Yellowgrass First Nation were arming themselves and forming a "Warrior Society" in response to the threat to their land claims.

Violence from within, and violence from without. Both were possible. The former would make it probable that the animal mutilator or mutilators were the same person or people as whoever decapitated Grim. The latter would mean that there were two different criminals or sets of criminals at large, similar to what happened in the swine barn case.

Peter slowed down as he crossed the bridge over the Brokenhead River. The bridge lights shone on the river, roiling black-brown just below, flecked with chunks of grey ice racing by like spinning plates.

It had risen considerably just over the course of the evening. An ice dam had probably developed downstream. A couple more metres and they would have to close the bridge, but that was unlikely. The province would break up the ice dam before that happened, with dynamite if necessary. Peter didn't think it was likely to be a flood year, but then he hadn't paid close attention, and in any case, just one major April storm can tip the balance.

Then it hit him. Utterly unrelated to floods and bridges, at that moment he remembered again that he needed to tell Kevin about the blackened partial skeleton in Grim's lab. Events had precluded passing this information on before. It started as the excuse to talk to Kevin, but the more he thought about it, it wasn't just an excuse, it was a legitimate clue. Especially in the light of what happened to Grim. But he had completely forgotten after the shock of seeing the head and Kevin unhinged like that.

He didn't want to wait until he got home. And it would be more dangerous to pull over on a dark highway than to make a hands-free call, so he said, "Hey Google, dial Kevin."

Peter expected his call to go to voicemail, but after just one ring Kevin picked up.

"Hey Pete, just the man I was hoping to talk to tonight."

"Oh? What's up?"

"No, you first. Why'd you call me?"

"We never had a chance to talk about why I came looking for you in the woods by the Favels' place yesterday."

"Right, yeah, I was preoccupied," Kevin said, with a small mirthless laugh.

"By the way, about that, how are you doing?"

"Fine. I'm sorry I freaked out on you like that. Unprofessional. But, well, let's just say that it was an unexpected find."

"I imagine it was. Grim stuff." Realizing what he said he added, "Sorry, I didn't mean to make a pun."

"Understood. But anyway, you were saying?"

"Yes, I wanted to tell you that I just remembered something about Sturluson's lab. There was half of a charred-looking skeleton in there. He said it was an archeological find. One that would be in the news soon. I assume now that he meant the Norse settlement, but he didn't mention it at the press conference."

Peter had just crested a rise. The lights of New Selfoss were now in view to the north. Traffic was picking up as more side roads fed into Highway 59.

"That's interesting. Kristine and Ryan searched his office and lab today. They didn't find any human remains. I'll get a more complete description from you when I see you tomorrow."

"You're seeing me tomorrow?"

"That's why I was just about to call you. I'm going to need to borrow that Thor's hammer."

CHAPTER
Thirty

Peter surveyed Kevin's office while his brother-in-law was out making coffee. The dubious qualities of what Peter called "Mountie coffee" were a standing joke between them. He generally refused when offered a cup but agreed this morning to try it again as Kevin had promised that it was a special new blend.

The office was in the same state of disarray that it had been on Peter's last visit. In fact, if possible, it was even more disorderly this time as four Bankers Boxes were piled on the guest chair when Peter came in. Kevin quickly moved them and stacked them on an already precarious tower in the corner by the window. While Kevin was out, Peter's reflexive curiosity led to him to lean forward to read the labels on the boxes, but they were just dates and file numbers. He quickly resumed a relaxed pose when he heard Kevin return.

"So, working on a holiday, Kev?"

"You know the saying — crime don't take no holidays. And anyway, isn't Good Friday all about a major crime for the Christians? Executing the Saviour without the benefit of due process?" He handed Peter a blue RCMP mug as he said this.

"I disagree. Jerusalem was under internationally recognized Roman jurisdiction, and the Romans followed their due process. You can't apply today's standards of Canadian jurisprudence to another country 2000 years ago."

Kevin sat back in his chair and grinned. "As is so often the case, you are right, Pete. I apologize for dissing Roman law." He took a sip from his mug, which appeared to picture two bears having sex. The words were too faded to read. "Shit, this is good. If I do say so myself."

It smelled like burnt plastic to Peter and tasted like bitter pond water, but he just smiled in response and nodded.

Kevin set his mug down and leaned forward. "So, I presume you brought it?"

"That's why I'm here, isn't it," Peter said, smiling while digging in his jacket pocket.

"Yes, that's why you're here. And to sample some kick-ass Mountie coffee, of course."

Peter pulled out a Ziploc baggie that contained a small red towel. He opened the baggie and unfolded the towel to reveal the Mjölnir.

"Can I ask why you need to see it again?"

"Not just see it — I'm afraid I'm going to need to keep it for a little while, Petey boy."

One trick Peter had learned when he wanted to find something out from Kevin was to just remain quiet. Peter loved to talk, so this was hard, but Kevin loved to talk even more and practically started twitching during long conversational pauses.

Peter silently handed Kevin the Mjölnir and sipped the coffee some more while suppressing a shudder. He smiled in a way that he hoped would be read as genuine.

Kevin scratched his big red beard. "You see, we have to send it in for testing."

Peter nodded and smiled. He sipped some more coffee.

"A professor from Sweden called. Sturluson's press conference made international news and there were pictures of the Mjölnir in some of the stories. This guy said he was pretty sure it's a fake. Some complicated reason to do with the design. Not from the right era."

Peter took a chance and asked, "Gustafsson?"

Kevin furrowed his brow and narrowed his eyes. "No, but that's a weird guess. Stenberg, I think. Who's Gustafsson?"

Peter took a deep breath. This was as good an opportunity as any to tell Kevin what he had found on the internet. It helped that Laura had been involved in the net sleuthing as Kevin was much more likely to give her the benefit of the doubt. Peter's involvement with an investigation, on the other hand, usually put Kevin on edge.

"Laura found a group called the Saga Study Society on an 8kun forum, which is a kind of semi-secret internet chat —"

"I know what 8kun is," Kevin interrupted. "Go on."

"Right, of course, so Laura found this local group of Odinists . . ." He paused. "You know what they are?"

"No, that I don't know. Odin lovers, I guess. But enlighten me on the details."

"They're modern believers in the old Norse religion, but not the New Agey naked-dancing druid flavour, but rather the right-wing white nationalist flavour. Also called folkists."

"Also called Assholes, I'm sure. But tell me more about these naked druids . . ." Kevin laughed.

"Ha! Not your type. Gnarly little old men with long beards and carbuncles."

Kevin made a face.

"So, I dug a little further and found that this Saga Study Society believes in a lost saga called the Bjartur that tells of a Norse settlement around here, exactly as Grim said the archeology proved. And this saga was apparently found by a Swede named Ingvar Gustafsson. That's why I asked. Although in retrospect it would be strange for the same guy to push a saga supporting the settlement story with one hand while trying to debunk the archeological evidence with the other."

"The whole thing is frigging strange."

"But here's the interesting and potentially useful part. That threat to Dan and Kim ended with the expression 'Muna Bjartur,' or 'Remember Bjartur.' The Saga Study Society group has the only electronic copy of the Bjartur saga I could find, and when you try to join the forum, they ask who sent you. The correct answer is 'Bjartur.' Funny coincidence, eh?"

Kevin frowned. "And you knew the answer was Bjartur? How?"

"Part lucky guess and part logical deduction."

"And you don't think it's a coincidence."

"No. It's too specific, and the mentions of Bjartur align too well, both temporally and spatially."

Kevin sighed. "Temporally and spatially? Really? You should listen to yourself sometime. But I get your drift. These Saga people are likely behind the threats."

"Threats, plural?"

"You haven't heard? That pony's head was dropped on the Favels' doorstep overnight with another note pinned to it."

"Oh no! Dan and Kim must be beside themselves!"

"They were pretty distraught for sure. The head was all gross and maggoty too."

"Jesus. What did the note say?"

Kevin smiled. "Even if I knew, Pete, I wouldn't tell you. Active investigation and all. You know the deal. You were just lucky that Dan showed you the first note. Or unlucky, depending on how you want to look at it." Kevin paused and took a big gulp from his coffee. Peter waited for him to say more. "Anyways, I haven't seen the note yet. Kristine's taking the lead on investigating the threats and mutilations, while I focus on the Sturluson murder side of things. She went out there earlier when the call came in."

Peter nodded and sipped a bit of coffee as well. It was even worse as it cooled off. He forced himself to stay quiet.

Kevin wiped his beard with his sleeve and went on. "So, I'll pass this saga group stuff on to her when she gets here, thanks, and in the meantime —"

There was the sound of a door opening from down the hall.

"Speak of the frigging devil, that's probably her!" Kevin stood up and walked to his door. He stuck his head out into the hall and called out, "Björnsdóttir! That you? Got a moment?"

"Yeah it's me. What's up?"

Peter felt his heart sink. He didn't relish talking to Kristine again.

"My brother-in-law's here. He's found something that might be useful."

When Kristine stepped into the office, Peter was amused to see her wrinkle her nose as she surveyed the chaos, presumably looking for a third chair that might be hiding somewhere under the mountain ranges of papers.

"Christ, Gudmundurson. Divisional command is going to be here tomorrow. You really want them to see this?"

Kevin shrugged.

"Anyway, whatever. If Bannerman has evidence for me, I'll take him to the interview room. You coming?"

"Nah, I heard it all already. And like you said, I've got some organizing to do. Once I get this mjolnir thingy packed up and sent to the lab. And I've got some other evidence to go through, and . . . well . . . you know how it is. You kids run along and have fun now!" Kevin grinned and waved his big hand toward the door.

Peter had never been in the interview room before. He always just talked to Kevin in his office. On the one hand, this was preferable as it was pristine and empty, and thus far less distracting or alarming.

On the other hand, it made him feel like a suspect. There was just a wooden table with a voice recorder on it, three wooden chairs, and a camera mounted on a tripod pointed at the table. The walls were painted a pale green and had no signs or decorations. There wasn't even a clock.

Kristine motioned to one of the chairs and then sat down across the table from Peter. She pulled a small coil-bound notebook out of her jacket breast pocket.

"I'm just going to take notes, unless you prefer I turn the recorder on?"

"No, that's fine."

"So, what have you got for me?"

Peter repeated what he had told Kevin about the discovery of the Saga Study Society and the connection to the name Bjartur. He again emphasized Laura's involvement as he had the distinct feeling that Kristine didn't like him.

"Is that it? Anything else?"

"That's it."

"Then thank you for your time, Dr. Bannerman. We've already investigated the Saga Study Society and they do not appear to be involved, although we continue to monitor their activities."

Peter raised an eyebrow. He knew he shouldn't comment, but he couldn't help himself when faced with something as illogical as this. "Really? The Bjartur thing is just a coincidence?"

"It appears so, yes."

"Wow, OK. What's your theory then?" Peter knew she wouldn't answer that, but, again, he couldn't help himself.

"I cannot comment on that." Kristine's tone was bland and neutral. She stood up and indicated the door. "If that's all, once again, thank you, and have a good day."

CHAPTER
Thirty-One

I t was early on a brilliantly clear day, the air clean as if fresh-scrubbed and the sun slanting low between the houses across the street from the RCMP station. A sunbeam bathed Peter's truck as if it were the particular highlight of the street. Peter was surprised and pleased by the weather. For some reason Good Friday had always been cold, windy, and grey in the past, or so it seemed to him when he thought back. It was almost the latest possible date for it though, so perhaps that was why. It was a perfect day to do a little scent work with Pippin and to collect some pussy willow branches at the same time. He and Laura had the tradition of decorating the house with pussy willows and other signs of spring such as fresh flowers for the Easter holiday. Given the climate, even in mid-April the flowers were almost always store-bought though. Sometimes crocuses were already blooming, but it felt wrong to pick those as they were rare.

First, he had to check his messages. The clinic was closed for the holiday, but he was on call. Peter woke his phone as he walked across the parking lot. There was one voicemail and one email. The voicemail was from Sarah Winslow. She was a young woman who, confusingly, lived with another Sarah, Sarah Brennan, up on Curie Road. They had recently moved from the city to start a meadery. Both Sarahs had long brown hair, were of similar height and both usually wore denim overalls. Peter had trouble remembering which was which, but Winslow was the more talkative one. They brought a pair of Shih Tzus to see Peter.

"Hi, Dr. Bannerman? Sorry to bother you on a holiday, but there's something seriously wrong with the bees. I don't know whether it can wait until Monday. Call me back when you get the chance, please. Thanks!"

Bees? Fortunately, Peter had recently attended a seminar on bee medicine basics put on by the vet association. In order to reduce the inappropriate use of antibiotics by beekeepers, the government had started requiring a veterinary prescription. Also fortunate was that Peter had planned to take Pippin up Humboldt Road, which ran parallel to Curie, north of town. Most of the major streets and roads in New Selfoss and district were named after famous scientists. Peter had to remind himself to say "Curie Road" rather than "Agassiz Road," as the name had just been changed after a heated debate. Louis Agassiz, the famed geologist and biologist, for whom the glacial Lake Agassiz that once covered most of the Canadian Prairies was named, apparently had also been fond of measuring skulls to prove the superiority of white people. Or so the thumbnail story went. The detailed story of his work was more complex and ambiguous, hence the heated debate, but it was hard not to give Marie Curie her due instead, especially as no other roads had been named after female scientists, so the opposition to the renaming eventually backed off.

Peter called back and let a Sarah know that he could be there within the hour. Then he opened the email. It was from Dwayne Lautermilch:

Hi Peter,

Thanks for the invitation. Clubs aren't normally my kind of thing, but I think I'll take you up on the offer to try out. I've always been curious about darts, and I've watched a lot of it on TV.

Thanks again!

Regards,
Dwayne

Peter smiled at the idea of the two of them being in a darts league together. What a strange world. What a strange life. He quickly sent a text to Chris to tell him about Dwayne's interest and to ask when the next practice was, and then he started the truck and drove home to pick up Pippin and the piece of Patrick's skin he had saved in the freezer.

Both Sarahs were outside when Peter pulled up. One of them, Sarah Winslow he thought, was wearing a full white beekeeper's suit and was attending to one of a cluster of a half a dozen blue rectangular wooden hives in a field beside their driveway. The other walked up to meet Peter, waving and smiling. He reconsidered. No, this must be Sarah Winslow, the chatty one. Not that it really mattered.

"Hi, Dr. Bannerman! Thank you so much for coming on a holiday!" She shook his hand and then bent down to greet Pippin. "Oh, what a beautiful boy you are!" Pippin wagged his tail vigorously. He always seemed to know when a compliment was being paid.

"It's no trouble. Pippin and I were planning to come up this way anyway. I have to tell you though, I'm not a bee expert!"

"But you're a vet, and you can get us drugs if that's what's needed!" Sarah said this with a laugh and then led the way across the field to where the other Sarah was pulling a large wooden tray out of the hive.

"Hi, Dr. Bannerman! Come look at this. It's fine, the bees are quiet right now." Beekeeper Sarah nodded toward something that looked like a metal watering can with smoke coming out of the spout. "Smoked 'em a little for you."

Peter approached and looked at the tray, which was covered in beautifully symmetrical hexagonal honeycombs. At least half the hexagons were open and black and greasy looking, whereas the rest had tan-coloured wax coverings. It had a nasty dead fish odour. Peter was relieved. He knew what this was.

"This is foulbrood," he said, savouring the wonderful medieval sound of the disease's name. "You'll have to destroy this hive, and I can prescribe Terramycin to protect the others."

"Damn it," the other Sarah said.

"At least you caught it early."

"That's why we bugged you on Good Friday! Thank you again for coming out. Where are you and Pippin off to now?"

"He's a champion sniffer dog, and I like to take him to different areas and challenge him with different scents. Today I thought we'd try the old Thorkelson land east of Humboldt Road. I know Dan and Kim Favel, who own it now."

"Cool," beekeeper Sarah said as she pulled her netted hood off. "They seem like good people. Thorkelson's home quarter section is up for sale now too, eh?"

"I didn't know that, but it makes sense."

"Yeah, we like to walk Barney and Flo that way and saw the sign yesterday. It's his son, Jim Junior, selling it."

"I went to high school with him. He lives in Calgary now, but I guess he must have kept his local real estate licence."

"Selling the old family home is always tough."

The original plan had been to drive up Curie and then turn east on a grid road across to the north end of Humboldt, where Crown Land abutted the north side of the old Thorkelson section, and find a path there, but now Peter was curious about the home quarter section, which meant driving back south, toward town, and then across to the south end of Humboldt Road. He assumed that this was where the Sarahs walked their dogs.

He didn't have any clients along Humboldt Road, and it didn't lead anywhere useful or interesting, so he wasn't familiar with it. The more he thought about it though, the more irritated he was at himself for not having come before. It was an obvious thing to check out. For one, Grimur would have accessed the property from that side as his car wasn't at the Favels'. In fact, the murderer would have had to have come in from the west too. Kevin didn't mention anything about finding Grim's car abandoned. He'd try to find a way to ask. It shouldn't be top secret police investigation information, should it? However, it was also possible that Grim, or his head, had been transported this way by his killer. Also, whoever was watching Peter and Dwayne would have entered the property from this side. It was definitely worth checking out. And as to the appropriateness of Peter poking around here? He was looking into the fate of his patient's genitals. A stretch to be sure, but enough of an excuse for him.

Peter pulled into the driveway in front of the old wooden farmhouse that had a realtor's sign out front. The house was two stories and looked to be at least 80 years old. The white paint was peeling and a few of the grey shingles were curling, but otherwise it appeared to be in reasonable shape. The for-sale sign listed "JTJ Realty" and gave a local 204 number. It promised a "6 Minute Callback" — "Guaranteed" and trademarked.

"What do you think, Pippin?" Peter asked as they climbed out of the truck and walked up to the house. "Should I give Jim a call?"

Pippin cocked his head for a moment and looked at Peter while he was speaking, but as it was obviously another one of those times when his master was just saying random words at him, Pippin resumed sniffing the overgrown grass along the driveway.

"You know what? I think I will. Why not? Kevin or Kristine have probably talked to him already, but maybe he'll let slip something to an old friend that he wouldn't think to tell them. You never know, right?"

Pippin was ignoring him now and continued sniffing.

Peter pulled out his phone and dialed the number on the sign. After one ring it went to voicemail, "Hi! You've reach Jim Thorkelson Junior of JTJ Realty! I'm busy helping someone else's real estate dreams come true, but I will call you back within six minutes. Guaranteed!"

Peter chuckled to himself. The temptation was strong to phone Jim on one of those mornings when Peter got up at five thirty. *Helping people's real estate dreams come true before dawn, Jim? Cool.*

At the beep he said, "Hi Jim! It's Peter Bannerman. We played D&D together in high school. I'm looking at your dad's old place right now. Give me a call when you get the chance. Which will be within six minutes I guess, eh? Ha ha!"

He glanced at his watch and noted the time, but his phone rang immediately, so Jim's guarantee was valid this time at least.

"Hey Pete, great to hear from you!" These days he only allowed Kevin to call him Pete, and that was under sufferance, but back in high school it was more common. Peter had much less self-confidence then and didn't speak up for himself.

"Thanks for calling me back!"

"No problem, buddy! It's been 20 years at least, eh?"

"At least. And you're in Calgary now? But this is a Manitoba number."

"Yeah. Been here something like seven or eight years, but I kept my Manitoba licence. I do a fair number of cottage sales, often to

Albertans with Manitoba roots. I come in every couple months, but I have Al Finnbogason working for me locally there. You know him?"

"Sure. Ken's brother."

"That's him. But I wanted to handle my dad's place myself. You know how it is. Anyway, what can I do you for, Pete? You said you're out there. You interested?"

"Maybe." Peter had his white lie ready to go: "Laura and were thinking it would be nice to get out of town and have more land."

"This is perfect for you guys then! House needs a pinch of love, but it is rock solid, and as far as more land goes, there's a whole quarter section of it. What've you got in town? Like a regular 8,000 square foot town lot?"

"No, we're at the edge of town and have a half-acre."

"Well, that's still, what? One-320th the size of dad's place!"

"And he had a whole section behind it too. Why'd you sell that separately?"

"I thought about hanging on to the home quarter. Sentimental, I guess. But it doesn't make sense. Cowtown is home now, so there's no point in keeping it. Even though I'm in the industry and totally get that it's just business, it's really important to me that the right people own Thorkelson land."

"And the Favels are the right people?"

"Totally. I had some pushy assholes jump to make an offer right away as soon as dad died. They wanted to develop the land and put a subdivision in. Dad would spin in his grave like a rotisserie chicken if anyone ever did that. I knew the Favels had recently set up on the southeast corner of the section, and I used to date Kim, so I gave them a call."

"Right. Makes sense. Who were these developers? Just curious?"

"Some lawyer for a numbered company. Never did talk to the actual interested parties."

Peter had to bite his tongue to stop himself from asking for name of the lawyer or the company's number. It would seem like a weird degree of interest. And no doubt the police had pursued this angle already. Instead, he said, "Oh, OK. Toronto money or something like that then."

"Probably. Anyway, I gave the Favels an awesome deal because that's what I do for the right buyers! And I'm going to give you an awesome deal too, Pete, because you're the right buyer! I'll send Al around with the keys so you can have look inside. Wait till you see the crown mouldings."

"Thanks, but I don't have much time today. I was just driving by on my way to a call and saw the sign. I'll chat with Laura about it when I get home."

"For sure, buddy. OK if I give you a follow-up call tomorrow?"

"Sure, but how about Monday, after Easter?"

"No sweat. Will do. Great talking to you, Pete! I gotta call somebody else back now. Hopefully they're not calling about dad's place and are going to snatch it out from under your nose! Ha ha! Talk soon, Pete!"

"Oh, one thing before you go. Why six-minute callback, not five or ten?"

"Ha! Both five and ten were trademarked already. And six is more memorable, right? It made you ask!"

Peter pocketed the phone and turned his attention to his dog. "That was intriguing, Pippin, wasn't it? Well, probably not for you — you couldn't hear Jim anyway. But now things will get interesting for you because it's scent hunt time!"

CHAPTER
Thirty-Two

Peter could see a rough track heading east from the small yard behind the house. There had once been a white picket fence, but it was mostly collapsed. The track looked like it was where a gate had once been; a post with rusty hinges still stood there. The path was grassy and overgrown, but two ruts were visible where presumably a small truck or tractor had once been driven. It disappeared into a large aspen bluff. With any luck it led to the section now owned by the Favels.

Before heading off that way, Peter pulled his phone out again and brought up a satellite view. The trees were too dense to make out the track, but the alignment seemed about right. He also saw the Dukovskys' place a little further north and then another, quite small house beyond that. Both of those also backed onto the old Thorkelson section.

Peter pulled out the little piece of the poor dead ram's skin and presented it to Pippin, holding it delicately between his right thumb and forefinger. Pippin didn't need to be told what to do. He knew the routine well. Peter only held items to his nose that he was supposed to sniff, remember and eventually seek when the command was given. Pippin sniffed deeply, flaring his lips slightly as he breathed in, making the faintest whistling sound.

Peter smiled as he watched his dog do this. He loved imagining what was going through his mind, knowing as he did so that it was in fact unimaginable. A wholly alien intelligence was at work, wielding a wholly alien skill. Proportionally, as much of Pippin's brain was devoted to decoding smell as Peter's was to decoding sight. Occasionally one of Peter's patients would go blind due to some disease or other and their owners would be greatly distressed, asking whether it was kinder at that point to ease the poor sightless pup into the next world. Peter would patiently explain the power and utility of smell in dogs and the distant secondary nature of vision. He would guarantee that their dog would learn to navigate quite well by smell, aided by memory, whiskers, and sound. It was astonishing. Dogs inhabited a world fully illustrated by scents.

We don't even have the language to describe how they experience and comprehend the world, Peter thought as Pippin finished sniffing. *We have to reach for visual metaphors like "illustrated," but most things we see are stable and solid, whereas scent is ephemeral and often on the move. Most objects we see are discrete and well-defined, blocking the view of what is behind or beneath, but their smells intermingle and interweave, often revealing to the nose what is hidden to the eyes.*

When Pippin was done, Peter put the skin fragment back in a baggie with an icepack and tucked it into his backpack. He smiled at Pippin, leaned down, looked him in the eye, and said "Seek!"

Dog and human moved quickly down the track and were soon deep in the forest.

The aspens were much further in leaf than just a few days before. It was still easy to make out some individual stands, as the trees within the stands were clones of each other and were uniformly in the same stage of leafing out. The stands that stood out were the few still bare ones, but most were bejewelled with a fresh pale green that glowed in the sunlight. The trees leaned into the track as if bending to whisper something to Peter.

The trail bent sharply to the north and then split in roughly east and west directions. As in the Robert Frost poem, Peter picked the one less travelled by — not for any philosophical reason, but because it seemed more likely to lead where he thought they needed to go, which was east. Pippin had other ideas, however. After ten metres up this path, he turned around and trotted to the other one, where he sniffed vigorously for a long moment and then picked up speed, heading west. This felt like a semicircular path that would lead them either to the Dukovsky place or the next property north, the one with the little house he had seen on the satellite view.

Pippin stayed several paces ahead, nose to the ground, never checking back to see if Peter was following. The path was straight enough that soon Peter could see an opening in the trees in the distance that had some sort of grey structure in it. He jogged a few steps to catch up with Pippin. He put his hand on Pippin's collar and whispered, "Slow, boy." Pippin gave Peter a sideways glance and slowed down to match Peter's speed.

The structure was now in view. It was not the Dukovskys' modern McMansion, but rather something that Peter thought would be best described as a shack. It was about the size of a two-car garage and was built of weather-beaten greying wood. Traces of red paint were visible here and there, especially on the shaded north side. There were a few small, grimy windows and a single door in the corner on the south side, facing a gravel driveway that led to Humboldt Road, 30 metres or so farther west, barely visible through overgrown brush.

Peter glanced around the weedy yard. It was a classic abandoned prairie farm tableau with assorted completely rusted ploughs and harrows and other implements lying about, as well as an equally rusty gutted truck that looked like it dated from the 1930s or '40s. A larger collapsed building, likely a barn, stood on the far side of the yard to the north. Willows had colonized its roof, pushing green-grey shingles aside.

It was a quiet morning with the only sounds being the distant trill of a red-winged blackbird and the faint rustle of aspen leaves in the light breeze.

While Peter was taking all of this in, Pippin had gone to the door and was staring at it fixedly. He gave a quiet woof and then looked back over his shoulder at Peter before going back to staring at the door.

"Really? In there?" Peter asked as he walked up to join his dog. "Are you sure?" Peter pulled the piece of skin out again and got Pippin to sniff it, which he did briefly and then resumed staring, letting out another low woof.

"OK, if you say so, but it's probably locked anyway."

The door swung open with a creak as soon as Peter tried the doorknob.

"All right, so it's not locked . . ." He looked carefully at the door. The doorjamb was splintered. "Correction, it was locked at some point in the past, but someone's broken in."

They stepped inside, finding themselves in a large room which occupied the western half of the house. There were two doors to the right, leading presumably to other rooms. The only light came in from the dirt-encrusted windows, but on this sunny day it was enough to see that there was very little furniture, just three wooden chairs, a wooden table, and a filthy couch with a spring protruding. A countertop with a chipped enamel sink stood against the far wall. A pile of beer cans lay on the floor between the chairs. To his disgust, Peter noted that most of them were Bud Light and MGD. There were also a couple of empty bottles of Five Star rye whisky. None of them was dusty, so they couldn't have been there very long given how filthy everything else was.

Pippin had been sniffing intently around the perimeter of the room and then stopped in front of the farthest door on the right.

"OK, coming," Peter said as he stood up from examining the cans and bottles.

The door led to what had once likely been a bedroom. There was a large empty wardrobe in the corner, its doors swung wide open. Otherwise, the room was empty.

"So? Ancient Norse blot rites were performed in here?" Peter said, chuckling. Pippin was excellent, but he wasn't perfect. The odds of anyone, human or dog, being perfect in any given skill were almost incalculably low.

Pippin stared at the floor in the near corner to his left and woofed again.

Peter bent down and had a careful look. The light was poor in there, so he brought out his phone to use the flashlight function. It was a hatch of some sort. The floor was made of pine planking, and there was a large knothole in one of the planks in the middle of this hatch. These old houses didn't have basements, but there was usually a crawlspace or a small dirt root cellar.

Peter pulled up on the trap door with the two fingers he could get into the hole. It opened easily. The flashlight revealed a low crawlspace with several Bankers cardboard boxes and green Rubbermaid bins. Amongst them was a large roll of paper that was evidently too long for any of the boxes or bins. By lying on the floor and leaning into the hole he was able to reach the roll and bring it up.

It looked like a set of drawings or possibly blueprints. He pulled the rubber band off and carefully unrolled it.

Pippin was still staring into the hole.

It was a map of the area done like a landscape architect's drawing with all the nearby buildings, wooded areas, marshes, rivers, roads, power lines, and so on marked with precise measurements noted in a neat draftsman's hand. The Favels' house was in the bottom right corner. The Yellowgrass First Nation reserve was at the top and Humboldt Road on the left. The middle of the map was dominated by the Thorkelson section of land now owned by the Favels. It was marked up with lines in a strange way that didn't make sense to Peter at first. Then he realized that they were property boundaries, roads, and utilities. This must be the subdivision plan Jim Junior had referred to!

In the bottom left corner, it said "Asgard Estates." Asgard, home of the Norse gods. Peter used his backpack and the baggie with the icepack to hold two of the corners down while he leaned back to take a picture with his phone.

Things were beginning to slide into place. He could almost hear the whirring and clicking in his mind as units of data rearranged themselves, like a kaleidoscope turning quickly, assembling an increasingly clear picture.

Then he heard the sound of tires crunching on gravel and an engine being switched off.

CHAPTER
Thirty-Three

Although Peter's natural style was to make decisions slowly and deliberately by weighing all the relevant factors and analyzing them in a framework of pure rationality, he was also capable of instantaneous, even instinctive, decision-making. In a series of swift and silent moves he rolled up the drawing, put it back in the subfloor, closed the hatch, and ran with Pippin across the room to the wardrobe. Pippin didn't need a command but followed Peter's moves. He had been in competitive agility before Peter discovered how good his nose was, and echoes of that training stuck with him. They climbed in, and Peter closed the doors behind them. The wardrobe wasn't deep enough to sit in or crouch, but fortunately it was tall enough even for Peter to stand with his knees slightly bent and his head pulled down. It wasn't especially comfortable, but he hoped it would only be for a few minutes. If it was the partiers coming back for another round, he'd have to figure something else out. Pippin stood beside him, lengthwise, nose to Peter's right knee.

A small gap remained between the two doors, but he reasoned that it was too dark inside the wardrobe for anyone to see them on a casual glance. Peter breathed a quick "shhh" to Pippin, even though he was already quiet. Pippin seemed to know that they were trying not to be seen or heard, or he was just very good at mimicking his master.

Peter heard the creak of the door opening.

"Hey! Anyone here!" It was a faintly accented female voice. He couldn't place the accent and the voice wasn't familiar, although that didn't mean much as Peter was terrible at recognizing voices. This led to numerous awkward telephone conversations with clients who assumed he knew who they were when they said, "Hi, it's Anne with Kitty," or something like that.

There was the sound of someone walking into the main room and then a quiet, "Fucking kids," followed by the sound of a bottle clattering after presumably being kicked. Peter reached down to place his hand on Pippin's head. He could tell that Pippin was silently panting.

Then he heard the door of the adjacent room open and close again right after. Peter held his breath. This room would be next. Sure enough, the door to this room opened immediately after, and through the gap he saw a tall woman silhouetted against the brighter light of the main room. He couldn't make out any features other than long blond hair as she turned to leave and closed the door behind her. He kept holding his breath for a couple of seconds longer and then exhaled quietly.

"Yeah, hi. It's me." It sounded like she was talking on her phone. "The door's broken and there's a bunch of cans and bottles. Kids partying, I guess. That's what the Dukovskys figured too when they called." She was quiet for a moment. "No, I think the stuff's OK. No sign anyone was in that room. But yeah, sure, I'll double-check."

Shit. She's coming back. Peter held his breath again.

He heard quick steps and then the door was flung open. The woman moved across the far side of the room in deep shadow and then bent down over the hatch. She lifted it and as she bent over the opening, she turned on her flashlight.

Shit. If she happens to swing it this way . . . Peter thought. He leaned to his left, away from the gap between the wardrobe doors, but this meant he couldn't see what was happening anymore.

"No, everything's there. Doesn't look like anything was touched. Like I said, stupid country kids. I'll get someone to fix the door, and we might want to think about a security system, although we don't want to attract attention either."

Silence.

"Yeah, I get it."

Peter heard the hatch being dropped back in place, but this was not followed by the expected footsteps to the door. Was she scanning the room? He waited for a beam of light to shoot through the gap.

"Sure. See you tonight."

Now the footsteps he had been waiting for, and the sound of the door to the room being closed. Then more footsteps and the creak of the front door. A minute later he heard an engine start and tires on gravel again. Everything that happened before, now in reverse as if rewound.

He waited until all he could hear was the blood rushing in his ears, and then he exhaled loudly. When Peter opened the wardrobe door, he looked down to see Pippin's happy smiling face looking back up at him and his tail wagging furiously.

As they walked back Peter couldn't help but be hyper-aware of every little noise, even though he knew it was irrational. Whoever had come to the shack was clearly focused on the shack and its contents and had spent no time walking around the yard. It would be bizarre for her to return now to specifically walk down this path. But fear, being an emotion, was by definition irrational. And who was she?

He really had no idea. He wished he could place that accent. But the development plan was a major find and very exciting, even though it presented a number of thorny questions for him.

"What do you think, Pippin? Should I call Kevin right now and tell him about Asgard Estates?" he said, using a quieter voice than normal.

Pippin glanced up at Peter without breaking stride.

"It could be the motive for the threats against the Favels, so he should know, right?"

This time Pippin didn't look up.

"It would be great to first tie this in with the Saga Study Society though, and with Grimur's murder and the mutilations, don't you think?" Peter smiled at the thought of presenting his brother-in-law with an air-tight theory, constructed of perfectly interlocking units of logic and evidence. He didn't like to admit to himself that he was competitive, but at moments like this he couldn't deny it.

"Yeah, I'll just hang on to the information for a few hours while we fine-tune the theory. Besides, I'm not sure how I'll explain how we found it without Kevin going Viking thermonuclear on me!" Peter chuckled at the mental image of Kevin's face turning tomato red and little mushroom clouds sprouting from his ears like in a cartoon.

When they reached the first T intersection where they would have to turn south to make their way back to the truck, Peter stopped and looked at the path ahead. This led in the direction of the section Jim Junior had sold to the Favels. He also suspected that it led to the archeological site that he still hadn't seen. The Asgard Estates plans didn't need to be connected to anything else, but Pippin had smelled Patrick down there somewhere in the crawlspace, so, the development plan was linked to the mutilations, and the mutilations were linked to the murder and the archeology because of what happened to Grimur's head. The shin bone's connected to the knee bone, and the knee bone's connected to the . . .

Peter stared down the path, undecided. Pippin looked up at him, evidently waiting for some indication of what was next, and when none was forthcoming, he sat down and began to lick one of his paws.

Peter prided himself on his calmness and ability to master his emotions, but he couldn't shake that sense of heightened vigilance and apprehension. Thinking about Grimur's death hadn't helped. The image of the head impaled on the nithing pole kept flashing into his mind, no matter how often he swatted it away. He felt a deep chill looking east down that narrow, grassy path.

"No, let's go home," Peter said.

CHAPTER
Thirty-Four

"**J**im Junior sent you this?" Laura asked.

Peter hoped the question was rooted in innocent surprise, not doubt. On the walk back to the truck he decided that he wanted her opinion on the map, but he couldn't tell her how he found it. The solution came to him when he backed out past the for-sale sign in front of the old Thorkelson place. Jim Junior had mentioned the development plan. It wouldn't be such a stretch to claim that he had then sent Peter a picture of it, just to show how absurd it was, would it? On the spectrum of white lies Peter had told over the years, this was only mid-range. Eggshell white rather than either pure snow white on the one end or old yellowed parchment white on the other. He would just have to edit his backpack out of the photo. He quickly did this on his phone while in the bathroom after arriving home.

"Yes, he was appalled by the idea. Couldn't stop talking about it. He knew I'd agree with him when I saw this."

"And why were you talking to him in the first place after, what? Twenty years?" The doubt was unmistakable this time. Laura peered at him over the tortoiseshell framed glasses she wore when knitting. Peter had only said, "I was talking to Jim Thorkelson Junior," without explaining why. He had hoped she wouldn't notice, which was silly, of course.

"I got called out to look at these bees, which was kind of cool, and while I was there Sarah Winslow, or maybe it was Sarah Brennan, mentioned that Jim Junior had finally put the old home quarter up for sale. I called him on a whim. I was just curious . . ." He trailed off and smiled in what he hoped was a charming and ingratiating way.

"Curious about what?" Laura's tone was neutral, but with a hint of warmth, so Peter took a chance.

"The whole thing. The Favels, Sturluson, medieval Manitoba Vikings, Skraelings, Saga Study Society, animal mutilations, blot rituals, all of it. I figured there was no harm in asking innocent questions to try to satisfy that curiosity. See if Jim might fit in there somewhere or know something. Scratch that itch, you know? I'm sure Kevin or Kristine have already asked the same questions, so I'm not stepping on toes."

"And Kevin has seen this map too?"

"Oh yeah, of course." An old yellowed parchment white lie. But Kevin would see it very soon.

"And what did you tell Jim Junior you were calling about? Did you pretend to be interested in the property?" Laura was smiling now.

"You bet! Said we were looking for more space."

"Hmm, well, I'll confess, I'm pretty curious about all of this too. I'm just glad you didn't go poking around in someone's attic or office to find this!"

"Ha! No. No attics or offices!" Not technically a lie, Peter thought while trying to keep a mischievous grin from showing on his face.

Laura sat up straight and put her knitting aside on the end table. Peter could see that she had been working on a navy-blue sweater with an upside-down parrot on the front, accompanied by the words "Pining for the Fjords." Monty Python themes were apparently selling especially well this year. She adjusted her glasses and then pinched and scrolled across the image on Peter's phone.

"Did you see the part at the top?" She turned the phone toward him and pointed at an area between the Favel section and the Yellowgrass First Nation marked Crown Land.

"Yes?" Peter wasn't sure what she was getting at.

"The Crown Land is subdivided too. The marked lines are fainter, but they're there. That's an active Yellowgrass land claim."

"Right! I totally missed that."

"It was part of the original reserve but was taken away in the 1920s because of pressure from the local timber lobby."

"Those, Finns," Peter winked at her. As a New Selfossian of Icelandic heritage, Laura was by tradition supposed to look down on the Finns, which were the next group to settle the area and who dominated the lumber industry. For a time, the rivalry was almost as intense as that with the Veni Icelanders in Gimli, but only almost.

"Yeah, those Finns," Laura chuckled, "but seriously, this is interesting. Messed up, but interesting." She resumed her pinching and scrolling.

Peter, who had been standing beside Laura's chair, stepped over to his own big green armchair and sat down. They were both quiet for a moment. Pippin, who had been watching them while panting quietly, settled down on his blanket by the fireplace hearth and fell instantly asleep.

"This is the link to the archeology finds and the threats," Peter finally said. "It's obvious now."

Laura looked up from the phone. "Yes. The presence of an ancient Norse settlement might complicate the land claim and the threats might chase the Favels away, freeing up all the marked areas."

"And since it seems likely that this Saga Society is behind the threats, they must be linked to the numbered company promoting Asgard."

"Makes sense. Find out who owns that company and find out who valkyrie-whatever-that-number-was and her friends are. But the company isn't identified on the map."

"No, and Jim Junior just said 'a numbered company' without

mentioning a specific number. It's possible he doesn't even know or remember, but Kevin could track it down through the lawyer's contact information."

Laura nodded. "Right. Good that there's progress on this. Kevin is coming for Easter dinner, so maybe we can ply him with drink until he lets a few details slip."

Peter laughed. He was surprised by Laura's enthusiasm for finding out more about this case. He wondered whether she had started to accept that he was unable to help his own curiosity, so her smartest strategy was to play along and stay close in order to be in a better position to prevent Peter from going too far. But the Icelandic connection probably made it more interesting for her too. And Pippin's near-death experience put bigger personal stakes into play.

Laura handed the phone back to Peter and picked up her knitting again. There was a text message from Chris Olson saying that it was great news about Dwayne and that he and Ken were planning on meeting at The Flying Beaver Saturday afternoon for a pint anyway, so that would be good opportunity to meet Dwayne if he and Peter were available.

There were also three voicemails from clients involving an extremely itchy cat, a vomiting dog, and a bloated and distressed looking horse. Peter sighed. Some days on call were dead quiet, and others were pandemonium. Rarely was it something in-between. Poisson clumping. The horse was probably the most serious as it could have a potentially fatal case of colic, but Peter called the cat and dog owners first to see if he could triage them over the phone before dealing with the horse. It turned out that both the cat and dog needed to be seen, so he arranged to meet them at the clinic in two hours, which he hoped would be enough time to deal with the horse, which was at a nearby hobby farm.

Laura waited for Peter to finish his calls before commenting. "One of those days?"

"Yup. One of those days."

CHAPTER
Thirty-Five

The Flying Beaver on an Easter weekend Saturday afternoon was dead quiet. As Peter was still on call, he looked at his phone nervously several times while waiting for the others. Peter had come on time, precisely to-the-minute on time, while the others had not, but he was used to the imprecision of other people.

Friday had been busy, but not too stressful as the horse did not have colic after all, and the itchy cat and vomiting dog were easily dealt with. There had been a few other simple calls through the afternoon, and then suddenly the phone stopped buzzing in the evening, and he hadn't been called once today yet.

Lloyd, the barman, called over to Peter, "You sure you don't want anything yet? Don't worry, this is one place where you won't be judged for drinking alone!" He laughed while polishing glasses.

Peter smiled, "Actually, I'm on call. Just a club soda, please."

"You got it, Doc!"

Just then, Dwayne walked in, weaving his shambling bulk between the tables and chairs as he made his way over to Peter. While they exchanged greetings, Lloyd came over with Peter's club soda and asked Dwayne, "And how about you? Manipogo Pale is on special."

"Club soda for me as well, please."

"You on call too?" Lloyd chuckled. Peter didn't know whether Dwayne and Lloyd knew each other, but Dwayne took it the right way and laughed.

"You bet. You never know when there might be a model train emergency! They derail all the time!" Peter assumed that Dwayne was either an ex-alcoholic or didn't drink for religious reasons, or both. He was curious, but he restrained himself from asking.

Chris and Ken entered together and picked up beers at the bar before settling around the table with Dwayne and Peter. Once all the introductions had been made and they'd had a few sips of their drinks, Ken invited Dwayne to join him at the nearby dartboard.

"It's not like a try-out or anything. I think we'll take just about anyone who has at least one arm and one eye right now! Just don't hit me or the beaver, and we're good."

Everyone laughed.

Chris and Peter chatted while the other two threw darts. Peter's instinct had been right, Dwayne was good. Dwayne was so good that Ken mouthed, "Get a load of this!" to Peter and Chris, with a thumbs-up and his eyes wide.

Afterwards they all sat together and finished their drinks while talking about the darts league, the rivalry with Gimli, and their prospects for taking home the Golden Dartboard this coming season. The Flying Beaver remained empty and quiet otherwise. Lloyd hadn't bothered turning the sound system on. Peter liked it this way.

They were just wrapping up when Ken yawned theatrically and stretched his arms out to the sides. This caused his sleeves to ride up. Dwayne pointed to Ken's arm and asked, "Nice three-dragon tattoo. Get it at Iron Feather in Winnipeg?"

Peter marvelled at Dwayne's eyesight as it was such a small tattoo. No wonder he was so good at darts. Peter's vision wasn't quite as acute, but he had an unusually powerful ability to focus and notice small details, which probably accounted for the Alan Evans.

Ken blinked and looked at Dwayne, a flicker of surprise playing across his face, "Um, yeah. You know the place?"

"I don't know whether Peter's mentioned, but I did time at Stony. This is a few years ago." Dwayne looked at the table as he said this, and then briefly glanced up at the three faces watching him. "Don't worry, I'm a totally different person now, but anyway, my last cellmate just before I got out had the exact same tattoo. I thought it was cool and asked him where he got it. He said Iron Feather."

"Huh, funny coincidence, eh?" Ken said.

Dwayne nodded and, warming to his subject, looked up and went on, smiling now. "Yeah, it is, I guess. And this guy, Brad, he explained about the three-dragon symbolism, but he also said that it stood for the three initials of a group he belonged to. Saga something. Said because I was of German background, I might be able to join, but I changed the subject. There are all kinds of ethnic gangs in the pen, and I wanted to stay clean before my release. Beautiful tattoo though."

Peter felt his stomach tighten. He looked around the table. Chris was oblivious, draining the last drops from his beer glass. Ken had a neutral facial expression. Dwayne was still smiling.

"It is," Ken said. "I picked it from their catalogue. Now you've got me worried that it's a prison gang design!" He laughed.

Peter quickly weighed his options but decided to forge ahead as something important had become clear to him just then. "It's not. At least I'm pretty sure it's not. There's a shadowy group on the internet called the Saga Study Society. The three 'S's, the 'saga something,' and Norse design could all be coincidental, but it sounds like them. They're white nationalists and Odin worshippers rather than convicts, although I suppose there could be overlap."

Ken let out a big woosh of breath. "Wow, Peter, now you're really making me want to laser this thing off!"

Ken looked sincere to Peter, but Peter knew that he was terrible at reading people. And Ken Finnbogason a crypto-fascist? Hard to believe. Earl Petursson, sure, but Ken? He doubted it. Yet, the coincidence made him uncomfortable.

"Remember Brad's last name, Dwayne? Just curious," Peter asked.

"Yeah, Thorkelson," Dwayne said as he began to stand up. Peter remained sitting and stared up at him.

"Did he have a father or uncle named Jim?"

"No idea."

Ken looked at Peter and shrugged.

Peter wished he had walked to The Flying Beaver. Walking helped him think, and it was the perfect distance to try to work out what he had just learned, but unfortunately, he had had to take the truck in case there was an urgent call. Instead, he drove down to the lake and parked at Suomi Beach, thinking that maybe either the drive or looking out at the softening ice would help, but he couldn't stop himself from wondering about how the shade of grey in the ice might correlate to its diminishing thickness rather than having any productive thoughts about Ken and Earl and Brad and the Saga Study Society. What would Ken's handle be on the 8kun chat? He couldn't guess. Maybe he just lurked quietly and didn't participate. Talking to Laura might be helpful. He should just go home.

Once Peter had greeted Merry at the front door and made his Earl Grey decaf, he went to where Laura was sitting with Pippin on the deck. Laura was reading and Pippin was napping.

"It's the first day where it's nice enough to sit outside," she said.

"With a sweater, mind you," Peter said as he settled into the Muskoka chair beside her.

"Sure, but at least not with a toque and gloves."

Peter took a few sips of his tea before telling Laura about Ken's tattoo and Brad Thorkelson. He also mentioned Earl Petursson's tattoo.

"Brad? He's Jim's younger brother," she said. "Much younger, I think. Half-brother actually, from Jim Senior's second wife. I didn't know he was in jail."

"I didn't know anything about him at all, so you're a step ahead of me."

"So, all these guys are in the Saga Study Society, including Ken?"

"I don't know about Ken. It's possible he just liked the tattoo, as he said."

"Has he ever given any hints that he might be into this kind of stuff?"

"None. But I barely know the guy. An acquaintance, not really a friend."

"Not like Tom then," Laura said, giving Peter a hard look. Tom was the owner of the swine barn that exploded last winter.

"That's not fair, but no, not like him. I knew Tom much better and was still wrong."

"My point exactly. But that's OK. Nobody really knows anybody as well as they think they do."

Peter nodded and took a long sip from his tea. The yard in front of them was more of a meadow than a lawn. Later, as it grew, they would let Gandalf graze on it to keep it from growing out of control, but for now it was still just the pale green and yellow of early spring. The meadow was fringed on three sides by a mixed forest of pine, aspen, and birch. Peter felt like he could stare across the meadow at the forest all day long. He never did because he was too restless, but one of these days he would try it, just to see.

Just then there was some motion in the tree shadows on the north side, to his left. Peter felt his stomach turn to ice. He nudged Laura and pointed silently. Pippin, who had been lying beside them, looked up, his ears perked.

There was more movement.

Then he saw it.

It was a yearling whitetail deer buck with fuzzy little antler stubs, a shiny black nose, and huge shiny black eyes.

All three of them relaxed.

"Were you thinking what I was thinking?" Peter asked.

The buck froze at the sound of his voice.

"One hundred percent." Laura gave a snort of a laugh. "But anyway, I've been wanting to show you something."

"Oh?"

"It's on the laptop. I'll bring it out here."

After Laura went into the house, the buck began to move gingerly across the far corner of the yard, taking each step as if his hooves were made of thinnest glass. He glanced at Peter and Pippin several times as he did so and then, as if responding to an invisible signal, suddenly bolted into the trees on the east side, disappearing from view almost immediately.

CHAPTER
Thirty-Six

"**E**ivor's Circle? Is this connected to the Saga Study Society?"
Peter asked after Laura opened a chat page on 8kun. The
laptop was set up bridging the armrests of their two Muskoka chairs.

"Yes." Laura paused for a second while she clicked a link and
opened another page. "Yes, it's connected. It looks like it's an inner
or elite subgroup of the Saga group."

"And you got in how?" Peter turned from the laptop to look at
his wife.

"It's not much higher security than for Saga. Just a few more questions that weren't that hard to answer, and I faked a very convincing
profile of a Norwegian extremist closely linked to Anders Breivik."

"Jesus, Laura. The mass shooter in the Norwegian summer camp?"
Laura shrugged. "Uh-huh."

"How did you think to look for these Eivor people?"

"I've been following the Saga chat, and it's mostly pretty dull
stuff. Typical knuckle-dragger right-wing drivel with a superficial
Nordic twist. But nothing about the Asgard development, or blot
rituals, or nithing poles, or animal sacrifices, or —"

Peter cut her off, "Or murders of professors?"

"Precisely. Then someone said that they had heard about 'Eivor' and how could they get in touch with him. But valkyrie3939 shut him down right away. Said we don't talk about Eivor here. So, I did some poking around and found this Eivor's Circle."

"Huh, wow. Well done! Did you find out who Eivor is?"

Laura smiled. "It's quite an unusual name, so it may not be a specific person in the group, but more symbolic, kind of like Bjartur is just a touchstone for the Saga people. As far as well-known Eivors go, it's either a Faroese pop singer, or the main character in the *Assassin's Creed Valhalla* video game."

"That would be the latter then," Peter said, smiling back.

"Agreed. Incidentally, it's a gender-neutral name. The singer is a woman, and the video game character can be either gender, but keeping the same name."

Peter sucked in his lower lip and nodded. "So, what have they been chatting about, these Eivors?"

"Nothing at all at first, but then when I logged in last night there was an active chat regarding a house this group uses. Apparently, some kids had broken in and partied in there."

Peter avoided looking at Laura and kept his face as composed as he was able. "Huh, really?"

"They were relieved none of their stuff had been messed with. It was all well hidden in the house, according to valkyrie3939 —"

Peter broke in, "She's in Eivor's Circle too?"

"Yeah, I should have mentioned. She's actually the group admin, at least from a chat forum perspective."

"Any of the other names from Saga show up there?"

"Yes, about half. Of the ones I mentioned to you, vesturvatnslander88, but not MBthorsbondsman. There's a lot from an asgardschosen and from egilsbow9."

"Egil's *bow*?"

"Yeah, I had the same thought," Laura said as she glanced down at Pippin's still hairless flank.

"You were saying? About the house?"

"Yes, well that was pretty much it. Just a debate about installing a security system."

"They didn't hint at what the 'stuff' was" — Peter made air quotes as he said this — "that they hid so well?"

"No."

They were both quiet for a moment. Peter stroked Pippin's back while Laura typed something.

"I'm logging in to Eivor's Circle chat now. Let's see what's new." Peter leaned forward as text began to appear in the box.

"It doesn't look like anyone's online right now," Laura said, "but if the admin keeps the chat live, the log will still be up. Once they close the chat, they can choose to delete the log, which it looks like Eivor's always does, unlike Saga."

Laura scrolled quickly through the chat, which appeared to be from a half hour ago, until Peter said, "Stop there. Look at this."

valkyrie3939: mbthorsbondsman called me

asgardschosen: on the phone?
he knows who you are IRL?

valkyrie3939: looks that way, small town,
but thats not the point

asgardschosen: fuck

egilsbow9: then whats the point?

valkyrie3939: he suspects something,
doesnt buy what we told everyone about G

asgardschosen: will he talk?

valkyrie3939: doubt it, otherwise
he would have talked already, not called me first

asgardschosen: why call?

valkyrie3939: wanted to warn me directly
he said, not through the group chat

asgardschosen: warn?

valkyrie3939: getting to that —
warn that some of his friends are
on to the SSS, saw the tat and figured it out,
one was in stony with mbodinsraven

asgardschosen: fuck

egilsbow9: chill, i got this

valkyrie3939: thx

At that point valkyrie3939 and egilsbow9 had logged out. That chat had been about two hours prior, which put it immediately after Peter left The Flying Beaver.

Suddenly text appeared on the screen.

valkyrie3939: vigridsspear?

Laura's fingers flew to the keyboard, and she logged herself out. "Sorry, I panicked. Vigridsspear is me. I should have stayed on so the quick logout doesn't look so suspicious."

"No, it's OK. We probably don't need to log on again. Vigridsspear can just disappear now," Peter said quietly, still looking at the screen, and then turning to Laura he continued, "MBThorsbondsman must be Ken."

"Sounds like it." Laura spoke quietly too. Both of them turned back to the screen, which was now blank except for the simple text heading, "Eivor's Circle," and the log-in box. Pippin was awake and seemed to sense a change in the mood. He glanced back and forth between the two of them. Peter was tense, his hands clasped tightly together on his lap and his brow furrowed. Laura just stared at the screen.

"And he's in trouble. I don't like the sound of 'I got this,'" Peter said.

"No, I don't like it either. Call Kevin."

Peter pulled out his phone but didn't dial. He looked at Laura. "Should I tell him everything? Like that you got into Eivor's Circle?"

"Yes. He'll understand. It's better that I did it than you. In fact, let me call him."

Laura fished her phone out of her jacket pocket and dialed.

"Voicemail. I'm going to call the duty desk at the station."

"OK." Peter could feel his heart begin to thump and his palms becoming damp with sweat.

Laura dialed again. Someone picked up right away. Peter heard her explain that because of an online threat she had discovered, she had reason to believe that Ken Finnbogason was in immediate danger. There was a pause while she listened to something, and then she said thank you and hung up.

She put her phone down and turned to look at Peter, her face a mask of tension. "Kevin got dispatched to Ken's already. A neighbour called ten minutes ago to report a disturbance."

CHAPTER
Thirty-Seven

Peter didn't know what to do with himself. Laura told him it was best that they just stay home and wait for word. She reasoned that if something had happened to Ken, Peter had been one of the last people to see him, so Kevin would be in touch with questions very soon. Then Laura went back inside, telling Peter that she was putting the laptop away and picking up her knitting. The dead parrot sweater was almost done. That would take her mind off things. It always worked.

Peter stayed outside, but couldn't sit still, so he got up and walked a circuit around their property, Pippin padding along behind him. He checked all the fences, doors, and gates, and he checked on Gandalf. The goat had been getting far more regular attention in the last week than ever before, and he seemed to like it. *Maybe he's not so much of an introvert after all*, Peter thought. Peter retrieved some old rubbery carrots from the kitchen to feed Gandalf while he thought about what else he could do.

Then he had a flash of inspiration. He went back to the kitchen and rummaged in the freezer compartment until he found the Ziploc baggies with the bits of Misty and Patrick in them. Laura normally insisted that such things be kept in the deep freeze in the garage, but Peter felt like they should be kept safer in the house, and they were small bags that he was able to tuck unobtrusively behind the tub of mint chocolate chip ice cream Laura never touched.

Pippin watched his master carefully, his ears erect and his tail doing a slow wag. Then they went outside, and Peter presented him with the two skin fragments and commanded "Seek" at the bottom of the deck stairs. Pippin moved quickly toward the forested edge of the yard, his nose to the ground, and then proceeded to do a circuit around the entire perimeter, while Peter followed. He wasn't sure what to expect, or even how it made sense to search here, but maybe if the perpetrator had some of that scent on him, and had been here, then they could track him or her back through the woods . . .

It didn't make a lot of sense, but despite the tension inherent in the reasons for searching, the actual process was relaxing and calming. It funnelled man and dog into a focused activity where all peripheral thoughts and inputs fell away, a little like "the zone" that athletes describe, Peter supposed.

But there was nothing. Pippin did a second round, this time away from the boundary and focused more on the house, gardens, and garage, but there was no "woof" or sudden sitting at attention.

Peter was beginning to formulate an excuse to leave the property with Pippin when Laura appeared at the back door.

"Kevin called," she said. Before she even said the words, Peter could tell from looking at her face that the news wasn't good. "They found Ken. He's dead."

Peter's mind went blank. This news should spark a torrent of thoughts, but instead, nothing. Blank. Wordlessly, he walked up to Laura. They hugged each other for a long time.

After they had gone inside and sat down in the living room, each in their favourite chair, facing each other, but not really looking at each other, she said, "Kevin's on his way to interview you. Wants you to stay here. He says he needs to interview me too because of my online contact with the possible killers."

"How?" Peter asked when he finally found a way to make his brain work and his mouth move. His face was pale and expressionless.

"An arrow through the eye, Peter," Laura said, still not looking right at him. "An arrow in the eye."

"Like Harold," Peter said, his voice flat.

Laura gave her head a small shake, as if snapping out of a trance, and looked quizzically at Peter.

"Harold, last Anglo-Saxon king of England. Killed by the Normans at the Battle of Hastings in 1066 with an arrow in the eye."

"Oh. That Harold."

Some colour returned to Peter's face and his voice became more animated. "Did Kevin say how it happened, like where Ken was? At a window or outside? I don't even know where he lives . . ." Peter trailed off.

"No, he didn't give any more details. If he's still in the same place he was with Cheryl before they divorced, then he's on the west side of town, Darwin Road. Cheryl used to be in the Craft Guild with me. A potter."

"Cheryl? Who's Eva then? He mentioned her to me once."

"Girlfriend. Reason for the divorce. Anyway, their place on Darwin has a lot of bush behind it, similar to here."

"Egilsbow9 among the trees," Peter said, his voice quieter again. "Just like with Pippin."

"Probably," Laura said, also quietly.

"Do you know who Egil is? In Norse mythology or Icelandic history, I mean."

"There are a few. In history, there's Egil Skallagrímsson of the famous Egil's Saga. He was a kind of anti-hero, violent even by saga standards. And in the myths, an Egil looked after Thor's goats. And in the half myth–half historical Thidrek Saga there's an Egil who has to shoot an apple off his son's head with an arrow, like William Tell."

"The last one then, I guess."

"Maybe . . . pretty obscure though. Skallagrímsson is much better known, and he knew how to handle a bow too."

"Not that it matters where the chat handle comes from," Peter said.

"No, not that it matters."

They lapsed into silence, Laura eventually picking up her knitting again, and Peter staring out the window, scanning the treeline.

When Kevin arrived his face was tight and grim, and his interview with Peter was brusque, businesslike, and efficient. Peter had seen his otherwise voluble brother-in-law slip into this mode before, always after a serious crime. He had asked Laura to excuse them and suggested to Peter that they sit on the deck while he took notes. He didn't offer any additional information about the murder. He just asked for a detailed recounting of the events at The Flying Beaver earlier that afternoon, which now felt like days ago to Peter. He seemed to be aware of the significance of the tattoo but didn't remark on it. When Kevin was finished with his questions, he asked Peter to send Laura out. Peter started to get up to go and get her when something occurred to him. He sat down again.

"Kevin, there's something else I meant to tell you. I honestly did. This Ken thing has acted like a control-alt-delete on my brain."

"Oh, what's that?" Kevin's tone was still sober.

"I found something that might help." He pulled his phone out, brought up the image of the plans for Asgard Estates and handed the phone over.

"Where did you find this?" Kevin asked, after examining the photo and handing the phone back. "And when?"

Peter took a deep breath. "This morning, at an abandoned house near the west boundary of the old Thorkelson property. I fully intended to call you today, and then —"

Kevin held up his hand to stop Peter. He sighed, rubbed his forehead, and looked down at his lap. Then he looked back up at Peter and said, "Pete, I'm not going to ask you why you were there, not yet anyway. The time will come for that. But I am going to ask you how you found this."

Peter was relieved that Kevin hadn't started shouting. There wasn't the slightest trace of anger visible in his brother-in-law, just weariness. "The how will actually answer the why anyway. In addition to scent training Pippin on Misty, I scent trained him on Patrick."

"Patrick . . . the goat?"

"Yes. My plan was just to enter the Thorkelson property from the other side and see if Pippin could pick up any of Patrick's scent there. Like I said before, he was my patient and —"

Kevin held up his hand again. "Spare me the justification, Bannerman. So long as you planned to stay clear of the taped off areas, what you did wasn't technically illegal. Just technically stupid. But no surprise there. Continue."

Peter nodded. "Well anyway, Pippin insisted that the scent trace did not lead into the Thorkelson property, but to this old house, a shack really."

"Yeah, I know the one. Just north of Dukovskys'."

"Yes, that's it. We didn't find any of Patrick's parts, but we did find these plans, in a cubby under the floorboards. Patrick's scent was strongest in there."

Kevin grunted. "Show it to me again."

Peter passed the phone back.

"This might be the missing piece," Kevin said quietly.

"The motivation?"

"No comment. But thank you for this, I suppose. We'll talk later about your apparent death wish. But for now, Laura, please."

"Kevin, one favour?"

"Maybe."

"Can you not tell Laura how I found the plans? I told her Jim Junior sent them to me."

Kevin stared hard at Peter for a long moment and then nodded. "OK. But you owe me big."

Peter understood that he was to leave Laura and Kevin alone, so he went into the kitchen with the intent of brewing some tea.

As he was filling the kettle, he suddenly changed his mind and set it back on the counter. Instead, he reached into the cabinet above the refrigerator and pulled out a bottle of 18-year-old Highland Park scotch whisky and poured himself a generous finger and a half in a small cut crystal shot glass.

Kevin found Peter sitting at the kitchen table, his drink almost finished.

"Scotch in the afternoon? Is the world coming to an end?" Kevin was visibly more relaxed now. The conversation with Laura must have gone well.

"Maybe. You tell me."

"Good point. We've now officially had more murders in this district in this one calendar year than in any other, even counting that murder-suicide nightmare on the Arneson farm a few years back."

"And we're only four months into the year."

"Yeah. I'd ask for a snort, but (a) I'm on duty, and (b) I don't like scotch." Kevin's tone was warmer now.

Peter just nodded in response.

"Look, Pete. I don't mind telling you that I don't fully know what we're dealing with yet, so I'm going to ask you and Laura to stay home for now."

"Shades of February and the pigs," Peter said, looking at the table.

"Yeah, weird, eh? Anyway, there's probably nothing for you guys to be worried about, but just do me a favour and keep your heads down."

"And away from open windows."

"Ha. Not funny, I guess. And one more thing — I might need Pippin tomorrow. Would that be OK? Has he recovered?"

"Yes, he's doing really well. Of course, you can use him. Anything you need. To sniff around Ken's place?"

"No, D Division's homicide unit is looking after that investigation. I might want to follow a hunch about the Sturluson case. Technically, they're in charge of that too, but they're not on site anymore. Everything's back at the lab."

Normally Peter would probe for more information about Kevin's hunch, but he felt like a deflated balloon, completely drained of energy and ambition. And he didn't want to push his luck.

CHAPTER
Thirty-Eight

K evin phoned later that evening. "OK, I do need Pippin. The division's canine unit are all out on a man-hunt in the Roblin area. I thought they might be done by now, but the sucker is proving to be good at evading capture. I could wait, but I don't want to. I'd even take General Brock if I had to, although I don't like Earl. Homophobic sack of shit."

Peter swallowed hard. "Kev, I forgot to tell you, but Earl's got a triple S tattoo too."

"Jesus, really?" Peter heard the sound of scribbling in a notebook. "Thanks, I'll get someone to interview him. Another reason not to like the S.O.B. Although the Saga guys are bush league compared to the Eivor crew."

"I think they both have the same tattoo, actually."

"Yeah? Well, anyway, can you meet me and Kristine with Pippin at the Favels' tomorrow morning at eight? I've got to bring you along as the handler."

"Easter Sunday? Um, sure, I guess. You going to tell me what your hunch is?"

"No. Need-to-know basis for now. You'll see soon enough."

Peter woke to find that a dense fog had slid in from the lake overnight. At first, he didn't notice it because he was awake before dawn and it was black outside regardless, but then he saw that the streetlamp at the end of their block was faint and smudged, with a dim grey halo around it. He loved fog. He loved it even more in the winter because once the sun rose and burned it off, the moisture from the fog would crystalize into hoarfrost, sugar frosting the world like a child's winter fantasy. Now in the spring it would just soften and blur everything, transforming hard reality into something more dreamlike and open to interpretation. Although these thoughts offended Peter's root rationality, they still had a hold on him. He supposed it was the same countervailing feeling that led him to enjoy fantasy literature. The logical and the illogical minds can live together in the same brain, so long as the illogical mind deferred to the logical for important decisions. Illogic is permitted to exist purely for entertainment purposes. Like cinema of the mind.

Pippin looked good. It was really as if he had never been shot or lost any of his liver. They would take things slower than normal as a precaution, but otherwise Peter felt comfortable taking him back to the Favels'.

Pippin ate his breakfast with gusto and was visibly excited to see that Peter was preparing to take him out. He became even more excited when Peter got the small satchel of supplies he used for scent training. Pippin wagged his entire hind end as he waited in the front hall, as it was clear that they weren't going to just be circling the yard again.

Laura came into the front hall, wearing her robe and slippers. Unlike Peter, who usually bounded awake, Laura was a slow waker. She yawned and stretched and rubbed her eyes.

"Going somewhere? It's Easter . . ." She had gone to bed early, so she hadn't heard about Kevin's call.

"Yeah, Kevin called again last night. He asked if Pippin was well enough yet to be used for some scent work. We're going back to the Favels' farm."

"Oh? He wants to involve you in the case now?"

"I was surprised too, especially after he warned us to stay home, but their own sniffer dogs are busy in Western Manitoba. I'm just coming along as the handler. I'm sure he'll limit my involvement as much as possible."

Laura yawned again and smiled warmly. "Well, anyway, I'm glad Kevin's with you, otherwise I wouldn't let you go."

"I wouldn't want to."

"Oh really?" Laura smiled again, but this time the smile was a little less warm.

"Seeing what I saw at the Favels' last time, no. And hearing what I heard about Ken, no. I still want to know about the mutilations of my patients, but I don't really want to know any more about the mutilation of people. I think I'm still trying to process both murders. The first especially because I saw the result, and the second because I knew the victim. It still feels abstract in the way of a horror film. And you know I don't like horror films."

"OK. If you're seeing Kevin anyway, I've got something you can pass on to him. I couldn't get to sleep last night. My mind was spinning." Laura talked as she walked over to where the laptop was in the living room, Peter and Pippin trailing behind her.

"I thought you weren't going back into those chat rooms?"

"I didn't. It's something else. When we were talking about the tattoos, it triggered a vague memory. I had seen something like that somewhere before. Then, suddenly at like two in the morning, I remembered."

She turned the laptop so that Peter could see the screen. It was a video clip of the press conference Grimur Sturluson had given at the university. Laura moved the scroll bar to near the end. "You stopped watching after Grim was finished talking, but at the end the camera pans to the grad students while the reporter is making his closing remarks. As they're turning away to leave the podium, you can see one of them has a tattoo on her leg. See?"

"Yeah, I guess. That's Jessica from Minnesota. The tattoo's not very clear."

"I had the reading glasses on that I use for knitting when we watched it, and it caught my eye because I was looking at her graphic Converse sneakers. Some kind of comic book design. I wondered whether the tattoo was related, but then forgot about it because it wasn't important or relevant."

"So, you think this is a triple Norse dragon? Looks like a black smudge to me. Maybe a triple black smudge, but a smudge."

Laura grinned at him. "You underestimate me, dear husband." She opened a photo editing program and brought up a still that had obviously been taken from the video clip. She clicked a few buttons and a zoomed-in photo of Jessica's lower legs appeared. It was brighter than the original and had much sharper contrast. They were blocky and pixelated, but there were clearly three spooning Norse dragons on her lower left calf.

"Wow. I do underestimate you."

Laura smiled and kissed Peter on the cheek. "Yes you do. Now just be careful and stick close to Kevin. And look after our poor boy." She ruffled the fur on Pippin's head.

The fog had become even denser as Peter drove up to the farm. Being Easter Sunday there was hardly any traffic. The truck was an island in a world of grey, the headlights causing the grey to glow ahead, whereas all around it was dim. He knew where the sun should be, but it was not visible, not even as a brighter patch of grey. Mailboxes flashed by, appearing suddenly out of the murk, and then disappearing again just as quickly, but otherwise there was nothing other than the road itself to indicate that he was not driving through the middle of a cloud in the sky. When he was a child, passing through clouds was his favourite part of flying, but driving on a country road it was nerve-wracking. He was grateful that the roads were straight and wide, so the chance of accidentally ending up in the ditch was low. He did have to keep his speed down though as the few vehicles that did come the other way emerged suddenly from the fog as if conjured into being directly in front of him. He worried about missing the turn-off to the Favels' place as the signs weren't visible, but he had been there often enough recently that he had a good sense when it was likely to be. To be safe he counted in advance on the map the number of driveways and intersecting roads he would have to pass first. After leaving town, one right and then two lefts.

At the third left he turned slowly and drove up the gravel driveway until his muted headlights played on the side of an RCMP Chevy Tahoe. The yard lights from the Favels' house were faintly visible off to the right, and Peter could just barely make out the fences bounding the ostrich and pony pens to the left. The white wood was particularly difficult to see in the light grey fog.

When Peter got out of his truck, he saw Kevin at the hood of their SUV, waiting for him. Kristine was farther away, leaning on the fence, intent on something in her hands — likely her phone, Peter thought.

Kevin took a couple steps toward Peter, smiling. "Hey, Pete — glad you and wonder-pooch could make it. My partner there" — Kevin gave his head a quick jerk toward Kristine — "thinks it's a waste of time, but I've done my Easter egg hunt already and holidays are pretty boring otherwise. Christmas brings some crimes, but people don't drink enough on Easter. I mean, how plastered can you get on those little liqueur eggs? Way less family tension at Easter too. Anyway, boring. Good time to be out here."

Peter chuckled to be polite, but Kevin's idea of what was funny sometimes didn't mesh well with his own. "Sure, no problem. We've saved our egg hunt for later. Then it's brunch, and after that, time for Easter games!"

"Easter games? Never mind. Forget I asked. And we're still on for dinner?"

"Of course. Looking forward to finally meeting Stuart."

"OK, let's get started before the ice queen over there freezes to the fencepost and blames me."

Polite chuckles.

Peter turned his attention to Pippin. "OK, boy, Uncle Kevin's going to give me something for you to sniff."

"Uncle Kevin? I didn't think I was that hairy and ugly, but whatever. Here it is, Pete." Kevin turned around and pulled a large clear plastic bag out of a black duffel that was on the ground beside the police vehicle. It had a large number written on it in black ink. The bag appeared to contain a blood soaked white dress shirt. Even though the blood had dried, the rusty red was vivid against the comprehensively monochrome world.

CHAPTER
Thirty-Nine

Peter glanced at Kevin and raised his eyebrows.

"Yeah, it's Sturluson's."

Peter nodded and waited for Kevin to say something more, but he didn't, so Peter took the bag from his brother-in-law, gingerly opened it wide so that Pippin would be able to smell the contents without Peter having to touch the shirt. He bent down and offered the open bag to his dog. Pippin pushed his nose into the bag and flared his nostrils for a few seconds. Then he took a step back and looked up at Peter.

"He's done already?" Kevin asked.

"Looks like it. The scent is probably extremely strong in there, so he doesn't need a very long exposure."

"OK, we're ready to roll," Kevin shouted to Kristine. She nodded but didn't look up from what she was doing.

Kevin grinned broadly at Peter. "But she's an excellent cop. Probably better than me."

"I know she's better than you," Peter said and grinned back. Then he turned his attention to Pippin, who was sitting beside him, looking up with what could best be described as naked expectation.

"Seek!"

Without looking at Kevin or Peter, Kristine turned and opened the gate beside her. She walked ahead into the mist, and the others followed.

"Shouldn't we let Pippin go first?" Peter asked as he and Kevin walked quickly to try to keep Kristine in sight. Visibility was no more than 20 metres.

"Nah, it's OK. We discussed the game plan. She knows where we're headed, but if our boy finds something earlier, like in the marsh, I'll holler and call her back."

The fence soon faded into grey oblivion behind them. The fog had varying density with sheets and tendrils of it moving slowly, creating occasional gaps through which he could see farther. There was no perceptible breeze, so Peter reasoned that it was an effect of subtly varying temperature and moisture gradients.

Then suddenly something appeared to their left. It was a large dark sphere hovering just a little above waist height. Peter wasn't sure what he was seeing at first until the fog loosened slightly to reveal legs and a long neck attached to the sphere. It was an ostrich.

"Look, Kev, I think it's Mr. Hooper," Peter whispered.

His brother-in-law glanced nervously at the enormous bird. "Should we be worried?"

Peter weighed mentioning Mr. Hooper's strength and bad temper but decided that there was no advantage in further alarming Kevin. It was good that he was a little nervous. "No, just keep walking straight ahead, don't make eye contact, and don't do anything sudden or loud."

"General bad-ass-animal safety advice."

"Yup."

The ostrich stared at them and then faded back into the grey as they moved forward, the fog thickening behind them.

After a few minutes they were at the far fence line, by the marshy area where Big Bird had found the Mjölnir. Pippin kept his nose to the ground the entire time and showed no interest in anything else.

"He's lucky to still have smell to go on," Kevin said as he clambered over the fence. "I can see sweet bugger-all, and this fog seems to muffle sound too. It's kind of cool, but mostly annoying."

Peter nodded in agreement as he encouraged Pippin to crawl under the fence.

They had lost sight of Kristine. She had evidently gotten over the fence much faster.

"She'll probably wait for us when she gets to the path. Either that or we'll meet her at the clearing where the nithing pole was." Kevin was out of breath, so he paused. Peter was interested to see that his red beard was covered in small beads of sparkling dew. He waited for Kevin to say something else.

"But before we get there, I have a question for you, Pete. The ground is soaked with Sturluson's blood, so I presume Pippin will home in on that. What if the scent is elsewhere too — can you get him to scent hunt again?"

"For sure. That's a common part of the scent trials. Multiple valid targets." Peter waited again. He was tempted to keep talking about scent training but sensed that Kevin was finally ready to reveal his hunch. He was right.

"Good. Homicide thinks everything happened right there, but we don't have a confirmed cause of death, let alone the murder weapon."

"Loss of head isn't a cause of death?"

"Ha, yeah it is, but the Norse killed their victims before beheading them, usually by strangulation. No doubt these wackos used a sword or axe to take his head off, and homicide is focused on finding that, but I think it was part of a ritual. Homicide doubts it. If I'm right though, I'm betting they used a garotte to kill him first. That's something more likely to just be tossed away in the woods, unlike a sword. If we can find the garotte, then we might be able to find prints or other clues and, well, it's worth a shot anyway."

They were moving gingerly through the marsh now. They were wearing rubber boots, as Kevin insisted on coming this way because the Mjölnir had been found here, but it was still slow going.

"But Kristine doesn't buy this theory?" Peter asked as he narrowly avoided tripping over a submerged log.

"No, my esteemed partner is with homicide on this. Thinks it was a straightforward killing with the head-on-a-stick to throw the scent off, so to speak." Kevin was quiet for a moment before he went on. "Did you know that Sturluson was killed on Sigrblot?"

"Sigrblot?"

"The Norse only recognized two seasons, winter and summer. Sigrblot in late April marks the start of summer."

"Marked with sacrifices?"

"Sometimes. And those would be in a sacred spot, like under a special tree or by a special rock. There's nothing like that in the clearing, so I was going to look for that nearby somewhere, but what the hell do I know about special trees and rocks. Then I remembered Pippin . . ."

"OK, makes sense," Peter said as he felt another data point slide into the mix, but there were several gaps still. "Any idea why Grim though?"

"My best guess is that he figured out that the Mjölnir was a fake, and that maybe the whole archeological find was fake. Maybe confronted the fakers."

"You don't think he did the faking?"

"Nah. I've seen the type before — flaky but sincere in his flakiness. Turns out old Sturluson was more of a rock star than an actual respected archeologist among his fellow eggheads. Talked to a guy in the field in England who said Sturluson was a fool and wouldn't know a movie prop from a museum piece, even if it was stamped 'Made in China.'"

"Huh, that's interesting." Another data point. A big one. Which reminded him about Jessica. He needed to tell Kevin about her. Suddenly an archeology graduate student who was part of the Saga Study Society or Eivor's Circle was much more important.

There was a loud "Shit!" from somewhere in the murk ahead of them. It was Kristine.

"You OK?" Kevin shouted.

There was an inaudible response.

"You and Pip are much faster. You better go ahead and find out what's up."

Peter nodded. He'd tell him about Jessica at the next opportunity.

Kristine wasn't very far ahead. She had reached the dry path and was sitting on it with one of her boots off.

"Got a booter?" Peter asked.

"Yeah," she said as she poured water from her boot and then wrung out her sock.

"It happens," he said, inanely. At that moment the first bit of sun he had seen all day appeared in a thinning of the fog in the east. It lit the path in an ethereal glow while mist still lay thickly on the marsh on both sides.

Peter was about to comment on this when saw it. Just above Kristine's left ankle there was a tattoo of three "S"-shaped Norse dragons.

CHAPTER
Forty

Their eyes met and locked. Peter's stomach tightened. It was obvious that she had seen that he noticed the tattoo and that the look in his eyes betrayed that he understood its significance. She knew that he knew. That so much could be conveyed by eyes alone astonished Peter, but he had no doubt.

He was about to say something, anything, to break the tension when Kevin appeared, looming bedraggled and bedewed out of the mist like some fearsome swamp thing from the sagas.

"Thanks for waiting, guys. You know it would break my heart if you raced ahead and solved the case without me, but I see you're enjoying some quality time together instead," he said, panting. He stepped up onto the path, gave Pippin a pat on the head, and grinned at Peter and Kristine. Kristine had put her sock back on and was in the process of pulling up her boot.

"Step in a wet spot, partner?"

"Yes." She spat the word out without looking up, stood up quickly and, without saying anything further, began walking up the path.

Peter's mind whirred like the wheels of a car stuck in the snow. There was a lot of noise and smoke, but no forward motion whatsoever. *Kristine. Jessica. Three dragons. Grim. Nithing pole. Arrows. Garrotte. Ken. Earl. Brad. Blood. Blot. Mjölnir. Eivor. Bjartur. Kristine.*

These words and names and more flashed across his mind in a rapid-fire mishmash.

Kristine. Oh my god, Kristine. He had to tell Kevin now, but he had no idea how he was going to do it.

Kevin and Peter were walking side by side on the path with Pippin a few steps ahead, nose still to the ground, and Kristine a few steps farther, about enter the woods at the western edge of the marsh. Only the first rank of trees was visible, the rest lost in the grey.

"Kevin," Peter said in a low whisper to get his brother-in-law's attention.

Just then Kristine whirled around, held up her hand for them to stop, and then motioned for them to crouch. "I hear something," she mouthed.

Peter strained to listen but couldn't hear anything other than the pounding of blood in his ears.

He and Kevin dropped to a crouch. Pippin lay down quickly and quietly, looking at Peter quizzically as he did so.

Kristine unholstered her pistol.

Peter's mind was in turmoil. This was it. She was going to shoot both of them. Probably Pippin too. He should scream or jump at her or both or . . .

Kristine crouch-ran toward them.

Kevin unholstered his pistol as well.

"There's someone in there, just past the first trees," she whispered, her expression fierce. Her eyes were an unearthly blue. Peter hadn't noticed their intensity before, even when their gazes had locked a few minutes before. She was lying. She had to be. It was a trick. But he couldn't make himself say or do anything.

Kevin nodded, peering intently at the treeline. "OK, Pete, you and Pip stay back. I'll go ahead down the path. You cover me," he nodded to Kristine.

Peter watched helplessly, feeling paralyzed, as Kevin stayed low and moved cautiously toward the trees.

Kristine kept watch, scanning the forest, her pistol drawn and pointed ahead.

When, after no more than 30 seconds, Kevin arrived at the edge of the woods, he motioned for Kristine to follow but held his hand up for Peter to stay. Kristine trotted quickly to catch up and then they moved into the trees and out of sight, Kristine just a couple steps behind Kevin.

It took every scrap of self-control for Peter to stay where he was, as he had been told to, but then he couldn't anymore. He had to help Kevin somehow. It was surely a trap. Just as he stood up, intending to shout and warn Kevin and make Kristine turn around, he heard two sounds in rapid succession from ahead. There was a faint sharp thwack, and then a louder dull thud mixed with the sound of small branches snapping, like a sack of cement had been dropped on a dry bush.

Kristine came sprinting out of the woods. "Run! Kevin's down!"

Peter's mind, which had been a maelstrom of disconnected thoughts, suddenly snapped into focus. *There had been no gunshots. If Kevin had been physically ambushed and knocked down by some mysterious third party, why was Kristine running away from that? Shouldn't she be engaging? Shouting, "Drop the weapon, police!" or something like that?*

No. Kristine had pistol-whipped Kevin on the back of the head to incapacitate him as a witness and now was coming back to deal with Peter. He was right. It was a trap. And he had acted too late.

He ran.

It was what she had told him to do, but it was also the only option. She had a gun, and he did not. She was a highly trained police officer, and he was not. He doubted that she would shoot as the Favels would probably hear that, plus finding a bullet from her gun in him would be complicated for her to explain.

Peter ran off the path, Pippin right beside him. He would make straight for the fence in the hopes that the marsh would slow

Kristine down. He could hear her sprinting and panting behind him, but he didn't want to waste the fraction of a second to look back. Also, he had to watch where he was going and aim his steps for the grassy tussocks.

He heard a splash as she entered the marsh behind him.

Just go. Keep going straight. Watch your step. You can't die out here like this. Laura would be devastated. Laura. He felt emotion rising in his chest. *You must survive. Go, go, go.*

Pippin was slightly ahead and to Peter's right, seeming to move effortlessly through water that came up almost to his belly.

The fog, which had seemed to be lifting, closed in again all around them, placing Peter and Pippin at the centre of a small dome of half-light, dull, grass-flecked water below, fuzzy grey to all sides and above.

Where was Kristine? He and Pippin were splashing loudly enough that he couldn't hear her splashing anymore.

Then he missed one of the tussocks and plunged his left leg into a deep hole and stumbled.

Before Peter fully realized what had happened, Kristine was on him. He had fallen on his side in a few inches of water. She grabbed his shoulder and yanked him onto his back. Her face was all fury and resolve.

"No!" Peter shouted, holding his hands up in front of his face.

She brushed his hands aside with her remarkably strong left arm, and dropped her knees onto his chest, knocking the air out of him.

This will be the last thing I ever see, Peter thought, as he watched her right hand come up, holding the pistol by the barrel and the handle, black like the night sky, poised high above his forehead.

And then in a flash she was off him. He saw fur and legs and then heard Kristine scream. Pippin had leapt at her arm and knocked the pistol down. Peter didn't know whether he had bitten her or not.

The world was a jumble of arms and legs, human and canine, and water, and grass, and fog, and shouting.

Then Peter was up, and he and Pippin were running as fast as they could toward the fence. Or at least where he hoped the fence was.

Shit.

There was no indication of direction, and after falling he had lost his orientation. What were the odds that he had chosen correctly?

But he hadn't chosen, he realized. Pippin had, and Pippin was probably right.

This time he did glance over his shoulder, and there she was, surging out of the fog, blond hair wet and stringy across her face, jacket sleeve torn, pistol out, panting, gaining on them.

And then they were at the fence. He thought he felt Kristine grasp at his jacket as he went over.

There was no way they'd make it across the paddock. No way. She was faster on hard ground.

But there was no other option. Just run.

He could start shouting to try to get the Favels' attention, but the fog was much thicker again, so it was better to be quiet and try to evade Kristine.

Peter turned sharply left, gave a burst of speed with what felt like his last reserves, and then stopped, stifling his urge to breathe hard. Pippin was silent as well. The fog swirled around them like cold damp ghosts brushing their faces. He heard Kristine's running footsteps for a few seconds, and then those stopped.

It was if the world had been drained of all sound. The silence was profound. Peter held his breath and waited.

Then there were some odd sounds. Something else was moving out there. It was almost a scuffing sound. Some rustling too. Then footsteps coming closer.

Peter stiffened. Should he run the other way?

And then there was an eerie hollow rumbling sound, so deep that Peter could feel it in his stomach. It was familiar yet he couldn't identify what the sound was.

The fog began to lift, parting like shredded gauze curtains.

Peter could see that Mr. Hooper was no more than a metre from Kristine. The ostrich had been "booming." It was his alarm call.

"Get!" she shouted, waving her pistol at him.

The ostrich's right leg shot forward and claws the size of small pickaxes raked the woman's stomach.

She screamed in a way Peter had never heard anyone scream before and dropped to the ground, bright red blood blooming across the dull brown earth.

Mr. Hooper turned and trotted off into the fog.

CHAPTER
Forty-One

Easter dinner was a week late. Kevin spent three days in the hospital in Winnipeg, two of them against his will. Kristine did not make it to the hospital. Mr. Hooper had disembowelled her so forcefully that one of the paramedics confessed to very nearly becoming physically ill when he arrived at the scene.

At first there was a serious worry that Kevin was bleeding into the brain, but the scans all came clear. Nonetheless, they wanted to keep him for observation, something Kevin pronounced to be "bullshit" because he was usually just alone and bored in his hospital room, with nobody actively observing him.

By the time he and Stuart came for dinner, the only aftereffects of being pistol-whipped were a persistent headache and profound sense of betrayal.

"Kristine," he said as he sat down in the living room, shaking his head slowly. "I still can't believe it."

"I can, but honestly only in retrospect," Peter said as he stood waiting for his guests to get settled. "Drinks, guys? Scotch? Beer? Wine? Tea? Water?"

"Scotch sounds nice," Stuart said, smiling at Peter. "Lovely home you have, by the way."

"Don't do it, Stu," Kevin said. "Pete's scotch is that nasty stuff that tastes like Satan's anus."

Peter laughed and Stuart raised his eyebrows and grinned. "You would know, wouldn't you, Kev? Didn't you used to date Satan? But that sounds marvellous regardless, so I'll have one of those, Peter, thank you."

Kevin grinned. "A beer for me, please, and none of that weird Belgian stuff either. Just a plain Canadian lager if you would."

"One dram of the nectar of the gods and one tall glass of yellow swill coming right up!"

After everyone had their drinks, Laura joined them from the kitchen. She and Peter were mostly vegetarian, but they didn't want any awkwardness for their first meal with Stuart, so Laura had prepared lamb. Normally Peter did most of the holiday cooking, but he couldn't bring himself to handle the lamb meat. He could eat it, just not touch it when it still looked like it came from the animal. He allowed himself this small hypocrisy, reasoning that in its raw state it reminded him too much of Patrick.

They sat quietly by the fire for a few minutes, with Pippin and Merry snoozing on either side of the hearth, until Peter said, "Yeah, Kristine. I mean, I never liked her, but to think that she was some kind of Odinist animal mutilator . . ."

"The top Odinist in the district: valkyrie3939." Kevin said quietly, looking at his glass. "But not an animal mutilator. That was Jessica Thorsteinsdottir. The grad student from Minnesota: egilsbow9."

"She shot Pippin?" Peter had a sudden flashback to the accent he couldn't place when he and Pippin were hiding in the wardrobe in that old shack. Minnesota.

Kevin nodded, still looking at his glass. Stuart was watching the fire. Peter smiled to himself when he considered that Stuart was precisely Kevin's type — tall, slim, and, inasmuch as Peter could judge such things, good-looking. In particular he noted Stuart's long, slender fingers and well-manicured nails, quite the opposite of Kevin's battered-nail sausages. Stuart was also very polite and cultured and had a charming Nigerian accent. Again, the opposite of Kevin, with his hoser bluster and diction. Peter didn't really understand the idea of opposites attracting, but he supposed it applied in his own life as well. As if on cue, Laura put her arm around Peter's shoulder.

"And Jessica cut up Patrick and Misty and drained their blood, and Stinky's too?"

Kevin nodded again.

Peter took a deep breath before going on. "For genuine religious reasons? I mean, did she really believe this crap?"

"It looks that way. Kristine maybe not have, but Jessica, yes. But I clearly had my head up my ass when it came to Kristine, so who knows."

"Nobody knew or even guessed, Kev. She did such a good job of hiding how much she was tampering with evidence to throw the scent off. Everyone always said that she was a good cop, and she was — but in the technical sense, not the moral sense it turns out. Smart but evil."

Kevin grunted his agreement while examining the lacing of foam inside his beer glass.

"And Grimur? Was he an Odinist?" Peter asked, his glass of whisky still untouched in his right hand.

"No. I don't think so at least. He was just so caught up in this archeological hoax the Eivor's Circle people put together."

"It really was a hoax?"

"Hundred percent," Kevin said, taking a swallow of his beer. "And a pretty good one. The Thor's hammer is excellent quality, but fake.

They tripped up with the Bjartur Saga though. Bjartur is a more modern name, and the whole story was full of holes."

"But it was sort of an unnecessary bonus feature anyway. What about the other stuff they found out there?" Peter asked, shifting forward on the couch.

"A few trinkets, some old nails, and a knife. All decent quality and professionally aged to look old. Good enough to fool Grim, but the truth would have come out eventually. Didn't matter though as it was more just a marketing tool for the real estate development. I don't think they really expected to have an impact on the Yellowgrass land claim."

"But the threats against the Favels might have worked."

"Maybe. The whole thing is messed up. I don't think we can expect people like this to have totally logical plans. Most of this was just pure hate and sick pride in some Nordic fantasy la-la land."

The room fell quiet again, other than the crackle of the fire.

Stuart smiled at Laura and Peter. "What's that I smell? Lamb?"

"Good nose, yes, it is!" Laura replied. "I hope you like lamb."

"I love it!"

"We can eat in about 20 minutes."

"Great!"

"More drinks in the meantime?"

"Yes, more drinks?" Peter chimed in. "What do you think of the Ardbeg?"

"It's wonderful, and yes, please," Stuart said.

Kevin groaned. "I would love to, but my head would not."

After Peter had poured another precisely calibrated ounce of scotch into Stuart's glass, he turned to Kevin and asked, "Two more questions?"

"Sure, go ahead. The T3s are kicking in. Mixed with that beer, it's putting me in a generous mood."

Stuart patted Kevin on the knee while Peter and Laura chuckled.

"So first, what was up with Ken? How deep was he mixed in?"

"The core group, these Eivor people, was Kristine, Jessica, that Norwegian grad student Jon, Brad Thorkelson, and two others I can't name yet as the investigation is ongoing." He said the last few words in a mock serious newsreader's voice. "But no one you're likely to know anyway. And then Ken, Earl, Grim, and a bunch of others were in the outer circle of Odin fanboys and fangirls, most only semi-serious and none, so far as we know yet, involved in anything criminal."

"Supplementary question?"

"So, three questions, not two." Kevin smiled.

"I suppose, but only because you reminded me to ask." Peter smiled back. "What's Brad Thorkelson's story?"

"We don't know everything yet, but he's old Jim's other son by his second wife —"

"That I knew," Peter interjected.

"Do you want to hear the rest, Sherlock?" Kevin asked with a gentle mocking tone.

Peter grinned and nodded.

"It seems that he and Jim Senior didn't get along. The old guy couldn't stand Brad's right-wing wacko politics, and Brad was probably already talking about future real estate development for the land while Jim was still alive. It also looks like he and Kristine were in a relationship."

"Huh," Peter said, "Kristine in a relationship? Weird. But talking about Brad reminds me, supplementary question to the supplementary question?"

Kevin rolled his eyes. "Sure, shoot."

"This numbered company and Asgard Estates, that's all Brad's doing?"

"Brad and Kristine, as far as we know. They wanted the land for this development but knew that having Brad's name involved would kill the deal, and Kristine's could raise questions because cops don't get paid well enough to buy that kind of land. A numbered company was the best way to do this, although if they had been smarter, they would have lied about the development plans. Brad should have known his half-brother better."

"Mostly about money and greed at the end of the day then. Real estate profits."

"No, you still don't get how some people tick, Pete. To me this looks like greed, and toxic family relations, and racism, and delusion, and malice, and hubris, and evil, and selfishness, and a whole lot of other messed up shit all rolled together."

Peter nodded and took a small sip from his whisky. "You're right. I don't get how some people tick."

Kevin grunted and nodded. "Your last question? I'm getting hungry."

Laura jumped up. "Thanks for reminding me, I better check on the lamb!" Pippin got up and followed her into the kitchen.

"The charred skeleton at Grim's lab — any idea who that is?"

"This is totally off the record, buddy, and between you and me because, as much as I hate to admit it, you were useful in this case, and maybe even helped save my life, although most of the credit goes to the ostrich."

Stuart stood up. "I'll see if Laura needs a hand."

"You can stay," Kevin said gently.

"No, it's fine." Stuart smiled, and walked toward the kitchen, comically waving goodbye.

"Forensics is pretty sure it's the missing Alexander kid from Yellowgrass. Probably killed at the last Haustblot, which is the autumn equinox sacrificial blot. We think Grim found the bones and was persuaded that they were ancient from an Indigenous warrior killed by the Norse because of the weapon marks on the bones and the way they had been aged. Ironic that the prof was then himself killed at the next spring blot."

Peter sucked his breath in and shook his head. "Unbelievable."

"Dinner's ready!" Laura called from the dining room.

Later, after the guests had left and Peter was done loading the dishwasher and tidying the kitchen, Laura came up and hugged him. Peter hugged her back, and they remained embraced for a long time.

"You know that I'm not superstitious," Peter said quietly, while they were still hugging.

"Mm-hmm."

"But if I were, I'd have to think the Pointsmen were cursed or jinxed."

Laura chuckled. "It's not funny, but you're right. It is weird how members keep dying in bizarre ways."

"It's going to be tough to replace Ken. Know anyone who can throw like that?"

Laura let go of Peter, stepped back, and reached for a napkin on the counter. She crumpled it into a ball and threw it across the length of the kitchen, past the tip of Peter's nose, landing it dead in the centre of Pippin's food bowl. Then she turned to face Peter, smiled, and shrugged. "No idea."

Here's a sneak preview of the next
Dr. Bannerman Vet Mystery:
Eleven Huskies

PROLOGUE

Atlas and his siblings and friends loved their food. Their master mixed it up fresh every morning. He brought it into the kennel room in a big pail and poured it into a half-dozen stainless steel bowls. They emptied the bowls before he even left the room. That's how much they loved their food. There were 11 of them, so they had to share, but they were used to that. Sometimes old Winter still snapped at the twins when they nosed into his bowl, but otherwise it all worked out fine. The best days were in the weeks before a race when they got extra. What dog doesn't want more food, especially when it's so good? It was always the same, but that didn't matter. It was food, and it was good. Then one morning it wasn't the same. It had a different smell and a different taste. It was still good, but it had changed, just for that one meal. The next day Atlas felt tired, so very tired, and for the first time in his life he wasn't hungry for breakfast. Then later he began to vomit. He couldn't stop. His master was very anxious. The world gradually became grey and hazy. The last thing Atlas remembered before he fell asleep was his master stroking his head and saying something he couldn't understand, but it was soothing.

CHAPTER
One

Dr. Peter Bannerman loved to fly. Ever since he was a little boy flying with his parents and his brother Sam to see relatives in Nova Scotia, he was transfixed by the beauty of the earth from above and by the magical nature of being suspended in the air. No matter how well he understood the physics, and he understood it very well, he couldn't shake that irrational sense of magic.

There were only two other passengers on the float plane as it headed northeast from Thompson toward Dragonfly Lake. They were a young man and woman, but they didn't look like a couple as both were wearing navy-blue jackets emblazoned with Government of Canada crests and the letters TSB. It was much too loud to talk, and Peter didn't enjoy small talk with strangers anyway, so he was pleased to leave the pleasantries at a smile and a nod, and then turn to look out the window. He couldn't stop himself from trying to puzzle out TSB though. It sounded very familiar, but he could only generate improbable guesses, like Terror Security Board or Technical Services Branch or, the one that amused him and refused to leave his head, Toxic Spice Bureau.

Northern Manitoba slid by under his window, an endless carpet of dark green flecked with blue. As he looked north, he marvelled that this went on for thousands of kilometres past the horizon, slowly turning into taiga, then tundra, and then the Arctic Ocean. Extending the line across the North Pole, the same would happen in reverse as it crossed into Siberia. Eventually somewhere there, on the other side of the globe, it would intersect with a road or a settlement, but before then, only wilderness, no sign of humans. *How glorious*, he thought.

The flight was short, and before Peter could turn his attention to figuring out which lake they were flying over, the pilot began to bank for a landing. It was Dragonfly Lake. Most northern lakes look similar when seen from the air, but Dragonfly Lake had a distinctive X shape. He smiled as the plane raced down toward the surface of the water, the trees blurring. This was one of his favourite places on earth, and it was where Pippin, his prize-winning sniffer dog and best friend, was originally from. He had thought about bringing Pippin, but it was too much fuss for what should be a quick visit. He would be back in a couple weeks anyway, and Pippin would come then. The plane seemed to clear the treetops by inches only but then hit the surface of the lake with surprising smoothness, smoother than landing on a runway.

He was met at the dock by his old friend John Reynolds, owner of the Dragonfly Lodge and Pure North Outfitters. John was a short middle-aged man with a ponytail and a bushy moustache, famous for his booming laugh and his iron handshake, his size belying his strength.

His grip was light today though, and his face was marked with worry.

"I can't thank you enough for coming, Peter, and on such short notice."

"You're welcome. It works out well because I had taken these days off to work on the garden, but it's raining constantly in the south. First drought, then flood. Nutty times."

"Beautiful summer up here, so long as the fires don't start. Do you want to stop by the lodge first?"

"No, let's go straight to the kennels. How's Atlas?"

"Still totally out of it. And Pretty and Gus are looking rough too."

As they walked up the dock, they passed the two passengers with the TSB jackets, who were still waiting for their bags to be unloaded.

Peter whispered to John, "TSB? Know what that's about?"

"You didn't hear? A plane went down yesterday. They're the Transport Safety Board folks."

Ah, that makes a lot more sense than Toxic Spice Bureau, Peter thought. "I didn't pay attention to the news yesterday," he said. "Any casualties?"

"All three onboard presumed dead. Plunged into the lake. Just horrible. RCMP dive team got here earlier this morning." John gestured out to the lake, where three boats were positioned in a rough circle.

"That's terrible," Peter said, while recalling his own experience landing on the lake. He hadn't been scared, and he wouldn't be next time either. It was all simple physics, and in good weather with a well-maintained aircraft and an experienced pilot, there were no random factors to consider. Luck shouldn't play a role. He would check the statistics later, but he was confident that landing a float plane on a calm northern lake was no more dangerous than driving on Highway 59, which was his customary benchmark for calibrating risk. He always marvelled at people who were swayed by anecdotes of horrible events, rather than by the statistics regarding their actual probability.

"Yeah, it is terrible. The plane was recently fully safetied, and the pilot, Ned Fromm, was one of the best. Young guy, but I'd trust him to fly me anywhere, through anything, in any aircraft. He could fly a chesterfield through a hurricane if it had wings and a prop." John chuckled at his own joke.

"Who were the passengers?" Peter asked as they climbed into the truck, Peter almost forgetting to duck his head. Being tall, normally he did this instinctively, but when he was distracted, he banged his head far more times than he could count. "Your clumsiness will be the death of you someday," his mother had often warned. But so far, so good.

"There's no official confirmation yet, but the hot rumour is that one of them was Brendan O'Daly," John said as he started the engine.

"Who's that?"

"You haven't heard of him?" John threw Peter a glance. "He's that hydro exec who quit last year to start a bitcoin company. TealCoin, he calls it . . . called it. Teal for blue and green mixed, as in the green energy from the blue hydro power."

"Ah, OK. I don't follow the business news."

John grunted. "Yeah, I usually don't either, but when there's a northern angle I pay attention. Plus this guy is, or was, apparently quite the character. Not the usual dull technocrat in a grey suit and a toupée. Bit of a high-roller wannabe, dating Monique What's-her-name from that band. Even got his picture taken with Elon Musk." He glanced at Peter, apparently expecting a reaction.

Peter just nodded. He found little more boring than celebrity gossip. "Was he supposed to be your guest?" he asked.

"No. I'm guessing he was booked at the Friendly Bear." John turned right onto the gravel road that ran along the lake shore toward the lodge, which Peter could now make out through the trees on the far side of the bay.

"And the other passenger? His girlfriend maybe?"

"No idea, haven't heard."

"Any guesses what happened? Bad weather last night?"

"A perfect evening, actually. A couple of the guests were out fishing and said they saw the plane suddenly wobble badly and then clip some trees. It then came in kind of sideways and flipped right over when it hit the water."

"Pilot had a heart attack?"

"Maybe. As I said, he was a young guy. But heart attack's as good a guess as any right now." John pulled into a gravel parking lot behind the lodge. "You sure you don't want to stop by your cabin first?"

"No, I don't need to. Let's go see your dogs."

●

The kennels were in the trees on the far side of the parking lot from the lodge. Whereas the lodge was a beautiful log structure, the kennel was a simple plywood building with a sheet metal roof, and with chain-link fenced runs attached to the sides, each with a wide-open door into the kennel building. A large open exercise pen, also fenced with chain link, was attached to the back of the building. No dogs were outside.

To reach the kennel, they had to walk past a couple of ATVs, four snowmobiles, several large metal barrels, a burnt-out truck, and a jumbled heap of unidentifiable metal and plastic objects that Peter could only describe as junk. Peter mused about the contrast between the front of the lodge, facing the lake, which was a postcard-worthy emblem of the Canadian North, and the back of it, which was a much more realistic view of what most of the settled North looked like in his experience. Aesthetics generally took a back seat to the practicalities of making a living and survival.

"Hail on the roof doesn't bother them?" Peter asked, looking at the gleaming sheet metal.

"We don't get much hail up here, but no, my dogs don't get spooked easily. Is that an issue for some of your patients?" John asked as he rummaged in his pocket for keys.

"Yeah, for some it's quite bad. Any sudden loud noises like thunder or fireworks set them off. I had one make a dog-shaped hole in the screen door and then run for miles cross country, presumably trying to escape the noise."

"Wow, no, no worries about that here." He found the right key and unlocked the door. "Here we are, Reynolds' Runners

Kennels, fastest team in Northern Manitoba the last three years in a row."

They stepped into a bare room with shelves and cupboards on one side, and various harnesses hanging on the wall on the opposite side. Directly ahead there was a wide hall with kennels on either side. Peter counted eight on each side. Each one of the 16 kennels had a stainless-steel cage-wire door and cement walls reaching about three-quarters of the way to the ceiling. There were a couple of skylights and several large fans. It smelled much cleaner than most kennels Peter had been in, but there was something else unusual that he couldn't put his finger on immediately. Then he thought of it.

"It's so quiet in here. With 11 huskies, I expected some singing."

"Normally you can't hear yourself think, especially at feeding time, but right now none of them are feeling well enough." John said this quietly. "Do you want to start with Atlas?"

This book is made of paper from well-managed FSC® - certified forests, recycled materials, and other controlled sources.